I0741408

IT WAS IN THEIR HISTORY

WHERE SILENCE LINGERS

KATHRYN TIJERINA NICHOLS

Red Penguin
BOOKS

It Was In Their History

Copyright © 2025 by Kathryn Nichols

All rights reserved.

Red Penguin Books

Bellerose Village, New York

Library of Congress Control Number: 2025920254

ISBN

Digital 978-1-63777-789-3

Print 978-1-63777-790-9 | 978-1-63777-818-0

All rights reserved. No part of this book may be reproduced, stored in a retrieval system, or transmitted in any form or by any means; electronic, mechanical, photocopying, recording, or otherwise, without the written permission of the author.

This story is fiction. However, nearly all the places mentioned in it exist. And many of the events woven into the story have been based on documented truth, although some of the names have been changed. The use of the Gettysburg College name and other business and family names is solely for literary effect, as well as historical accuracy, and without permission.

To my dad,
The man who filled my world with wonder, mystery, and love through his own inspired stories and tales.
The one who taught me never to fear where my imagination might lead, to take risks, to be brutally honest and relentlessly human. Because of you, I became the woman, wife and mother you always knew I could be.
Thank you, Dad. I love you!
Kat

"With God all things are possible, and without Him nothing is."
Matthew 19:26

Contents

Prologue

Hannah's Nightmare

I t always starts with the screaming.

A shrill cry piercing the darkness, sharp enough to shatter glass, and suddenly, I am running.

Always running, barefoot through endless corridors. As I am being chased by a shadow, I seem to never escape.

My breathing ragged, my feet slapping painfully against cold, wet tile. The hallways twisted, stretching impossibly long, the doors locked tight, slippery and useless beneath my frantic grip. Death lingering in the stagnant, rancid in the air.

Then silence.

Terrible, deafening silence.

Nothing sings pain like that. In that very silence, I stand alone. I am small and shivering, frozen in a spotlight of aching memory. Always the same moment, always the same cruel joke playing repeatedly in my mind. My youthful hand reaching toward someone who should have protected me, someone who never turned around. Someone who never even noticed.

I wake with a violent gasp, lungs heaving, heart battering against my ribs. Sweat soaks the sheets beneath me, the fabric tangled around my legs like restraints. For a moment, I stay paralyzed, caught between a nightmare and waking, until the dim reality of my bedroom slowly comes into focus. The soft glow of moonlight trickles through curtains that flutter gently, stirred by a breeze whispering secrets I don't want to hear. Memories best forgotten.

The terror still pulses beneath my skin, raw and consuming. It surges with a poignant urgency and an over-whelming aching, as it always did after dreams like these. Nightmares, really.

My throat tightens, grief and panic twist painfully together, mimicking the very knots in my stomach, leaving no room for rational thought.

I push myself upright, chest aching from shallow breaths, the floorboards creaking softly beneath as I move to the window. The lake stretches out silver and serene in the moonlight, calm water mirroring the perfect stillness of the sky above as crickets play their symphonic music.

I see their house across the lake, its dark silhouette both comforting and torturous. Grand in stature, ironic through the vacancy felt. The house represents everything I desperately need, everything I'd always been denied: family, connection, even love. Everything that was stolen.

My pulse quickens, an obsessive ache fighting as it desperately rises to the surface.

My movements become impulsive, driven by a force stronger than reason. The screen door groans softly behind me as I step outside into the cool night air, the dew-covered grass slick beneath my toes. The sweet smell of the foliage around me momentarily holds me.

Without thinking, I move toward the still lake, twigs snapping underfoot as my white nightgown moves ghostly in the moonlight, billowing around my knees, my thick strawberry-hued hair dancing behind me.

The water welcomes me with an icy embrace, the chill biting yet cleansing. I swim fluidly across the shadowy lake, my strokes rhythmic and steady despite the quiver running through my bones. My nightgown clings heavily, wrapping me in its innocence, its fragile purity an aching symbol of everything I'd lost. Everything I had been robbed of years ago.

As I reach the shore, the house looms, vast yet familiar. Water drips from my pruned fingertips, pooling around my feet as I move closer. My heart thrums painfully, my breath quick and uneven. I stop near the porch, shivering and silent.

Standing there beneath their window, raw and vulnerable, tears slip silently down my pallid cheeks. I stare at the home before me, through a window into her soul. It's warm, whole, alive with love, and I feel my heart crack open and ache once again.

Because deep down, standing here broken and yearning, I know there is no turning back.

There will never be a way back, not for someone like me.

Chapter 1

Charlotte – The Fight

"Damn it, Charlotte, I can feel your eyes on me. I need space."

Will's voice cracked like a whip inside the confines of the car, sharp and sudden, but not unfamiliar. There was a crackle to it, tension simmering beneath every word. His knuckles were white against the steering wheel before he let go, shoving the door open.

He looked at me, and for a heartbeat, something in his green eyes softened remorse, maybe, but it passed in an instant. The car door slammed behind him with a finality that made me jump. The setting sun cast a warm glow as I tilted my head to gaze out of the window at the vast countryside lined with soaring trees.

The argument with Will had begun during our drive home and gained momentum with every passing mile. Subtle feelings of resentment and uncertainty lingered, casting shadows over our marriage, leaving me despondent and lost.

The silence between us had felt thick, almost tangible,

like humid summer air before a storm. Each tick of the cooling engine resonated loudly, punctuating the space between us.

My fingers gripped the armrest as I sat frozen, the hush in the cabin pressing against my skin. Outside, the sky above the sunroof stretched in a cloudless canvas of blue, too vast, too peaceful for how small and out of place I felt. The trees along the edge of the road swayed in the summer breeze, but inside the car, it felt like winter.

Our quarrels burn out after a few days, but this feels different. My diagnosis had come weeks ago. *Relapse.* That single word had decimated my new bill on health. I didn't tell Will immediately because I didn't see the point. I knew what his reaction would be, and I didn't want to do that to him.

Tonight was supposed to be different. I had planned it for weeks, a night for just us. No crying kids, no work calls, no distractions. No sticky fingers or whining. Just Will and I, the way it used to be. But life has a cruel way of unraveling even the best intentions.

It wasn't for his lack of trying, but my insecurities had turned into a stone wall. I couldn't figure out how to break it down. I had looked forward to this night, anxiously anticipating the wine, the laughter, the conversation. But Will had been stressed more than usual, often lost in thought, his temper sharp. I could feel him slipping away, and it worried me.

William and I had always had our most cherished conversations during moments like these. He was my best friend. Oftentimes, we would play a game where we would ask each other thought-provoking questions like, "If you could fix one thing from your past, what would it be?" or

"If you could have any superpower, what would it be and why?" These dialogues not only engaged our minds but also deepened our connection to one another.

When I was in tune with Will, I felt invincible. His green eyes pierced through me, and his coy smile would ignite passion within me. Nothing could bring me down from that euphoria. However, after the kids came, that connection became elusive. Max, eight, had been our rainbow baby, an expression I'd learned during my pregnancy while reading about fertility issues. Max's arrival brought us immense joy, but the pregnancy was difficult. Bed rest, complications, all of it had tested us.

Max, now with an ebony mop of hair and a radiant smile, is emotionally sensitive and empathetic. Then there is Molly, our five-year-old with a tangle of messy golden-brown curls and hazelnut eyes, she rivaled the likes of Shirley Temple. Molly has a sweet demeanor, but she is no pushover.

Lately, with summer break, both kids had worn me thin. I was struggling to balance their education and extracurricular activities, feeling like I was failing on all fronts. Even my self-care had taken a backseat. I hadn't colored my roots in months. And now, with my diagnosis confirmed, I might not need to worry about my hair for a while.

My mother, a schoolteacher for almost fifty years, specialized in behavioral issues. I couldn't imagine how she managed to handle kids with psychological or behavioral challenges, yet she thrived in her work. She was often called to speak at school district meetings, and I admired her professional success.

When she had time off, she would take the kids. She loved those moments, soaking them up, and the kids loved it, too. She would whisk them both away to what she called "Camp Nana" for overnight stays. Those brief excursions were a Godsend. If she could, she would take them for an entire summer.

With summer ending, those stays became less frequent. The idea of reconnecting tonight with Will sounded heavenly, but there was a distance between us now, a disconnect I had not anticipated. I had become so enthralled with the kids, their activities, and my work that I had not noticed how far apart we had grown.

I often found myself in a sick cycle—picking up kids, volunteering, shuttling them to ballet or baseball, acting as their personal chauffeur. Will and I were like two ships passing in the night. At the end of the day, we would collapse next to each other on the couch, too tired to even speak.

I felt like one of those Stretch Armstrong dolls, visibly strained from being pulled in opposite directions. The days my mom had them, I would throw myself into other projects, much to Will's frustration. He would make snide remarks, "Do you even know what it's like to stop moving, Charlie?" I'd just roll my eyes, tension mounting again.

Marriage had morphed into a ball of unsaid words and miscommunicated feelings. There had to be an invisible push to continue being intimate and in tune with each other. Our history of verbal altercations had always been sparse, the thick stench of marital decay waiting to creep in. If we did not attempt to escape it, the fog would inevitably consume us.

My head spun from our fight. My jaw clenched tightly, blocking any other emotions from resurfacing. I recited Bible verses in my mind: *Set a guard, O Lord, over my mouth;*

keep watch over the door of my lips. The words echoed as I clung to the comfort of God. My arm still throbbed with a pulse where Will had given me an unintended bruise when I tried to stop him from changing the song on the radio. As childish as it seemed, music had always been a way for me to express my feelings.

The fight had started small but grew in magnitude. Music had always been my way of speaking, my way of saying what I couldn't find the courage to say aloud.

"Why do you always do that?" Will had snapped. "I get it, okay? You don't have to play a damn song to tell me how you feel."

The sting of his voice was worse than the words. He wasn't just angry, he was unraveling. And so was I.

I hadn't told him yet about the relapse.

Weeks ago, I got the call. The one I had dreaded but somehow expected. The cancer had returned. Ovarian. Again. As if once wasn't enough.

I had carried the news like a hidden stone in my chest, heavy and cold, refusing to let it spill out. Not yet. Not until I had the strength. But now, I wondered if I ever would.

We were already drifting, each of us holding onto our own sides of a rope that was fraying at the center. I didn't want to add more weight to it. Not yet.

Our marriage hadn't always been like this. Will used to be my home, the place I ran to when the world hurt too much. We used to stay up late, tangled in sheets, talking about everything and nothing. He was the only one who could pull me out of a spiral with a single word, a single look.

I missed that. I missed him.

Our kids, Max and Molly, were miracles. Max, eight

years old and so perceptive it scared me sometimes, with eyes like mine and a heart as wide as the sky. Molly, five, wild and sweet and entirely herself. They were our pride, our joy, our reason for trying so hard. But they were also part of the exhaustion. Parenthood changes a marriage. It twists it, stretches it, sometimes even breaks it.

I had thrown myself into motherhood after the first diagnosis. Every ballet class, every school project, every doctor's appointment. I showed up like it was a performance I had to nail.

Somewhere in that endless effort to be everything for everyone, I lost the version of myself that knew how to be a wife.

Will retreated, too. Into work. Into silence. He hated mess and chaos and the unpredictability of illness. He didn't say it, but I saw it in the way he flinched when I coughed too hard, the way he avoided my prescriptions on the kitchen counter.

I sat for what felt like hours in the car, the engine off, the silence a steady roar in my ears. The sun dipped lower behind the trees, casting long shadows across the gravel driveway.

I reflected on the events of the night, battling with myself for my inability to hold myself together. I scrutinized every detail, mulled over every word. He probably did the same, but I couldn't be sure. I analyzed his tools in the garage, labeled and compartmentalized in individual plastic tins, the opposite of how I felt.

I placed my hand on my chest, feeling the rise and fall of each inhalation. To an untrained eye, I appeared fine, not a hair out of place. However, if someone were to peer closely, they would have noticed strain on my blood vessels and the salty liquid that primed my eyes. My unavoidable habit was to seek refuge behind a locked door to cry in solitude. I despised vulnerability, hated that it made me feel inferior and weak.

I finally reached for my phone, hands trembling, and called him.

Voicemail.

"You have reached the voicemail of William Rose. Leave me a message, and I'll get back to you as soon as possible. Thanks."

"Will, it's me. I just… I don't want to fight anymore. Please call me back. I love you."

I hung up and exhaled slowly, the words echoing back at me. They felt small, insufficient. But they were all I had.

I would think of my father, who used to tell us that crying was good for the soul. It was the body's way of letting go of the emotions that weighed us down. Sometimes, when things got hard, I would say, "Oh, Dad, I miss you." As if he could emerge out of thin air and make it all right. I imagine his long, gangly arms embracing me, and it provides temporary relief.

I hadn't told Will about my cancer relapse. He hadn't given me an opportunity. I hadn't seized any opportunity either. The first time I had to tell Will, the silence had been deafening. My mother had come with me because you never know what you might be told. I had wanted Will to be there, but when he asked, I didn't speak. I didn't want to be disappointed if he said no.

The silence between us stretched for what seemed like an eternity. I could tell Will was attempting to process the news. His beloved grandmother had passed from breast cancer when he was eighteen. It was a difficult death for him, as she had watched him every day while his mother went to work.

When Will had finally broken the silence, his tone was firm but had a slight hint of unease. "You don't need to have surgery or chemo if we can avoid it." I had visibly sat up straighter, frustrated at the notion of him thinking I would entertain unwanted, unnecessary treatment. Still, it hurt.

I read a pamphlet on how loved ones can cope with a cancer diagnosis. It listed fear, denial, role reversal, and more. I couldn't figure out which one Will was struggling with. I had a crazy plan to tell him I was going to pen a memoir about my experience with cancer. Then I planned to gently tell him the news. Except, before I had been able to transition into my diagnosis, he had balked at the idea.

Will and I both struggled at the beginning with our ability to communicate clearly. Every time we spoke, we each wanted to be in control of the conversation. We wanted to be on top of every situation or conversation. It didn't matter what it was. Essentially, it just mattered who ruled the roost. It sounds ridiculous when I think about it or say it out loud. We have come a long way, but our marriage counselor is always telling us it's a deep-rooted issue with each of us due to past relation-ship traumas, and our self-awareness of where we are in the process. It can be frustrating because at times we are both knee-deep in the process of connecting, and other times, we're so frustrated that we revert to old habits. Old habits die hard.

That initiated a downward spiral. It unintentionally brought up past emotions of our arguments. One time, he had the audacity to yell, "You use cancer as a spotlight for attention." The moment he noticed my tears, his face fell. "Charlotte, I didn't mean that." However, deep down inside, I wondered if he had. Was I really the type of person who would use cancer to up my rank in life or gain pity? It was true, I had always thrived on attention. I would be a liar to say otherwise. I was the middle-born of three competitive girls; how could I not be? I was smack dab in the middle of educational excellence and distinguished accomplishments.

Ten years and I had come to know every pattern and every jab to throw. No one had been able to throw a sucker punch like I could. It had always been an embarrassing achievement, one I had secretly prided myself on. Has his mood always been swayed by his heavy workload? Has it been manipulated by the mounting pressure and lack of employees to fulfill their contractual obligations? I had assumed at the time that his actions toward me had somehow been rooted in a scenario much like those. The thought that he would have left never crossed my mind. I had never thought that I would ever fully understand his mindset. However, God made every person different for a reason, right?

As I stepped out of the car, the breeze hit me. Warm and fragrant with honeysuckle, but it did nothing to chase the chill clinging to my skin.

Then I saw it.

Across the lake, just for a second, I thought I saw someone standing near the water's edge. A figure, tall and still. But when I blinked, it was gone.

Goosebumps rose along my arms.

The wind picked up. The trees rustled. And in the distance, a dog barked once, then went quiet.

I backed up toward the house, eyes scanning the lake. Still nothing.

Still, the feeling remained.

Will was gone.

And something else, something I couldn't name, was here.

Chapter 2

Will – Private Eye

Will did not know who this bastard thought he was. He had to have been crazy. Will had started to see how wild-eyed Charlotte had become. She hadn't been herself in a while. At first, he'd brushed it off, but the threats had grown more frequent, more intense.

He always tried to stay five steps ahead. That was his job, his duty as a husband and father. To protect. To anticipate. It was in his DNA after all. His tactical upbringing had been deeply instilled by his father, who was a high-ranking officer in the Navy.

He stood up and cracked his neck, wincing at the sharp pop. His eyes glazed over a framed sepia picture of his father in uniform placed upon his bookshelf. He was a hard man, but his words rang true to date: *Never turn your back. Always scope out the field. Everything in life is a battle; it's just from a different point of view, son.*

Will chuckled to himself. *Dad, you were one hell of a soldier, but an even better man. Miss you.*

Charlotte used to roll her eyes at his habit, a nervous tic left over from football. Pacing the office, the click of his leather boots echoed against the wood floor, barely louder than the city's sirens and car horns outside. It was moments like this that reminded him of why they'd moved out of the city in the first place.

Despite the chaos, despite the exhaustion, he had to prepare. He stared at the overflowing folder on his desk: photos, logs, printed emails, call histories. A dossier on Baker. A man who should've stayed buried in the past.

He had been unable to focus; too many cups of coffee had been consumed. Perhaps it had been the pile of contracts lying on his desk. He had never known how to completely turn off his brain. He had always tried to be as efficient and effective as possible. However, he had always felt as if he were failing as an employer, as a spouse, and as a father. He had always felt like a clown juggling bowling pins in the air. However, in his case, instead of pins, it had been the weight of his little world. His family, his company, his friends, and his need to be present at the top of his game. It had become exhausting, and at any time, the cards would crumble.

He had been preparing for this meeting all morning. He had been up the previous night pondering what would transpire. He had even fallen asleep in Max's room. It had been a habit Max loved and Charlotte detested. She had felt it created a sense of dependency upon the kids, and it was proven when Max was three. He had slept in Max's room every night due to late nights at the office, and when he attempted to revert to a normal sleep schedule, it had taken months to wean Max off. He had woken up in the middle of the night at one point, and Max was still up playing a video game in bed.

He had assumed Charlotte had tiptoed in and quietly tucked Max to sleep while covering him at the same time. She was the type to always seek ways to make him and their children more comfortable.

Everything around him was being compounded by the imminent arrival of his appointment. Will didn't want to do this. He hated the idea of going behind Charlotte's back, of hiring someone to follow her. But something about her recent behavior—her eyes constantly scanning, the notes, the gifts, the silence had triggered every instinct in his body. And when instinct and fear aligned, he acted.

He reached for his phone and scrolled to the detective's contact. Maria, an old friend on the force, had recommended him. She hadn't asked why, just passed along a name and warned, "Be careful. Nothing good ever comes from secrets."

Everything had been organized and structured in a way that he couldn't possibly slip up with Charlotte. If she only knew that he was about to have her tailed. All so he could have confirmation that his suspicions had been, in fact, Baker. If she knew, she would have his head. He had been a sly one, too. Charlotte always said that for every bit of his charisma, he was just as cunning.

It had been years of anonymous calls and an unsolicited spotlight. Neither of them had yet to catch him. It had been the damn elephant in the room for years, and it was seated smack dab in the middle of their lives. They both knew he was there, hovering over them. Yet they never sat down and discussed him. Nor had they spoken about the boundaries that Baker daringly crossed. What couple wants to talk about their ex violating their privacy and essentially the very sanctity of their marriage?

A knock tapped at his door. He called out, "Come in."

His assistant, Marla, peeked in. "Mr. Rose, there's a Mr. Larson here to see you."

He looked up and smiled at his assistant, Marla. She was in her late thirties, the same as he. Marla, his ever-optimistic assistant, bustled in with her usual energy. She was a lifesaver at work and had always been loyal to him. Never letting anything slip through the cracks, she had been by his side ever since he first established his software company. She had been his first hire, recommended to him by Charlotte. He never once regretted bringing her on board. In fact, he often doubted he would have achieved the same level of success without her ingenuity and mindfulness.

Marla and Charlotte had met while taking a writing class, and it hadn't been long before they became friends. Although Marla was awkward with a dry, sarcastic sense of humor and came off as weird, she was someone whom Charlotte was genuinely able to let loose with. They still met for lunch once every few weeks just to touch base. Marla became like family to them. No, correction, she <u>was</u> family. She was invited to their parties and events and always arrived with a warm casserole or freshly baked cookies. Her husband was David. He was in the Marines and constantly on tour. He radiated American pride. He helped shed light on what it was like to serve one's country from a soldier's perspective and had been a positive influence on Max. Max always trailed alongside him, asking endless questions. David would casually respond as if he were talking to a friend, making him one of Max's favorite and most cherished people. It had to do with the level of respect that he had shown one of his closest friends and someone he could trust wholeheartedly.

"Send him in. And bring two bottles of water, please."

"Certainly," she said as the door shut behind her, a little harder than Will anticipated. Running his fingers through his hair, he stared at his desk. Strewn across its mahogany wood top was a messy array of paper and files.

What a mess. I just can't keep up, he thought. Will took a deep breath, raked his hand through his hair again, and tried to make the desk look somewhat presentable, not that it mattered.

On a neon yellow post-it, he made a note to have Marla file things in order of urgency and then attached it to his monitor, knowing full well that just because he wrote it down didn't mean he'd remember. Will grabbed a legal pad, a pen, and a discolored file folder filled to the brim with documents. He had started the file years ago after noticing random items being left at their door

Thick and ripping at the seams, it contained everything he had compiled about Baker thus far. It also contained photographic evidence, an array of old pictures from when Charlotte dated him, as well as a phone log, meticulously compiled, listing years' worth of calls Charlotte had received from untraceable numbers. Will even went as far as printing all the social media he could find, and references to conversations he had with Charlotte. His type-A personality could be visible in the stockpile laid out in front of him.

Moments later, Marla entered and stepped over to the side to reveal behind her an older gentleman in his early fifties. He strode into the room with a firm step and a neutral expression. A tall, silver-haired man with a neatly trimmed beard, he sported thin silver-rimmed glasses on his distinguished nose. Dressed in a tailored grey suit that high-lighted his athletic build, he looked like he stepped out of an eyewear advertisement, complete with dazzling white teeth. Larson. He looked like a detective—lean, quiet, eyes that didn't blink more than necessary.

"Mr. Rose," he said, shaking Will's hand. "Mark Larson. It's a pleasure to meet you. You wished to meet with me regarding a personal matter?" His eyes drifted to Marla as he stepped farther into the office. Marla placed the water bottles on Will's desk and turned to face Larson. It took no more than an awkward moment for her to realize she was dismissed. She walked toward the door but hesitated before moving across the threshold. That was Marla's body language for eavesdropping.

"Thanks, Marla. Please hold all my calls for the next hour." She nodded her head before replying, "Certainly, Mr. Rose." Then she shut the door behind her.

Will gestured to the seat across from him. "Thanks for coming. I appreciate discretion."

"Mr. Rose, if you could share more details about the matter you need my assistance with, I can better explain how I might be able to help, assuming it's something within my capability."

Larson leaned back in the leather chair and crossed his legs. As he did, his pant leg rose enough to allow brightly colored argyle socks to peek through. Clearly, this was not his first rodeo. He wore no wedding ring or the faint circle of a suntan alluding to one.

I wonder what his story is, thought Will. As he considered this, Larson fixated his eyes on Will and gestured to him to answer his question. *Well, he is assertive and direct, I'll give him that much.* It was almost intimidating, but he reminded himself to be confident in his accomplishments.

Will hesitated, then spoke. "Oh, yes, I apologize. It's been a long day. I've yet to drink an adequate amount of coffee this morning, and this matter involves my wife. The individual in question was her boyfriend for most of her time at university. It ended on a very sour note. He hated that she had begun to develop an interest in me and started to pursue me. At the time, I had been in a serious relationship of my own. Well, it was more than serious; we were engaged to be married. After both our relationships had dissolved due to our affection for one another, we ended up getting engaged ourselves. I guess it did not settle well with him, because he never left us alone after that. This is all an assumption, of course. However, I cannot think of anyone else who would possibly want to harm Charlotte like this. For years, he's been calling, watching, and stalking her. Now, it's beginning to involve my children, and that's where I have to draw the line. It's no longer a game I can ignore. This has become too intimate for me. I take it as a personal attack. However, I can't for the life of me understand his motives. So, step one for me is to be sure it's him. Before I head to the cops, I need substantial proof that can be upheld in a court of law. I have to be careful, of course."

Larson didn't react, just opened a small notepad and waited.

Will continued, his voice low. "His name is Baker. We've had incidents over the years, you know, but nothing we could ever prove. But it's escalating again. I need confirmation. I need to know if it's him."

"You want surveillance."

"Yes. Discreet. She can't know. She's already looking over her shoulder enough."

Larson nodded. "Any recent signs?"

Will tapped the folder. "These are just the ones I could document. But I know her. I know when she's afraid, even when she tries to hide it."

"Understood. I'll need to know her routine—where she goes, who she sees, times, and dates. I'll also need access to these materials."

Will slid the folder across the desk. "Take it. Just—" he paused, lowering his voice further. "If it is him, I want to know exactly what he's planning."

Larson stood. "Then I'll start tonight. You'll hear from me soon."

Will walked him to the door. Marla pretended to look busy at her desk as they passed. He caught her sideways glance but said nothing. She'd ask questions later, no doubt. He'd have to be careful.

Back at his desk, Will drafted a text to Charlotte: "Hey, hon, working late. Meeting at The Davenport tonight. Be home later."

He hit send and leaned back, stomach tight with dread. He hated lying to her. But he needed the truth first. Only then could he keep her safe.

And God help Baker if he were behind any of this.

Chapter 3

Will – Suspicions

"Thanks, Marla, I hope you have a good night," Will said with as much cheerfulness as he could muster. He grabbed his keys, ready to cut the awkwardness with movement, averting his eyes as he did so.

"Big meeting, huh?" Marla says lightly, though her eyes lingered too long.

"Just dinner," I replied, reaching for the door.

She tilted her head, voice softer now. "How is Charlotte lately? Everything going okay?"

Will hesitated. *Does she know something I don't?*

"Why do you ask?"

"Well, I know the kids are involved in quite a few things, and she seemed frazzled the last time I met her for pilates." Marla pressed her lips together, something unreadable in her expression. Then, almost like an afterthought, she murmured, "Some people aren't built to be mothers. Not really."

Will furrowed his brow, his glance narrowing. "Excuse me?"

23

But Marla had already shifted her tone. "That came out wrong, Will. I just meant that some people are stronger with structure and routine, that's all. It's a lot for anyone, really." She waved off the comment with a broad smile, but the words hung in the air. She hesitated, biting down so hard on her bottom lip that Will anticipated blood trickling down her chin. He studied her, unsure as to what thoughts were swirling in her head. Will didn't have time for these games. He stopped what he was doing and cocked his head slightly, waiting for her to talk. He'd been in business for a decade, and Marla had been his assistant for the same amount of time. Will knew how she took her coffee and that she kept socks in her drawer for when she was cold. He knew this woman inside and out. He also knew that when she bites her bottom lip, that meant that she had something brewing in her head. She was never one to not say what was on her mind either.

Like a cat that ate a canary. Will stifled a laugh because it was incredibly predictable. *I'm shocked she doesn't have a permanent scar on her lip as many times as she does this.*

"Marla, just spit it out already. I need to finish up this project before heading out to my dinner. I can't waste my time playing charades with you." She flashed a smile nervously. Her eyes shifted from where Larson had sat to me.

"Are you going out with Charlotte tonight, or is it the whole family?" She squinted, analyzing every movement. Sometimes, Will swore she could read his mind.

He paused for a moment. *Crap. I just messed up. She's on to me. I must be careful how I deliver my next response.*

"No, it is not with the family or with Charlie. I have a meeting."

Marla pondered this for a second, squinting her eyes in deep concentration. Will could almost see her going through the files in her brain. She didn't meet my gaze.

Marla had been his assistant for over a decade–sharp, loyal, and fiercely protective of his calendar. She wasn't just organized; she was intuitive. She'd once predicted a board member's affair based on a missing golf outing. She wasn't the flirtatious type either–Will had always seen her as a work sister, not someone to toy with. Which made this moment more unsettling.

He could barely see the pigment in her faded eyes behind the glare from her glasses, which were perched back on her nose. "You have a meeting? With whom? I didn't see anything or schedule anything on your calendar. I must have missed it. But that can't be right because I just checked it before I signed out of my computer." It came out as more of an accusation than a comment, and Will recoiled.

In turn, Marla stepped back as she realized her brazenness.

"Marla, I must have forgotten to tell you."

She pushed away the curtain of fringe from her eyes and smoothed down her blouse, clearly still unnerved. Perhaps she was even slightly offended. Marla's fingers tapped nervously against the desk, her eyes narrowing slightly as if weighing her next words carefully. "Are you sure it's nothing more, Will?" Her tone was edged with restrained curiosity. "Perhaps you did. Hmm." She resembled a wounded dog after a fight. "Well, then, I will leave you to it. See you tomorrow at seven."

Will waved as she turned to leave. "Sounds good, have a great time with your daughter tonight."

Marla lingered by the door, smoothing the files in her hands. He looked up, waiting for her to speak.

"Are you and Charlotte still good for the fundraiser next month?" she asked lightly.

"Yeah, assuming we survive Max's practice schedule," Will replied. "David still heading it up with you?"

"Of course." Her voice was too bright, too clipped.

Will murmured under his breath. "Guy's got the personality of a filing cabinet. Always polite. Never says much. Stiff neck, that one."

Marla's smile didn't reach her eyes. "He's … dependable, which is good."

Will nodded absently. "Yeah. Dependable." Then he paused, squinting. "Didn't he go to college or something with you?"

"For undergrad," she said quickly, already turning back to her files. "Years ago."

Something about her tone made Will hesitate. But only for a second. "Alright, see you tomorrow, bright and early."

"Always bright and early," she echoed, not looking up, her voice low. She waved and closed the door behind her.

Damn it. I feel like I fumbled that. Marla does not forget about anything. I know better than to mention having a meeting when she is the keeper of all my events. Why did I have to open my damn mouth? I am such a crappy liar.

Will pulled at the little hair on his head. *First thing tomorrow, she is going to ask how it went. Note to self, have a story. A solid backup. I need something, anything.* He tried to recount what number lie he was on now. Will leaned back in his chair and thought about how he was going to cover his tracks. He worked for about an hour and then got cleaned up for dinner.

He opened his closet and put on a fresh button-down shirt and switched out his shoes. The restaurant was known for its steak and was a bit more upscale than he would have preferred. Will hated going to these kinds of places, but he didn't pick it. Anyone who was anyone in our small town went to The Davenport, and it was her favorite spot.

As Will got in the car, he received a text from Charlotte. "Hey, babe, mind swinging by Max's baseball game on your way back from your meeting and bringing him home? Mandy said she can't carpool tonight." *Great, as if I need this on my plate, too. It stretches me even thinner. Hopefully, dinner is not long-winded. Extracurricular activities have always been a monster to contend with.*

It was one of the things that Charlotte always had a good handle on. She was militant as she moved seamlessly from each event without breaking a sweat, and she rarely complained.

If anything, I'm the one who was lucky in this situation, Will thought. *I get to enjoy a hot meal cooked fresh daily. It's just one of the many qualities that made her a super mom in my eyes. Sometimes I wonder what she needs me around for.*

He joked about it in the past, and she always quipped back, "Wouldn't you rather me want you than need you?" If he were being a hundred percent honest with her and himself, Will would rather she want <u>and</u> need him. That is where his masculinity and vulnerability collide.

Once at the restaurant, Will cringed at the idea of valeting, but had no choice. He took the ticket and handed the valet a couple of bucks in exchange. The lights were low, and the ambiance moody. It was aromatic and rich with the aroma of fine meat. The low hum of chatter from the dining hall greeted him as I approached the hostess.

"My party is here. Back corner, I believe." She smiled and displayed a set of gleaming teeth as she moved her hand in the direction of the seating area. Will always wondered how people were able to get that white of a smile. It seemed unnatural to him. Not to jump on the bandwagon, but Charlotte and Will had tried so many products, and they just never worked one hundred percent.

He felt like turning around and asking her about her hygiene practices, but before he knew it, they were narrowing in on a burgundy leather booth tucked in the corner of the room. That was when Will saw her.

"Thanks," he said as the hostess nodded and walked off. He took notice of her Victorian profile, her perky nose, and short brown crop brushed neatly behind her ear. She wore a simple pearl stud designed to go perfectly with her ensemble. A taut collared shirt was neatly tucked into her navy trousers, giving off an air of elegance.

As Will approached, her green eyes widened, gleaming back at him. "Hey! I was beginning to wonder whether you were going to stand me up." She let out a laugh and stood to embrace him. She had a fresh scent, clean and refined.

"Traffic was a bear getting here. Just be happy that I made it at all." Will sounded more petulant than he intended, and did his best to try to shake off his mood. She waved off the comment with a flick of her hand and took a sip of her wine. She sat back in the leather chair and analyzed him.

"So, how is the family?" She drew out the sentence, giving off a casual vibe but insinuating that something was wrong.

Will looked at the menu, scanning up and down.

"Great, actually. Last we spoke, I think Max had begun to play basketball. Well, now the kid is dominating."

She burst into laughter. "Dominating? Really, Will? He's eight."

He shrugged dismissively. "My son is going to be great. I just have to continue to work on his basics."

She rolled her eyes. "How is my sweet Molly?" She asked as she tapped away at her phone.

"She's a whip, that one. Never a dull moment nor a quiet one at that. She's currently into arts and crafts projects. So, there's been an excess of colorful pictures that I've been instructed to bring to work. Basically, there's some remnant of destruction throughout our entire house. It leaves Charlotte with the monumental task of picking up every single scrap of paper. It honestly drives her mad. The quandary is that if her art is not fully on display for all to see, then there is hell to pay. She is a bit of a dictator, that one."

She let out another roll of laughter. "She is an absolute doll. I can't wait to see them again. I love how exacting she is with everything she does. Perhaps I can take her to the next art exhibit that comes into town. I don't know when my schedule will allow for it, but I would like to hang out with both of them."

Will ordered a beer from the waiter and then grabbed a dinner roll. "Sorry, I'm starving. I ate late this morning after an intense workout. The protein shake I drank just wasn't enough. These rolls are insanely good." He licked his lips in satisfaction, the buttery bread curbing his hunger. "I do my best to eat healthy, and thanks to Charlotte and her svelte figure, she has made my diet regimen easier to abide by. So, what did you want to meet me about anyway?" Will took a sip of beer, cleansing his palate from the bread but oddly making him hungrier for more. Resisting the urge, he placed his hands in his lap and leaned back in his chair, fully engaged in what she was going to say.

She looked directly at him, took a breath, and then grabbed her phone. It displayed a custom-crafted image of her kids, Addison and Allison. She scrolled for a bit without looking up, pursing her pink lips together, and analyzing a picture in intense detail. She then refocused her gaze on Will.

"So, as you well know, I never deleted Hannah from any of my social media accounts. I've noticed in her last few posts some oddities, if you will. They caught my eye because it seems as if she's back in town. Have you had any run-ins with her? It's not like the suburban town you live in is big, after all."

Will's eyes bulged at the mention of her name. His body grew tense.

"Hannah is in Crescent? How is that possible? I thought she had gone East?" he exclaimed in an accusatory tone as if she should know before presenting him with this knowledge. She shrugged dismissively. Lindsey was used to his emotions and his tendency to get a bit abrasive during times of stress.

"I don't know, Will. I just noticed and figured I would give you a heads up since your last conversations or run-ins with her have been bad."

Will's mind rushed back to that terrible encounter years ago between Hannah and Charlotte outside the library where Charlotte was working. Hannah accused Charlotte of roping Will into marriage by using her son, whom Hannah had accused of not being mine. It had gotten ugly, to say the least. He remembered having to physically pick up Charlotte and remove her from the scene because, in that moment, the intensity radiating from her had made him nervous. Will had to tell Hannah to leave or he would call the cops. Words had been said, and bodies had been pushed.

"I didn't want to be the bearer of bad news, Will. But better me than someone else, right? I didn't want to tell Charlotte directly because I didn't want to stress her out."

She showed Will her phone where the image was displayed. It was no doubt Hannah's Instagram. The image displayed was of Hannah on a swing in our town's local park. This park is directly across from the kids' school. She was laughing and seemed to be enjoying herself and the company that she was keeping.

"Why would she have come back? She has nothing here but sour memories."

Lindsey grabbed her phone and put it back in her purse. "I recall hearing from you about her abuse as a child after her father passed away. I still can't believe what she had to endure at such a young age. I don't understand why she would come back here. I have not spoken to her in years, so I really can't tell you anything other than show you the picture."

Will nodded a thank you as the waiter handed him another beer. He took a long sip, not realizing how quickly he had finished the first.

"I appreciate you telling me, Linds. I really need to process everything before I figure out what to do. Anyway, enough about me. Tell me how everything is going now that you have Mom and Dad living with you, Carson, and the girls. I bet that has been interesting."

She laughed and rolled her eyes playfully. "Oh, it has been a real trip."

A little while later, he received a text from Mandy just as they were wrapping up dinner. "Will, game is in the top of the 7th. Charlotte told me to give you a heads up."

He looked at Lindsey and chugged a quarter of his new beer. "I hate to do this to you, but I must go scoop Max from his game. It's the top of the 7th."

She smiled at me and waved her hand. "Not an issue. You go. I have this."

As Will got up, he gave a snort of laughter.

She quickly responded, "You're kidding me, right?" She looked frustrated and playfully leery.

"I paid when I went to the bathroom earlier."

She faked a punch to my arm. "Damn it, Will. I got you next time."

Will hugged her. "Nah, no worries whatsoever. See you later, and thanks for the tip. Tell Mom and Dad hi for me."

She smiled and waved as he rushed out the door.

Chapter 4

Charlotte – Missing

The moment I realized Will's car wasn't in the driveway and that it was he who drove away, my heart dropped. I rushed back inside and began the relentless pursuit of tracing Will's essentials. His charger was gone. His toothbrush and overnight bag were missing, too. I ran around the house, anxiety rising as Baxter's barking ensued.

There was no sign of him, not even a note.

I collapsed onto the bed and stared blankly back at myself through a floor-length mirror in the corner. Dumbfounded, defeated, I looked like absolute crap. I looked dreadful, in fact. My skin itched everywhere. Standing up and walking closer to the mirror, inspecting the welts peeking through my collarbone, I instinctively pulled at the dress. *Stupid polyester*. This dress was a bad choice. Unable to control my emotions, I pulled at the dress hard, popping off one of its dainty gold buttons. It hit the ground rolling, then began to spin around in place until it stopped. Curious, Baxter went to inspect it, nose to the ground.

He looked up, staring at me blankly as he cocked his head to the side. He could feel my anxiety. *He probably thinks I'm crazy.* I then quickly changed. He began to bark, his almost human eyes smiling with affectionate eagerness. He bolted to the laundry room, and before she knew it, he was back with a leash clutched tightly in his mouth. He dropped it at her feet and proceeded to bark again.

"Want to go for a walk, buddy?" He barked again, but this time he twirled as he did it. "Let's go then."

As I walked out the door, I popped my AirPods in and set my phone to the relaxing music of Chopin. I closed my eyes, each inflection of the melody instantly soothing me.

The neighborhood was eerily silent, and the evening crisp. The quickly fading sun cast a pink strawberry haze across the sky. I stopped and looked up. Taking a deep breath, the crisp air filled my lungs. I gave praise to God for all that I had, regardless of whether I was fighting with Will right now. The engineered lakes sparkled in the dying sunlight, their fountains casting ripples across the surface. However, the serene backdrop felt sinister, and my pace quickened as I struggled to shake the overwhelming feeling of being watched. The wind blew a bit more fiercely as we walked, the heaviness of the breeze piercing my body.

As we began to approach an old playground, Baxter and I slowed our pace. Baxter took it upon himself to relieve himself. While I waited, my anxiety grew. I got my phone out of my pocket to see if I had any missed messages.

Where on earth is Will? Where could he possibly be? Could he have gone to his parents or maybe even his sister's house?

Before I knew it, my fingers were flying across the screen, sending a text to his family to check in. I didn't really know what was going on after all. However, I felt a sense of dread deep down inside. Time must have passed because I was jolted to the present by Baxter pulling at his leash.

As I continued to walk, my sense of unease grew. Every fiber in my being told me something was terribly wrong. I looked up and was startled by a movement in the woods. As I looked ahead to the trail that lay before me, a dense fog loomed in the distance. I could feel the burning sensation of eyes seeping into my skin. I quickened my pace. For years, the tension of this apprehension had built. What should be that of an unwelcome friend felt off somehow. Not that it had been daily. It wasn't even as often as every month. It had been through the extension of time, though. Each unsanctioned visit always felt different. It had never been exactly like the one before. My stalking had varied from the time to the place, to even the raw emotions that I feel with each.

Somewhere deep inside, I always feared it was Baker. The last time he showed up, he carved a single word into our mailbox: *Mine*. Will had covered it before the kids saw it, but I never forgot. He was never violent, just calculating. The kind of man who smiled when he made you feel unsafe.

I pushed my emotions deep down and bore the only armor I yield. My fingers grazed the dainty cross that was cradled between my collarbones. I recited, *Our Father, who art in heaven, hallowed be thy name. Thy kingdom come, thy will be done, on earth as it is in heaven. Give us this day our daily bread and forgive us our trespasses as we forgive those who trespass against us and lead us not into temptation. Amen.* Growing up a cradle Catholic, I've always known my prayers. I had memorized them before I had even learned my alphabet. Even now, a rosary is soothing, never far away from my reach. On my worst nights, I fade into my dreams with it tucked right under my pillow.

As we returned, paranoia terrorized my mind. Baxter's ears pricked up, his head lowered as he growled, baring his teeth. I walked more slowly and reassured him by giving him a gentle pat.

Once back home, the house felt colder than before. I heated up leftover pizza and buried my emotions in a glass of red wine. I checked Will's email, our bank accounts, and his social media. There was a withdrawal from a nearby bank, but nothing too crazy. He also had a gas transaction and a Starbucks run. Nothing that would arouse suspicions. His social media was devoid of activity, not that he was particularly active. *Where is he? Where could he be?*

I took another big bite of pizza, but before I could stop it, the sauce spilled on my shirt.

Ugh. Story of my damn life.

I looked at Baxter, and he tilted his head to the side, analyzing me. Annoyed, I raised my voice at him.

"What? I know I'm a mess. Cut me some slack, will you?" He sighed and put his head down back on his paws.

Great, now I'm fussing at the dog for no apparent reason.

Chapter 5

Charlotte – Knock Knock

I was juggling too much: my keys, my phone, and Molly's coat when a man appeared beside the cart with a calm, casual air.

"Hey, is Baxter still limping a little from the vet visit last Thursday?" he asked, smiling and nodding toward the tote bag where the dog's leash peeked out.

I blinked, my heart rate increasing rapidly. "How did you know he went to the vet?"

He laughed lightly, rubbing the back of his neck and averting his eyes.

"Oh, you know, Charlie, love. It's a small town. People, well, they just like to gab. Plus, I think I saw your SUV parked out front while I was grabbing coffee next door. Pretty easy guess."

I offered a polite but tight smile. Something about his comment made my stomach shift. The timing felt too precise, too easy.

I thought about that brief moment, how his eyes

lingered too long on the car seat in the back. How he knew just a little more than he should.

It's unnerving.

But at that moment, I chalked it up to neighborhood coincidence. I told myself I was being paranoid. That I'm just tired.

I won't make that mistake again.

Once back at the house, I began brewing a cup of tea. I set the kettle aside and poured the glass of wine I needed instead, hoping it would settle my nerves. Just then, Baxter's head perked up and he started barking furiously, scampering toward the front door. I followed tentatively, far less eager than he was.

"Baxter, hush. Calm down, boy!"

I peered through the rippled window, catching the distinct silhouette of an officer's cap just outside.

My heart sank at the sight of him. Something told me this was not a visit of good cheer.

"Officer Cortez," I said as I opened the door just wide enough to keep Baxter from lunging out. "Hi, um, is everything alright?" My voice cracked in fear.

Why is he here?

"Oh, no," I blurted. "Is Martha okay?"

Cortez waved dismissively, calming my nerves only slightly. "My Martha's just fine, Charlotte. No worries." He crouched to scratch behind Baxter's ears. "I've got two labs at home, remember? What breed is this big guy again?"

"Irish Wolfhound," I replied, my voice still shaky. "A giant teddy bear he is. He'd probably lick an intruder to death."

Cortez chuckled, then straightened, his posture tightening as his tone grew serious. "I'm here on another matter.

One of your vehicles was found near the north side of the city, submerged in a river."

His words knocked the air from my lungs, and I gripped the doorframe to steady myself.

"What? Submerged? How?"

"It appears the vehicle struck a light pole and veered off the bridge. We pulled it out about an hour ago."

My stomach flipped. "Was there anyone inside?"

"No," he says, his voice measured. "But we found your husband's insurance card and an overnight bag. Is Will home?"

He gestured toward the house as if expecting Will to walk out at any moment. A bitter laugh escaped me. "My Will doesn't act on impulse," I whispered. "He's a planner. This ... none of this makes sense."

Cortez jotted something in his notebook, his face unreadable.

"You said bridge," I added, horrified at the idea of Will's vehicle crashing and going over. "You mean Will went over the bridge. In his car. Into the water. And now he's not home?"

"Charlotte," Cortez said gently, stepping closer. "He wasn't inside the vehicle when we pulled it out, but it looks as if someone was messing with his brakes. He seems to have lost control."

That should have brought relief. It didn't.

I staggered back. "Is that supposed to make me feel better?" I snapped before covering my mouth, ashamed. "I'm sorry, Officer. This is just ... it's too much."

He reached out, steadying me. "Let's get you inside."

"Was he hurt? Is he okay? You don't know, do you?" My voice broke. "If someone told you Martha was missing and her car was found in a river after a fight, would you be calm? I'm not okay."

"I understand," he said softly. "Let's sit down and get you some water. Then we'll head to the station."

I sank into a chair, numb. My thoughts were spinning in frantic circles. As he handed me a glass, I noticed a new email on my cell phone. The cancer center. A reminder for my upcoming chemo appointment. One Will should be attending.

But Will was missing.

I closed the message and drank the water he gave me.

"Charlotte, I will be waiting for you outside. You can follow me to the station."

I watched him leave. I wanted to badly to pretend this was all a dream, but I knew it wasn't. I grabbed my keys; Baxter padded up, ears perked. I gave him one last treat and a pet.

Once in the car, my eyes landed on Will's to-go cup, his peppermint teabag still hanging from the side. My chest caved. That cup. One of the many he leaves around the house. Normally, it annoyed me. Now, I'd give anything to find another.

He's alive. I'd know if he wasn't. I'd feel it.

I followed Cortez's cruiser down the road and called Sadie. She answered on the third ring, chipper and oblivious.

"Hey! What's going on? Does Mom still have the kids?"

"Sadie," I interrupted, trying to keep it together. "Will is missing." It was the only way I knew how to get it out.

"What?!" she gasped.

"His car was found in the river. The police think someone messed with his car."

She spiraled into a string of questions, but I barely heard her. My mind replayed our fight. How he walked out. The way I let him.

I focused on the road, trying not to tail Cortez too closely.

"Did you call Marla or any of his friends?" Sadie asked.

"No. I didn't even think to. I just ... I don't want to raise alarms until I know more."

"Remember the last time he vanished for a night? Slept in a hotel parking lot because you were fighting?"

"I remember."

I pulled into the police station lot. "I have to give a statement. I'll call you after."

"Love you, Char. I'm praying. It'll be okay. God always has a plan, even if it isn't what we want."

"True. Love you, too," I whispered. Even though I knew the words were true, I still ached for him.

Chapter 6

Charlotte – Eyes Upon Us

I felt it before I saw it, that bone-deep awareness that something was terribly off. As I brushed Molly's hair upstairs, there was a feeling lodged within my chest that someone was watching.

I dared not glance at the window just to the side of the mirror, but it was like a magnetic pool.

Instead, I focused on tangled locks. Gently and methodically running the brush through each strand of curls.

But that feeling grew intense. It was subtle but certain.

Look. Now.

I peered out the window, my eyes searching through each tree branch and shrub.

Nothing. Just the oak trees swaying, the shadows trembling along the gravel path.

The bathroom light buzzed behind me. I clicked it off and strained my eyes in the dark.

"Hmm. That is weird." I turned to look out the door.

Something was there. It was not a shape but a presence.

Heavy. Watching.

I couldn't explain how I knew, only that I did.

It wasn't the unease of a stranger; it was the specific dread that I hadn't felt in a while.

I pulled the curtains tight.

"Mommy, are you okay? You're acting weird," Molly asked as she clutched her doll in her hand.

I forced a smile. "Of course, sweet pea. Mommy is just tired, is all."

But my heart wouldn't slow.

I tucked Molly in early, kissing her twice, and then walked out of the room to peek in on Max. He was fast asleep, a book about dinosaurs on his lap.

Then I walked the perimeter of the house, Baxter at my feet. Every lock was set. The cameras showed nothing unusual, but Baxter was staring at the door, his ears alert.

"Baxter, what is it, buddy?" I asked, walking toward him.

"Easy," I whispered and knelt to scratch behind his ears. But he didn't seem calm. Instead, his body was stiff and unyielding. He let out a low growl, baring his teeth, and bolted for the back door, barking with an intensity that sent shivers down my spine.

"Baxter!" I called sharply, but he didn't stop. Once out the door, he took off into the yard, ears pinned.

I ran after him, flipping on the floodlights.

He skidded to a stop near the edge of the property facing the tree line, tail rigid. Then suddenly he froze mid-growl and backed up, whining low in his throat.

My stomach dropped as I scanned the shadows. Nothing moved. Neither the wind nor the air vibrated. Just a terrible stillness.

Then—*scrape.*

My head jerked upward.

A soft, dragging sound. *Above.*

The roof.

I backed toward the house, breath hitching, my fingers trembling as I dialed 911.

Ten minutes later, Deputy Cortez arrived. Old, serious, and far too calm for my spiraling nerves.

"I didn't see anyone," I explained quickly, "but my dog's behavior changed fast. First alert, then submission. And then I heard something … on the roof."

Cortez circled the property while another officer walked the perimeter. Charlotte stood with her arms wrapped tight, watching the trees as if they'd shift.

They found nothing.

"No footprints. No signs of forced entry. Roof looks undisturbed," Cortez reported gently.

"But something *was* here," I insisted. "I *know* it."

Cortez hesitated, then offered the card she had already memorized. "If anything feels off again, call. But tonight, perhaps you should have someone stay with you. A family member, maybe?"

I nodded absently.

As soon as the cruiser disappeared down the road, I double-checked the locks again, just to be sure. The camera feed still showed nothing. But when I glanced at the lawn, a strange chill swept through me.

Someone had moved the planter on the back porch. Barely, just a few inches, but enough. Right beside it, a scrap of paper was half-tucked beneath the welcome mat. It was a cartoon flyer for the kids' school fundraiser.

Frowning, I thought, *Funny, I don't recall bringing that in yet. Had I?*

I told myself a gust of wind must've blown it over there, but a thread of unease tightened in my chest.

Then I called Sadie.

"I need you and Geoff here tonight," I said, my voice low, slightly trembling. "Something's not right. And I don't want to be alone with the kids."

"Why, what's up? Wild animal again by the lake? Last time it was that coyote, right? Or was it a tiger? I can never remember."

Despite the situation, I couldn't help but laugh at my sister; her commentary was always comical. "Sadie, there are no tigers that roam freely in the United States, especially in this part of the West Coast."

"Oh, duh, I mean cougars." She scoffed. "Well, no worries, we can come." Then she paused and yelled, forgetting to remove the phone receiver from her mouth, "Geoff, we're going to Charlotte's for the night!" Charlotte held the phone away from her ear.

"Thanks, Sadie."

I sank onto the couch, Baxter curled tight at my feet, still watching the back door, still tense.

The cameras filmed nothing. But I still couldn't sleep.

I knew better than anyone to trust the silence.

Chapter 7

Will – Saved

W hen Will woke up, he knew immediately whose bed he was in—and that terrified him.

The sheets smelled like lavender and smoke. The kind of smoke that clings to clothes, to memory. A soft hum floated from somewhere outside the room, a record player, probably. Classic jazz. Miles Davis, maybe. Something experimental, something intimate.

His body ached in places he didn't remember injuring. The bandages on his arm were tight, professional. The painkillers had dulled the sharper edges of the accident but not the dread. That was growing.

Will sat up slowly, careful not to disturb the tray on the nightstand: a glass of water, a bottle of ibuprofen, and a note in narrow cursive:

Rest. You're safe here. H

Safe. The word pressed down on him like a lie wrapped in silk.

Will swung his legs over the side of the bed and stood, wincing, his ankle throbbing. There were clothes laid out, his, or at least they used to be. A hoodie from college. Sweatpants that looked familiar. She'd kept them. That detail curled something uneasy in his stomach.

He moved slowly into the hallway, the wooden floor creaking underfoot. The house hadn't changed. Not really. Same creaky steps, same framed record covers on the wall, same yellowed map of South America by the front door. It was all the same yet somehow different. Nostalgia tried to crawl in, but he slammed the door on it.

Then Will saw her.

Hannah.

She stood in the kitchen, back turned, stirring something on the stove. Hair pulled back in a messy knot. A different version of the girl I used to know. Older. Wiser, maybe. Definitely more guarded.

"You're awake," she said without turning.

Will didn't respond right away. Just watched her.

"How long was I out?"

"A day. Maybe a little more. You had a mild concussion. Some broken ribs. Bruised ankle. Could've been worse."

She finally turned around. There was something unreadable in her expression. Not joy, not malice. Something between obsession and concern.

"Why didn't you take me to a hospital?"

"Because he was still out there. I didn't want him to find you. Or worse—follow you back to your family."

Will sat heavily at the small dining table. Everything in him wanted to scream, but the rational part held tight.

"You saw Baker?"

"Yes. He tampered with your car. I caught him in the act. I was watching from the trees."

Will closed his eyes. Not because he didn't believe her, but because he did. That was somehow worse.

"You're still watching us."

She didn't deny it. "I didn't know where else to go, Will. Watching you, your family ... it helped. Kept me steady."

"That's not healthy, Hannah."

"Neither is almost dying. And yet here we are."

Silence stretched.

She placed a bowl of soup in front of him. "Eat. Then we can talk about what happens next."

Will didn't touch the spoon. He just stared at her—the woman who once said she loved him, crying in the middle of a storm on a windswept beach. The same woman who might now be the only thing standing between him and a killer.

A familiar stranger.

Chapter 8

Charlotte – Red Flags & White Coats

I t was always in the evening when the pain began, originating in my lower abdomen. It started on the right and then pulsated there for a while before radiating downward toward my legs and my back. For months, unexplained exhaustion and pain had haunted me. I tried to dismiss it as another cyst, but deep down, I knew this was different.

One morning, I had woken up with bags under my eyes after a difficult night's sleep. I grabbed my computer and dropped myself on the couch. The news was something I watched routinely. It provided a sense of nostalgia at the muffled crime being reported. Coffee was how I jumpstarted my day. Wearily, I started researching each symptom slowly, scrolling through each ailment with intense precision. I had at least an hour before my oldest softly patted down to the foyer, rubbing his lashed eyes with his bed head on full display.

I had experience dealing with stomach pains, ulcers, various muscle tears, cysts, cancer, etc. I started to mentally list each affliction as if at the grocery store. Those that occurred daily and those that came and went were marked with an x or a check mark. Tiny nails hammered at my head. My energy had become so depleted that just walking to the bathroom would make me feel as if I had run a marathon.

As a child, my mother dismissed my ADHD as mere restlessness. Now, facing a fatigue so profound I couldn't pour a cup of coffee, I wondered if I'd always been battling something deeper.

The sudden feeling of being winded and tired from the moment I woke up had struck me as incredibly odd. It had been happening for several weeks now, and the paranoia had been deafening. Next to the cacophony of voices bellowing in my head, I had been experiencing a new aversion to food. The official terminology for this was satiety. I had no more wanted a beloved cheeseburger than I wanted a slap to the face. It was as if my taste buds were on strike. I would take a bite of food and then instantly be satisfied. I had become a dieter's dream.

To add to the list of oddities, another symptom was the constant sensation of having to go to the bathroom. I had been experiencing the urge to pee worse than post-pregnancy. The sprint to the toilet, followed by an Amen, had waved a red flag, as well.

Sex felt like a dark, ritualistic act, as if a knife had been thrust inside me. The intense, pulsating pain was always followed by my verbal groans of agony.

My checklist had been providing substantial evidence pointing directly at the "C" word. Forums under the title of ovarian cancer, with others experiencing similar symptoms, had reported the same satiety and cold chills. Some had boasted stories of success, while others related sob stories of their impending demise. It had painted a far too realistic picture of what my future could hold.

My mind had spun out of control. I closed my eyes for a moment to picture myself bald and hooked up to an IV, and recoiled at the thought. If I had been asked to take a personal stance, I would not have succumbed or accepted this fate. I would have stood up, instantaneously determined to equip my brain with a defense mechanism to defeat the incoming negativity.

I had finally relented and decided to call my gynecologist to schedule an appointment. Post research, I knew what questions to ask the doctor. Will came home exhausted from his workday, gave me a peck on my cheek, and cracked a smile. He grabbed a dinner plate and sat at the table, chewing as he talked out of the side of his mouth, "How was your day today?" He had salsa dribbling down his chin and was stuffing another bite in his mouth. I turned around so as not to face him.

"Oh, you know, it was the same old. I took Max and Molly to the park. Then we had a play date with Sam and Annie in the afternoon post-nap."

I had paused for a moment, trying to contemplate whether to tell him my cancer theory, and surrendered.

"Babe, that pain was bad last night, and it's been consistent throughout the day. Lately, I've practically been forcing myself to eat. I'm absolutely exhausted every damn day."

He looked up, the three tacos had somehow vanished. Then he sat back in the wicker chair as if contemplating my comment.

"Hon, you just had Molly like six months ago. You're fine. You're just super tired, that's all. She hasn't slept since the moment she was born. Now she hits the twelve-hour stretch, and your body is all askew. Just give it time to get back to its old self."

Just like that, he had single-handedly made me feel crazy. I sighed aloud, hoping for him to backpedal, but to no avail. Will always hated my tendency to overreact. The need to defer to the web for my diagnosis drove him crazy. I hadn't thought of myself as a hypochondriac per se, but rather in tune with my body.

"Well, regardless, I decided to check in with Dr. Pazano to have a quick check-up. Anyway, I was supposed to get checked after I had Molly, and I never went. So, I am long overdue."

He got up and washed his plate. As he walked out, he stopped and gave me a quick kiss.

"If it makes you feel better, then by all means. Better to be safe."

Later that week, I had my appointment with Dr. Pazano. It was on a Friday morning. I had been able to get Marla to watch Molly and Max while I went to get checked. She didn't exactly know why I was going. I had decided not to tell her my neurotic thoughts just in case everything turned out fine. Marla had been more than eager to help, but I could tell that, despite her best efforts not to ask, she visibly wanted answers.

After I had checked in at the front desk, I grabbed the book I had brought and began to read. Fifteen minutes later, the side door opened, and a nurse called my name.

"Mrs. Rose, we are ready for you now. Please follow me to the exam room. Number two. It is the second door on the right."

The nurse had perfect bone structure, a smooth

complexion that hinted at Botox. I estimated she had at least a decade on me, but her love for needles cast a shadow on her age. She was busying herself setting up when she turned to ask, "So you are due for your wellness check. You need both a pap screen and a breast exam. Are you okay doing it all now, or would you like for us to schedule you to come back later for them?"

She stopped and looked at me. She noticed the void in the air and forced herself to make eye contact with me, despite her efforts to remain fixated on the screen. I recall her eyes being a darker shade of brown. I was able to tell that she had not slept much the night prior, as the bags under her eyes were a dark shade of purple. In the right light, it looked as if she had taken a hit.

"I am okay doing all that is needed today. I might as well." I smiled softly.

"Great. I will need you to go ahead and change out of your clothes and put on this gown. When you are done, just have a seat on the exam table. The doctor will be in shortly."

Before she walked out, I hurried to interject, "Excuse me, Nurse?"

She had stopped and turned around; the door was slightly ajar.

"Might I get a CA-125? I have been having some intense pain in my lower right abdomen. I seem to have all the symptoms of ovarian cancer. I also am pretty sure I have another cyst."

She came back inside at my words. The hall was still visible through the open door. She stood a bit closer to me, and I inhaled a whiff of onions. It was repellent.

"Ma'am, we do not administer those tests unless the doctor thinks you need one. It is highly unlikely."

I had been patient enough, but to make me feel as if I was melodramatic was the tipping point.

"Excuse me, but I know my body, and you do not. I know I have a cyst, as I have a history of them. This is not typical of my previous ones. I have a right to ask for the test to be completed, and I expect you to request it."

My heart was racing as if I had just been sprinting. I had been too forceful, so I forced a sweeter tone.

"I would appreciate having closure. I would also request that an ultrasound be done to determine how big my cyst is."

With a huff and an exorcist roll of her eyes, she clearly had been annoyed.

"I will ask the doctor and see what she says. By the way, it is Dr. Sanders today. Dr. Pazano will not be able to attend to you. Unfortunately, she is out sick." She spun on her heels at that.

A few minutes passed when she knocked and asked me to follow her. "This is the ultrasound room. Please lie on this table and put your feet up in these straps. I am going to use this machine to have a look inside."

I had absolutely hated this part of the exam. To me, there had never been anything so invasive. No one had bothered to buy me a drink. Nope, it had been straight to the table with my legs spread wide open.

As I did what I was told, I began to feel a pressure in my lower abdomen as she had proceeded to move the probe around.

"I'm sorry if this is uncomfortable. Just give me a few

more moments to snap some images for her." I had not been able to help wincing at the pain.

"Is it a cyst after all?" I had asked.

"From what I can tell, possibly. The doctor will go over your results in a few minutes. Just get yourself cleaned up and go back to the original room you were placed in."

She sanitized her equipment, ripped off her gloves, and exited the room. I stood up, cleaned myself from the sticky lubricant used to ease the probe in, and walked back to the exam room. I put my clothing back on and then sat and waited. When the doctor came in, I sat back at attention. She had white-blonde hair in a French twist and thick, plastic reading glasses. She appeared to be holding my chart in her hands.

"Good morning, Mrs. Rose. My name is Dr. Sanders. I have been partners with Dr. Pazano for a few years now. We were both at the same practice years ago, before once again joining forces here. She is out sick today, so I am going to fill in for her. I'm sorry she is unable to see you today, but rest assured, you are in good hands. By the looks of it, you have some concerns as well as a pretty decent-sized cyst in your abdomen. Do you mind going through all your symptoms for me?"

She proceeded to sit down in the stereotypical round chair perched high on wheels and started typing into her computer as I began.

"Yes, certainly, I've been experiencing changes in my sleep patterns and difficulty waking up. I'm also dealing with persistent fatigue and a sense of fullness after eating. Additionally, I've noticed increased frequency in needing to use the bathroom, changes in my bowel habits, and pain during sexual intercourse. I've also had abdominal pain, which may be related to the cyst, with the pain radiating down my lower back and legs."

Dr. Sanders finished typing and looked at me, her eyebrows drawn together in a serious manner.

"Charlotte, due to your symptoms and the cyst that is showing on your imaging, I would like to move forward with your request for a CA-125 draw. It will not take very long, and we can do it right here. We can even give you your results prior to you leaving if you have an hour or so."

I felt a weight being lifted and smiled. "That would be great, thank you."

She stood up and grabbed my chart as she began to exit the room.

"The nurse will be back to walk you to the phlebotomist, and then you will wait in a different room near my office."

I nodded gently. "Sounds good, thanks."

The nurse came back just as the doctor was leaving. "Go ahead and follow me; there is no line, so you are up first." I followed her down the hall, decorated with abstract art portraits. A younger black woman with beautiful light brown eyes stopped to greet me as I approached. "Have a seat, Sweetie. It will only take but a minute, and I promise it won't hurt."

She grabbed her plastic string and began to tie it around my arm.

As the circulation abruptly cut off as if on cue, she flashed a warm smile. Rainbow colored braces filled her mouth.

"Squeeze your fist shut. Make it tight for me. Okay, yes, perfect, yes, that's great." She capped the small tube and covered the area with a swatch of gauze. She then pulled the needle out gently and discreetly placed a band-aid on the tiny hole. "All is good, Mrs. Rose. You are free to go wait down the hall to the left. It is that very last door on the right. This should take about thirty minutes at the very most."

I got up and turned to walk down the hall. Doctors, nurses, and admins filled with the buzz of the daily grind flashed past me without noticing the fear in my eyes. I made my way to the room and closed the door behind me, desperately needing a little peace and quiet to pull myself together. I didn't want to sit on the exam table with the medical paper already drawn for fear of ruining it since I wasn't getting examined. So, I turned and sat on the chair adjacent and pulled out my phone to fill my time with a cancer prompt on my A.I. generated assistant.

Thirty minutes had easily gone by when I received a text from my older sister. *"Hey, how is it going? Any news yet?"* I heard my sister's concern in her voice. It brought an easy smile to my lips. She had always taken the role of big sister seriously. She knew my concerns. Although positive, her words had not been able to mask her nervousness.

My response was quick. *"Just finished my labs, ultrasound, and am post-checkup. Waiting on blood work."*

Ellipses had appeared, and with a sharp ding, the next text had appeared. *"Keep me posted. I'm at work, but can take a call if you need me. Don't worry, Charlie, you'll be okay. Have faith."*

I added a quick thumbs-up and exited the screen, then went back to my depressing internet search. I read article after article about cancer, and I was about to click on the forum that had been started in 2012 with the title, *"Help, I Have Weird Symptoms,'* when there was a light rap at the door. I placed my phone back in my purse.

Coming back in, Dr. Sanders once again took a seat on the rolling stool that had been hidden just under the computer desk. She opened the file in her hand and tilted her gaze downward toward the data that lay before her. Taking off her glasses, she placed them on her lap.

Without a glance back up, she had begun, "Mrs. Rose, as I reviewed your labs, both the ultrasound and your blood markers indicate that there's a need to have a further check conducted by a different kind of doctor."

She paused and looked up, pushing her glasses back onto the top of her head. This pause for effect gave me all I needed to mentally focus on what she was about to say, and I suddenly realized I'd been holding my breath. When I finally exhaled, a long-winded and labored attempt, a look of concern swept across her face. I knew that my suspicions had been right.

"I highly recommend that you make an appointment with a good friend of mine. Dr. Berkley is an oncologist at the cancer center here in town. She is fantastic, and I think that she will be able to assist you best at this point. You see, your CA-125 came back at a higher level than I would prefer for your age and stage in life. Paired with your cyst, which is reading at a ten, I believe it could be indicative of a form of cancer. Now, I don't want to alarm you; however, I do think she can provide you with the answers that you need. So, here is her card. I want you to call her tomorrow. I will shoot her an email shortly after you leave and let her know you will be contacting her shortly."

She handed me a business card, dark card stock embossed with blue lettering. I ran my fingers over the information as if it were braille. I felt the words and envisioned my future. At this premonition, the hairs rose on my neck, and I nearly dropped the card, the weight of its words almost unbearable. I had been hoping for a sliver of information, but the doctor was a Jedi at masking emotion.

"Thank you. So, um, does this mean I have cancer since you are referring me to her? To, I mean, an oncologist?" My words came out as a string of stuttering. I was able to feel the pulsating of my own heart as my anxiety began.

"Not necessarily, Mrs. Rose. I am referring you strictly as a precaution, due to your results. Dr. Berkley is more equipped to do your surgery and biopsy the cyst, should it require that. I am in no way referring to whether it is or is not cancer. I have no way of knowing that information at this point."

She smiled in an offhand kind of way. She lightly placed her hand on mine as she rose from her stool. "Please be sure to give my office a call and let me know what the doctor says." She walked to the door and held it open for me.

I stood up robotically as if a switch had been turned on. She pointed to the door on the right. "This is a quicker exit. Check out on the other side." I nodded as I walked in the direction she had indicated.

As I exited the building, the fresh breeze was what I needed to alleviate the pressure that had been building within me. I greedily sucked in the cool air, exhaling slowly as I walked to my car. Once inside, I let the heat of the day envelop me in its warmth.

The next couple of days were a blur. It was almost as if they had morphed together until I found myself sitting in the oncologist's office at the cancer center, waiting to be seen.

The beige room was bland and offered nothing to focus

on while I waited. I took out my phone and once again began to Google various cancers. It had quickly become a habit.

A tall, slender woman around my age walked in. She sported a medical coat over a light blue blouse and a navy pencil skirt, wearing matching navy flats and very little makeup. She seemed to be nice at first glance. She smiled and put out her hand for me to shake. "Nice to meet you, Mrs. Rose. My name is Karly Norman. I will be your nurse during this entire process."

Immediately, I zeroed in on her terminology. *What process had she been referring to?* "We will be determining what is going on internally with your body that would cause your CA-125 marker to come back elevated." She grabbed a chair and sat down with the office computer in front of her. "You mind running me through your current symptoms?"

So, I started to ramble off every ailment that I had since early in the year up to my current woes.

"Does it always hurt when you have intercourse?" She paused and looked at me mid-type.

"Come to think of it, yes. It's like a sex game gone wrong. It's excruciating at times. It feels like a knife jabbing into me, and at other times, it is more of a sandpaper feel."

She winced at the analogy I used, but recovered quickly with what seemed to be her trademark smile. "I can only imagine what that feels like." I gave her a half-smile and a shrug at that.

"Okay, so I have your allergies listed here as codeine. What does that do to you exactly?"

I cocked my head as I recalled the side effects. "It makes me extremely out of it, very drowsy, loopy." She wrapped up her report and stood up, grabbing a pink gown from the shelf on the left of the room. "Go ahead and put this on. I'll get you some warm blankets, so you can use them to cover yourself until the doctor comes in. It is always so cold in these buildings, so they might help."

She exited and quickly returned with two dryer-warmed blankets in hand. "These feel amazing. I could just roll up in them and fall asleep." She laughed at that. "Dr. Berkley will be in shortly, Charlotte." She drew the curtain before stepping out of the door and closing it behind her.

I changed into the gown and sat down on the examination chair. The warmth of the blankets penetrated my goosebumps and relaxed me. About fifteen minutes went by when I heard a light tap on the door. I turned off my phone and placed it down by my side.

Dr. Berkley was flanked by Karly. "Charlotte, it's wonderful to meet you. So, tell me, what has brought you in today?" After a few moments and mindless banter, the irritation within me began to grow. She knew what prompted this visit and was taking her sweet time getting to the point. I went through my history to bring her up to date.

She went on to say that she would need to remove the cyst to see what else she could find. This way, if there was something in there that didn't belong in my body, she had the experience to take care of it right then and there. We wrapped up the visit with an invasive pelvic exam, which I delighted in.

Dr. Berkley asked that I go downstairs and have a few more samples of blood drawn prior to my future surgery. Once I had been scheduled for it, I decided to text Will to get him up to speed.

Will: I went and saw the oncologist. She doesn't know anything further at this time, other than she would like me to do the surgery with her as my primary surgeon. We went ahead and scheduled it for next Tuesday, so be sure to take off work. I might need your mother to watch the kids, as my mom will want to be there with us. I'm doing blood work right now per her request. See you later.

I hit send and waited for the lady behind the window to call my name. The chat bubbles immediately emerged.

Okay, I will be sure to take off, just add it to the calendar. I will tell my mother, you just worry about getting healthy. It will all be okay, Charlie. Love you!

Eight vials later, I left with a slew of worries and hot pink tape on my arm.

Fast forward a couple of weeks post-surgery, and I received a call from the oncologist that my results had come in. I didn't have the nerve to go alone, so I called for backup since Will had back-to-back work meetings he couldn't get out of. I subconsciously thought I would want him there, but I didn't want to add additional pressure. I knew if I asked my mother, that it would be equally as comforting as if it were Will. Having both Will and my mother would be superfluous. I couldn't deter her from attending; I would never hear the end of it. I could also see the ball of nerves she had become in the days before the surgery.

My mother grabbed my hand and squeezed it tightly as we walked into the doctor's office. I was keenly aware that our roles had reversed. My mother lingered in a shroud of ignorance. I knew deep down inside that my mother, who had always been a pillar of strength, was scared. I sensed it on a different level. Her anxiety and angst buzzed with a loud energy.

We had been making small talk when there was a light knock on the door. I recognized that soft tap from my previous appointments. My assumption was correct when I caught sight of Dr. Berkley's smiling face. "Hi, Charlotte, and you must be her mother?"

My mother stood and gave the doctor a handshake. "Yes, I am her mother, Susan Escamilla. You can call me Sue for short." Her quick response gave away her Spanish accent.

She extended her slender hand to Nurse Karley, who was standing directly behind Dr. Berkley. Karley had always been keen on attention and was ready with a bright smile that displayed a row of glistening teeth. "Hi, I'm Nurse Karley. It's a pleasure." She then turned and started to busy herself as she fussed at the curtain and gathered things for Dr. Berkley.

She then took a seat in front of her computer and began to ask a few questions. The tension started to build within me. I wish that they would hurry it up. Was I riddled with cancer or not?

I started to go back down the pessimistic, vacant path of no return. I began mulling the possibility of cancer and other scenarios. My thoughts were graciously interrupted by Dr. Berkley. "Charlotte, Charlotte. Did you hear me?"

I shook my head and was brought back to reality when my mother snapped in front of my face. "Charlotte, the doctor is asking you a question."

I looked at my mother and then at the doctor. "I am so sorry, Dr. Berkley. It's just that my mind is so distracted lately. In all honesty, I just really want to know what my results are."

She clasped her hands together in her lap. "Yes, I was just asking if you were okay with your mother hearing, as well, before we begin going over everything." I felt my cheeks transition to a red hue in embarrassment. My mother was looking directly at me, and her perplexed face displayed embarrassment.

"I am so very sorry, Doctor. I hadn't realized, nor did I hear what you were asking."

Dr. Berkley waved her hand at that. "No need to apologize. I am very much aware of how patients become tense when they enter my office. There is no way around the anxiety of it all, I am sorry to say."

Looking at my hands twisted together in knots, I quietly stated, "Yes, she can stay and listen."

She opened my file and looked me square in my eyes. Before she had even spoken, my stomach dropped. I already knew. I began to get tunnel vision. Her words stopped registering. I was able to catch one statement that would change my entire life. "I regret to inform you that you do, in fact, have cancer. It is a very rare one at that. Clear cell papillary ovarian cancer, to be exact."

It faded to black then. Her voice had gone. I turned and tried to focus on my mother. I heard what might very well have been the wind being taken completely out of me. My brain was unable to recognize the words that had just been spoken.

As I looked at my mother, she stared blankly. In that moment, sheer terror overshadowed her with immense pain for me. As instantly as her vulnerability had displayed itself, it had gone. She turned and looked at the doctor as if she had made up her mind that this outcome was unacceptable. The alternative of my not surviving was simply unfathomable to her; therefore, the notion had been dismissed in her mind.

"Doctor, with all due respect, cancer is not a death sentence. God is the one who will determine the outcome."

Caught off guard, the doctor turned, looked at Charlotte, and then back at my mother. "Yes. Mrs. Escamilla, faith has a lot to do with how people can deal with this entire process."

My mother interrupted the doctor. "God is the only one that has to do with the outcome, with all due respect." She looked at me, intent on telepathically communicating that if I had cancer, I would be okay no matter what.

So that had been it. Cancer. Six rounds of chemotherapy, a full hysterectomy, and removal of my appendix and gallbladder. My new normal now is that I have cancer. Damn. Weeks later, I woke to find a big envelope tucked under the windshield of my car. I had an intense feeling that I had been followed. The envelope had been dampened from the morning dew, shown through a red hue. Slowly, I opened the tab for fear of what might be hidden within. Inside the envelope was a knit beanie. The scroll tucked inside had said:

"Keep warm, X."

Chapter 9

Charlotte – Strange Curiosities

There had been times when I received strange packages, a blue teddy bear left on my car one morning, and many other stuffed animals. Random books and, one time, even a book on parenting. There were times when Max or Molly mentioned seeing someone lurking near the lake, as well. Due to the distance, they had never been able to completely describe the individual. Will chalked it up to a local fisherman or bird watcher. I never felt it was an innocent passerby.

Months would trickle by before another sighting would occur. These unexplained, unnerving visitations had taken place sporadically during their formidable years. These had warranted little rationalization. How does one go about reporting such a thing? An upper-middle-class family in the heart of suburbia was being stalked. Sounds far-fetched.

Everything changed the day that the principal of Molly's school called to report that she had been talking to a stranger. My heart sank immediately. I had answered her call mid-run with heavy breath. Principal Stanton at their

Catholic school was frantic. She told me that Molly's teacher had seen her talking to a stranger during recess. When I asked who this individual was, she paused before stating that the person fled before they could get an identity. Mrs. Kayson, Molly's teacher, had reported that the individual was wearing an oversized hoodie that concealed much of their face. When Mrs. Kayson asked Molly who she had been talking to, Molly simply stated that it was a friend. She went on to say that her friend visited often and that they had met throughout the years, ever since she could remember. It puzzled Mrs. Kayson and caught her off guard. She decided then that she should notify Principal Stanton.

That same afternoon, when I had gone to pick up Molly, I asked her about it. "Hey, Molly Polly, what did you do at school today? Did you have fun?"

Molly smiled in the rear-view mirror. She grabbed her markers and began to draw. "Yup, Mommy. We learned about shapes today, and I was in charge of Simon Says."

I offered a smile in hopes of picking up on any nuances. I fixated my eyes upon her as she sat coloring, hoping that my concentration would allow me to infiltrate her five-year-old mind. "So, who did you play with or chat with today? Did you play with Olivia or Hazel?"

She continued to color, answering without looking up. "Yup, we played princesses on the playground today. It was fun! Then my friend came to tell me 'Hi' and that she wanted to be a princess, too."

I pressed on, "What was her name?" Molly shrugged.

With every moment that went by, there was a deep drumming of my heart. I swerved off the street and barely missed a truck with a landscaping trailer hitched to the back. I managed not to screech to an abrupt halt. I focused on slowing my breathing and began to regain my composure. The tremors in my hands would have given me away to any passerby. "Molly, what friend are you talking about?" My voice wavered despite the showing of my teeth.

"My friend, the one who always stops by and talks to me."

My knuckles turned pale white from the tight grip I had on the steering wheel. "Umm, honey, tell Mommy what friend you're talking about."

Without missing a beat, she responded, "Her name is Anna. She is sweet."

Anna. My blood ran cold. I hadn't heard that name in years, not since Will told me that was what Hannah sometimes called herself when she was trying to blend in. A childhood nickname. Back when she still clung to soft edges. My brain screamed with clarity. *Anna was Hannah.*

"I like her. She's pretty, and she is always nice to me. Every time I see her, I ask her to come talk to you and Daddy. She tells me she is too shy, and she doesn't have very many friends." At that, she paused in reflection, the red crayon hovering over the page in mimicry of her thought process. "I tell her that you are nice and that you can play together, but she always shakes her head no and tells me that we are okay being secret friends. So, I told her, Okay." At that, her crayon had begun to dance across the page once again.

I internally screamed at the information my daughter had so innocently just shared with me. I had always been afraid of this scenario, and now I had come to live and breathe it. Warning signals had gone off like a signal lost at sea. Where had my parenting failed? Why had Molly felt that this woman could be trusted so easily? I thought about my history, her history, their history. I cringed at the thought that this had taken a turn for the worse. I wondered what she looked like. It was the only way to be sure. Hannah had been Will's ex-fiancée. They had dated for years. When I came into the picture, things had not gone the way they had originally planned. We had known of each other, Will and I. It had been through mutual friends and family. We had merely been a product of our environment. Will and I had married right after he had called off his engagement to her. One could say it had changed Hannah forever. How could it not? I had then given birth to Max, not long after that. People had specu-lated that it was an impromptu shotgun wedding.

It had nothing to do with the sweet bundle of joy I had given birth to. Alas, people talked. I guess in her case, vengeance had been born. We'd always been starkly differ-ent. Rumors began. I was like a rhinestone megaphone; Hannah had been meek and shy. Sometimes, I thought that was what had initially drawn Will to me. That was years ago. What had prompted Hannah to come back? Why had she decided to target Molly? For how long has this been going on?

I glanced in my rear-view mirror, where Molly had her head down, intent on coloring. "Molly, can you look up at Mommy really quickly so I can see your pretty eyes?" Molly's doe eyes had caught my reflection in the rear-view mirror.

"Yes, Mommy?" I paused the podcast to ensure that I had her full and undivided attention. "Can I ask you a question about your friend, Anna?"

Molly turned her head innocently to the side, perplexed

at my question. She continued to stare at me, blankly, eyes void of emotion.

"You said you always talk to Anna. So, can you tell me how long you have known and talked to her? Where do you talk to her? Can you tell Mommy what Anna looks like?"

She blinked before she had reverted to coloring, "Okay, Mommy."

I smiled and patiently waited for the rest of her response. "I've known Anna from when I was small. I don't remember how old I was. I just remember she would come up to me and talk during playtime at school or when I was out in the backyard with Max. She's always nice to me. She always asks how school is. She even asks about you, Max, and Daddy. I think she was friends with Max before me. Baxter even loves her. He especially loves the treats that she brings."

I clenched my teeth together, thinking of Baxter. What a sellout, even my own dog betrayed me. In the process, I had bitten my tongue and had drawn enough metallic taste in my mouth to know it had been bad. Every nerve exploded with a sensation I had never felt before. "Ouch." I grabbed a Kleenex from my purse and dabbed at my small injury.

"You okay, Mommy?" I smiled awkwardly with the tissue sticking to my tongue.

"Yes, darling girl. Mommy just bit her tongue. Have you ever done that? It hurts when you do."

She let out a giggle and acted like I had been silly on purpose. "No, Mommy. Why would I bite my tongue?"

I attempted to continue the conversation and tried to pick up where we had left off. "So, Molly, what does Anna look like? What color hair, skin, and eyes does she have?"

As she looked down, she nonchalantly said, "She has long curly, red hair, like Rapunzel. And big blue eyes, like a Barbie. Her skin is like mine, though not like Max's. She kind of looks like Moana. She doesn't wear pretty clothes, though. I don't ever see her in dresses like you. I don't think she likes make-up either. She also has little polka dots on her face like Max and Daddy." She scrunched up her nose to make her point, and I had to smile at that. She had visibly shrugged in Hannah's disinterest and was clearly disappointed.

I kept driving, wondering how she had aged after so many years had passed. Her social media had always been private to me, but had shown a distinct following. I was curious, but always refrained from succumbing to temptation and googling her. I knew nothing of her as a result. There was no real social media footprint other than her Instagram. To me, when people had zero social media outlets under the age of fifty, it warranted a red flag. What were they trying to hide? Had she been riddled with valleys under her eyes? Had there been cascades of white tresses hidden within her mangled mane. I had always wondered what I would do and say if I ever saw her again.

I had always wished her well. The last time I saw her, she had approached me at my bachelorette party. It ended in a heated altercation. She had been inebriated. Adorned with ostrich feathers and a corset that had stifled my breathing, I told her that she had crossed the line. When she proceeded to say that I stole her life, my sister, Alex, usually extremely patient, had heard enough. Like a bull off a leash, Alex, mere inches from her face, stated she had best depart. Since then, I have yet to see or hear from her. I caught Hannah murmuring under her breath that I'd burn

in hell. Those words, unknowingly at the time, had penetrated my skin and cinched away at my soul. Hell wasn't a
place I had ever yearned to be. Quite the contrary. I had
always assumed I would make the trek to heaven's gates
one day.

Once back at the house, I resembled an octopus with
items draped every which way as I walked in the door. With
labored breath, I threw our things onto the mud room
console. I instructed Molly to feed Baxter. She obeyed my
instruction, as I heard Baxter's excitement at her arrival. I
had a bit of time before Will and Max were to arrive, so I
had decided coffee would soothe my oncoming headache.
My body continued to remain on edge. I was in desperate
need of something stronger, but the hour was too early to
warrant a glass of California's best.

I fixed my coffee with a splash of cream and made my
way to my computer. I melted onto the tufted chair, and my
eyes drifted upward before I started typing. The lovely
weather had a way of instantly putting my mind at ease. It
was a beautiful day, the sky a blanket of blue devoid of
white. The woods were clear of fog and framed the lake
perfectly, with water so still that it resembled glass. The
image of the woods lay mirrored in water.

A ripple, ever so slight, had begun to make waves. Any
lake, I wouldn't shudder at the thought of a single ripple,
but this wasn't any ordinary lake. It seemed as though a
boat had caused it. I immediately stood, alert to the movement—but I hadn't seen anything that could have triggered
it. Still, I had to push the thought aside. My imagination
was clearly getting the better of me. *Too much excitement,
Charlotte, it's nothing.*

I logged into my computer and went straight to the

search engine. I typed in *'Hannah Charles California'* and instantly received thousands of results. I balked at the work that had lay before me. Frustration hit me. I then attempted to lessen the results by adding *'Crescent City, California.'* The thousands of hits had suddenly been minimized to twenty-three. Twenty-three hits were doable. I began to go through birth years and finally came to one Hannah Charles, born in 1981. I clicked on the link to find the last known residence. That of which had been Crescent City, California. Despite my desperate pleading with my computer, the actual address could not be disclosed. It had been a small blessing. Had it shown, I would have impulsively showed up at her house.

Sitting back, I wondered why she had stayed in Crescent City. I had to know why she decided not to leave. I pushed away the gnawing feeling in the pit of my stomach that told me it was Will. Had she been stalking my children regularly, unbeknownst to me? I wish I had known each time she had come to visit with them. If I had known from day one, I could have prevented it. This was a parenting failure I knew I would never get over. I had not wanted to ask too many questions for fear of Molly becoming overwhelmed. It had not been as bad as it could have been.

I heard a door slam and knew that Max and Will had arrived home. I headed toward the kitchen, where I knew that Max would be raiding the pantry in search of rations. Sure enough, when I walked in, all I saw was his backside and his face buried in the bins.

"Max, I got those crackers you like. They're underneath the chips." He barely looked up as he grabbed for them.

"Thanks, Mom. I found them. I'm starving. I could eat

a cow." He turned around with a big smile so full of teeth and crackers that I had to suppress a laugh.

"Max, wash your hands before you eat those crackers, please." He gave an eye roll and walked to the sink. "How was school, bud?" He began to air-dry his hands, swinging them back and forth dramatically while offering up a smirk.

He knew how this action irritated me, but I relaxed as he began to respond.

"Good, good. I got to partner with Sam today for a project, so I am excited about that. We get to research an animal, and we picked the sloth." I couldn't contain my laughter at this revelation.

"What made you both pick the sloth?" I asked as he cracked a smile at my show of amusement.

"We both think they're funny-looking creatures, but they're still kind of cute in an ugly way. Sam is going to ask his mom if he can come over here this weekend to work on it. Is that okay?" I nodded in approval.

"Yes!" he raised a fist pump at his excitement as he walked out to the back porch, where Molly was playing with Baxter.

As he had closed the door, Will walked in, his hands full of various items. I quickly ran over to help him. "I swear you can say this boy's name a hundred times, but the selective hearing is strong with him!" I laughed.

"I understand that struggle. It's every single day." I paused slightly before continuing.

"Hey, babe," I started putting up the groceries he had brought in. He turned around as he had been about to walk toward the mud room with his gym bag in his hand.

"Yeah, what's up?" I turned around to look him in the eyes.

"We need to talk, so go put your things away and just come back over here. Okay?" His face had instantly dropped with both disappointment and worry.

"Is everything okay? Oh, yeah, you mentioned you wanted to talk when I got home. I completely forgot. Oh no, did the kids get into any trouble?"

I shook my head and repeated what I had said prior. "Go put your things up."

He turned to go, and before he had time to walk back, I grabbed him a beer. I was about to pop the top when he came back. I held the beer out to him and directed him to sit down at the bar. I poured myself a glass of wine and sipped it gently before starting.

"Uh oh, this must be serious. Everything okay?" His face had suddenly turned solemn. I didn't know why I was nervous. Maybe it had been the mere mention of her name. I wasn't sure how he would take it all.

"So, Molly's principal called me this afternoon. She said that Molly was caught talking to an adult outside the fence during recess today. Before she could confront the person, they turned and ran off." His eyes widened with astonishment.

"Did the cameras catch their face? What did Molly say? Was it a man? What the hell?" He started to visibly get upset, rightfully so. I waved my hands to calm him down.

"Firstly, no to all your questions. I did have a small chat with Molly on the way home. I didn't want to alarm her or get on her either. She's a good kid and always has the sweetest intentions." Will nodded.

"Yeah, but we need to make sure she knows the definition of a stranger, too." I closed my eyes and nodded my head.

"Yes. I know. It's a fine line when you are her age. Anyway, she told me that this person is a woman. A pretty woman. Her name is Anna, and she has brown skin and crazy red hair. She also said she has big blue eyes."

With that, he stopped moving completely and stared at me, confused as if he had been in deep thought. Slowly, the puzzle pieces had moved into place.

Click.

I visibly witnessed the connection. I nodded in approval to his realization that Anna was, in fact, Hannah, his ex. His face flushed red. If he had been a cartoon character, he would have been immortalized by flames.

"What on earth? What kind of sick game is this? I mean, what is she thinking?" I looked up at him and grabbed his arm gently in my attempt to soothe him.

"Will, calm down. I don't want Max or Molly to hear you. Bring it down a bit. Let me finish." He began to compose himself and took a swig of his beer. Immediately, he had slammed it down, almost cracking the bottle. Beer had bubbled up and spurted all over the counter.

"This is insane." I got a paper towel to wipe up the spill that he had made and continued.

"So, Molly told me that apparently Hannah has been talking to her for a very long time. Since she can first remember. My first instinct is that it has been years, Will. Years that Hannah has been stalking us all. Not just us, though, obviously the kids, too. She knows where we live because Molly said she has been here. She knows where they attend school. Everything. What is the point? What does she want? I'm scared, Will, that she is aiming to do something to hurt them, to inevitably hurt us since we got together. She was supposed to be with you, marry you, and have children with YOU!"

I didn't realize how emotional I was until tears ran down my face. Will brought me in for a tight hug and soothed my hair.

"Listen, she will never touch our kids. I would be damned if I ever let that happen." Max and Molly walked in then, with Baxter trailing behind them.

"Uh, what is going on, Dad? Mom, is everything okay?" He looked at me as I rubbed the tears from my eyes. Molly clung to my waist to console me.

"Mommy, you okay. Don't be sad." I bent down and looked at them both.

"Mommy is okay, guys. I just get emotional every now and then. I love you two very much. Now go wash up for dinner." They hugged me and told me they loved me as they ran upstairs.

I heard Molly ask Max as they had walked up, "I don't understand why Mommy is upset."

Max quipped, "Well, sometimes it happens to women." I wanted to laugh through my tears, but found it hard. He must have heard Will say something in passing.

Will looked at me, his eyebrows drawn together with consternation. "I'm going to have to ramp up the security around here. Did her teacher say what the protocol is now that they know a strange person has been talking to Molly?"

I shook my head, "No, she didn't mention anything, come to think of it. I was so emotionally confused by what she was telling me at the time that I failed to even ask. I should probably call and inform her of the new information. I'll make it a point to tell Max's teachers, as well. Should we go to the police and notify them?"

At that, Will had stopped as he finished his beer and tossed it into the recycling bin. "I don't know. I mean, I just don't know about that. I want to say that Hannah would never hurt anyone, much less a child. Then I stop and remember her past. She didn't exactly have a good upbringing. Things change, though, and people, too. Life has a way of transforming people and making them do things they would not normally do. It has been a decade; we don't know anything about Hannah, really. I didn't even know that she lived here." I cocked my head at that statement.

Analyzing the lines strung across his face.

"She lives in Crescent, too. I couldn't get the exact address, though. I searched it right before you got home. So, she goes back and forth when she wants to drop in. It's freaking creepy. Who does that? I feel like we need to notify the cops, Will. Just so they have a record." Will nodded..

"You're probably right. I can call my friend's sister, the one who's a cop. She's been with the force for a long time now." He turned and started to walk out of the kitchen toward the office.

"I'll start dinner. It should be ready in about an hour." He signaled okay as he turned. I had pulled the chicken from the refrigerator and had begun preparing it when I experienced an intense sensation of being watched, raising goosebumps on my arms. My phone rang, and I jumped, almost dropping my wine glass on the floor. The waves of burgundy churning around the base of the glass. I closed my eyes, and no sooner had I begun to compose myself when my cell phone lit up. It said "private." When I picked it up, all I heard were the echoes of a dog somewhere in the distance. I shuddered and hung up. With my reflexes on edge, I rushed to lock the doors and set the alarm. I put on music to calm my nerves and began to slice the clean chicken into strips. Before I knew it, I had fallen into a deep, methodical cooking groove. My concentration was only interrupted by Baxter as he barked incessantly at the back door. I instantly jumped, and the knife cut into my skin. My finger flowed sticky goo from the wound.

"Damn it, Baxter! I could have chopped my whole damn finger off. What is it, boy?" I tried to clean out my wound and wrapped a paper towel tightly around my finger. I placed pressure on it as I walked toward the back door nervously. Peering through the glass, it had gotten so dark outside that I could barely make out the tree line in the distance.

Bam! A rabbit collided with the back door. I stared in horror at the bleeding ball of fur slumped over to the side. Its tiny body convulsing as if an imaginary hand was shaking it. Whatever it had been injured by had severely wounded it. There was no way that it was going to survive. I heard a blood-curdling scream fill my ears and suddenly realized that it was my own voice. Instantly, my throat felt strained, my air flow constricted. The movement had ceased, and all that had been left was a mound of wet hair in a ball.

Baxter had barked madly, getting Will's attention. "What's wrong? Is everything okay?"

I guess I forgot to keep the pressure on my finger because blood had splattered onto my cream blouse. It had dripped onto our oak wood floors. The patterns resembled little psychedelic flower bursts of deep, crimson red. My thoughts were interrupted by Will's voice.

"Charlotte, Charlotte, what on earth happened? Your

hand! Baxter, calm down! Cage!" The electricity of the moment made me lightheaded, or perhaps it had been the loss or sight of blood from my almost decapitated finger. I heard Baxter as he sprinted at Will's command to his cage in the mud room.

Will hurried to grab a towel and dampened it with water. He rushed over to find me frozen, the stiff cottontail lying before me. He wrapped the cloth gently around my wound, my finger throbbing as pulsing waves of pain surfaced like little knives at the injury site.

"What's happened? Charlotte? How did you cut yourself? What is with the rabbit? How did that happen?"

He sat me down at the kitchen table and poured me a glass of water. Suddenly, smoke tickled my nose, and panic set in, but my motions were slow and robotic. Will quickly picked up on the odor and ran to turn off the stove. Half the chicken and vegetables lay in the skillet, burnt to a crisp, while the other half lay sprayed with blood.

"I'm so sorry about dinner and about the floor. I don't know what came over me."

He went to look outside the door at the carcass of the unfortunate animal. "I mean, Jesus, this day has been filled with surprises. None of which has been very good."

I let out a derisive laugh, not directed at anyone. Mid-laugh, I felt out of sorts. The room started spinning, and my equilibrium was off.

"Ha, you're telling me. I was fine until Baxter started barking. It scared me. Then, I heard the sound of something hitting the door, and then I saw the rabbit. Well, you've seen the result of it all." I waved my finger in the air so he could see the wound clearly.

"It was out of nowhere that it ran into the screen door.

Good thing M&M have not seen it. Molly would have a fit and start crying."

He quickly walked to the cabinet and pulled out a trash bag and disposable gloves.

"Yeah, good thing they're too occupied with Disney to bother. He pulled on the gloves as he walked outside, and with a look of revulsion, grabbed a bunch of fur in his hands. Then he walked toward the garage where our trash bins are tucked away to prevent wildlife from getting at them, and discarded the lifeless bunny. He walked back inside, grabbing the spray cleanser and a roll of paper towels. He then proceeded to clean up the patio area and began scrubbing at the concrete as I stared in disbelief.

"Mommy, what was that noise? We heard a scream," Molly asked with concern.

Max walked toward me and noticed my hand and the blood on my clothes. He placed his arm around my waist, eyes locked on the cloth tightly wound around my hand. "Mom, are you okay?"

I looked at his sweet, freckled face and then back at Molly's flushed skin, their expressions reflecting deep concern.

"I'm okay, guys, I promise. Mommy cut herself because Baxter went nuts, and there was a dead animal outside, and I cut myself. Pretty stupid, huh?" Both kids had drawn their attention toward Will, who had just wrapped up cleaning and was now locking up.

"What was it? What kind of animal was it? How did it die?"

Will had let out a stifled laugh, his hands held up as if he were being arrested.

"Okay, guys, enough with the five thousand questions.

Let your mom breathe; that was a lot of excitement she just went through. First off, let's talk about dinner. Who wants pizza because Mom burnt our dinner?" he smirked, his boyish good looks had warmed me inside. We locked eyes a moment too long, telling me he had caught my thought somehow.

I mirrored him with my own burst of laughter. "I'll call for delivery. Who wants cheese and who wants the one with the yummy vegetables?"

They had squealed in rejection at this notion. "No, vegetables. Ew! Cheese! We want cheese! Lots of cheese! We are cheese monsters!"

All I had heard was Molly's monster sounds followed by a ripple of laughter from Max.

"Great, let me give them a call and make sure they put extra olives, mushrooms, and peppers!" Both kids had smiled widely at that. "Dad! Stop! We just want plain cheese."

Will laughed some more as he walked toward the office.

"Okay. Okay. Vegetable pizza with no cheese it is! You don't have to yell at me, guys. I heard you loud and clear." The kids ran behind him, and a crescendo of yelling and laughter followed. Will had the ability to playfully joke around with the kids. It was always one of my most cherished traits about him. No one could rile them up better.

I gently opened the cloth to check the severity of my wound. It seemed like Will's quick reflexes had helped to curb the intensity of the bleeding. It still had a vibrant hue seeping through the severed skin. I grabbed the first aid kit and rummaged until I found a cotton ball, Band-Aid, and hydrogen peroxide. Once my makeshift medical station was complete, I proceeded to remove the cloth around my finger. I placed my finger under the sink and rinsed it off completely. Then, I air-dried it for a bit. After a few moments had passed, I noticed the tattoo on my finger had been sliced perfectly in half. The inked words "Gambled Love" had been symbolic of Will and my relationship. Now it reads "Gambled" and then "Love." The irony was not lost on me. I had cut myself deep, but had not thought that I would need stitches. I poured a bit of peroxide on my wound and dabbed at it with a cotton ball.

I walked back through the house toward our room while I yelled out that I was going to take a quick bath.

I drew a hot, foamy bath, then stripped away my soiled clothes. As I had slipped into the tub with ease, I melted into the hot water and allowed myself to be cradled. Almost immediately, I relaxed. My heart rate slowed, and my breath calmed. The water was a bit too hot, and I could feel the intensity of the heat burning my skin. Somehow, the pain made me feel alive. It was exactly what I needed to fixate on to stop me from reliving the last hour. My mind had released memories as it spiraled backward in time. *What did Hannah want from Molly? Was she the one calling our home over the years? Had she left random things at our doors and windows? But if it was her, why? Why had she decided to come back after all this time? It had been over a decade. Had she not been able to secure her own life yet? Hadn't she been able to find her own happiness?* Then it had flickered to Hannah, my injured finger, the dead rabbit. If I were superstitious, I would call it a bad omen.

I shivered despite the heat, suddenly gripped by an instinctual urge to glance toward the small frosted bathroom window. Had I imagined the faintest shift of shadow through the glass, a passing shape that vanished silently into the night?

I was then pulled back to the present, my thoughts dissipating as quickly as they flooded in. The doorbell sounded, and seconds later, Baxter barked. I heard Will yelling, "Pizza is here!" Kids! Charlotte!" followed by a choir of cheers as the tiny feet padded from above to down below.

Hannah had grabbed my attention again. I had to make it my goal to find out more about her. I had to talk to Will again about implementing a new security system. We had to make sure Max and Molly always had GPS watches. I could not take any chances with them being left vulnerable and prime for attack. She had crossed the line, and I'd be damned if she had tried to hurt my kids. I quickly dressed in my pajamas and slathered cream on my face before walking into the kitchen to sauce-covered faces. Will was laughing at something Max had said when he patted the seat next to him for me to sit. I had a strong sense that something was approaching. Something that had an ominous vibe.

Chapter 10

Charlotte – Chemo Session

T his time, I remembered my own pillow. Last time, I forgot it. This was a game-changer, as hospital pillows were scratchy and stiff, and a trick I learned the first time I had cancer. As I lay back in my hospital recliner, I pulled my beige knit sweater tighter. It was chillier than I had anticipated. Fun fact, I had forgotten that due to chemo, I was susceptible to the cold. I felt like an eighty-year-old in a young person's body yet again.

I took in my surroundings. The room was small, but at least it had a few outward-facing windows that allowed me to see the vibrant display of trees, making me feel less like a lab rat and more like a human. The room smelled of disinfectant, and the fluorescent lights flickered to an inaudible beat.

I guess this is home for the next several weeks. I analyzed my veins and tried not to allow anxiety to feed my mind.

My head shot up as I heard, "Hello, hello, if it isn't my favorite ex-patient." Mariam, my nurse from my first chemo, walked in briskly. She was wearing her curly hair in a long ponytail and sported a bright smile.

"Mariam! I have missed you. I love the pink scrubs," I said, bubblier than I felt.

"Why, thank you, Sweetie. Are you ready?"

I forced a smile and shrugged, "I guess I have no choice."

Disregarding my comment, she busied herself. She grabbed me a warm blanket and tucked it around me. The warmth engulfed me. This small comfort somehow felt indulgent.

"How are you doing so far, my dear?" She touched my hand lightly. Her wrinkled, cold fingers were a contrast to my own. She was unlike any nurse I have ever had. I offered a smile at her genuineness. It was hard not to; she had an inviting disposition. I caught a glimpse of the cross hanging around her neck, and it instantly gave me relief. It helped that Mariam was faithful; it's something I wish more hospitals placed emphasis on, as statistics have shown an increase in overall morale in the face of a medical or tragic disaster. Mariam was my very own angel, my vigilant saint who adamantly prayed for my well-being, and it will never be forgotten.

"This session is five hours from start to finish. So, I'm starting the IV now. If you need anything, just let me know. This button right here calls me at the nurse's station right outside." She handed me a beige cord with a bright red button at the center.

"I'll check on you at the top of every hour. However, if you need anything at all, please press the call button. My job is to ensure that you are comfortable during this arduous process. The doctor will be in to check on you toward the end of the day."

Smiling at me with a kindness so profound, she dimmed the lights before closing the door gently. My body knew this shiny metal object didn't belong. It was going to continue to send pain signals until removed from my arm. The jab of the cold needle made me wince, and I felt lightheaded at once.

Taking a breath, my gaze met the glowing lights ahead. I closed my eyes and felt the heavy weight of the prescription drugs seeping into my veins. *Drip. Drip. Drip.* The poison snaked its way through my body rapidly. The medicated cocktail feeling more like a venom than a remedy.

I slowly allowed myself to drift away into a past time filled with adolescent love and lust. I slipped as far away from my present nightmare as possible until I was back to being the girl who stole Will's heart.

Chapter 11

Charlotte – Captivated

The day was crisp and cold. The Christmas season bringing forth a buzzing of anticipation that can be felt in the air like electricity. Earlier, when my boss asked me to work late, I had reluctantly agreed. After twelve hours of measured customer banter and a falsified disposition, I am spent.

I grabbed my phone, scanning it for the latest messages. I didn't expect to see anything other than the time glowing back at me. It was then that I caught a glimpse of a missed call, as well as a text from my older sister. *John is back. Only for a bit. Hurry home. William is coming, too.*

My eyes bulged at the three-syllable name on my screen. I raised my phone a bit closer to my face. Did I read that right? My beating heart was like hooves on a racetrack as I reread the message. The excitement filled my belly with nerves. His name was a trigger for the lustful anxiety that I felt.

I scanned the black letters again and stopped when I hit

his name. I read the text again and again for fear that his name would suddenly vanish as if a hallucination.

I conjured up his face in my mind and imagined his green eyes staring back at me. Pulled into the past momentarily, I recall his dark mass of unruly hair and his sharp features, intent on imprinting his face onto my heart. His eyes, those incredibly intense, kind, piercing green eyes, make me gasp.

I took a breath and whispered his name. Maybe on some level, he could hear me. Exhaling, I stood up, walked over to my locker, and quickly grabbed my purse. I walked the store, making sure I had everyone on my checklist completed before closing. As I went, I turned off the lights in each of the sections. One by one, I locked up and then set the alarm. Walking to my car, I could feel an energy in the air. Before getting in, I let the wind encircle me, the burst of cold sending a current running up my spine. Tonight was going to be perfect. If I will it, perhaps it will be. He will talk to me. I need him to see me in a different, non-platonic way, not as the insecure kid with bottle-cap glasses and rainbow braces that I once was. I need him to be drawn to me as much as I am to him. If I am going, then I am going to try my damnedest to get him to notice me. I hesitate at my thought. Some part of me unsure as to what I am thinking is right. I ponder this a moment longer, but overcome by an urge of impulsiveness, shrug it off.

I drove home with fierce determination. Tonight will be the night that catapults me into a whole new chapter of my life.

As I walked into my home, I was instantly hit with the aroma of Colombia's finest. My mother was stirring a freshly brewed cup of coffee while the boisterous banter of both Sadie and Alex could be heard in the distance. I gave mom a quick peck on her cheek as she gave me a finger to her lips. She mouthed, "It's your Aunt Elise. She's on the phone." I winked and headed toward the back rooms.

Sadie was sitting on her knees, leaning toward the floor-length mirror, applying her makeup. She was almost touching the mirror as she leaned in closely at a right angle to wisp mascara along her lashes. Her hot breath left a fading mark with each exhalation.

Alex was spread-eagled, lying on the bed with vintage albums scattered before her. Various fashion magazines were open to the likes of Cindy Crawford and Christy Turlington. "Hey now, here she is, the lady of the night."

I crinkled my nose up. "Lady? Come on now, I'm in college, that makes me sound ancient and grotesque. Who says that these days, anyway?"

Alex rolled over onto her back with laughter. She stared at a magazine in her hand and began to whine. "First off, Dad says it all the time when you both wear dark eye make-up." She pouted, "I'm bummed I can't go see this front and center."

She lay back with the back of her hand to her forehead, pretending she was a damsel in distress.

"Ma grounded me, so I must serve my sentence." I swatted playfully at her and then plopped down on the bed beside her.

"Hey, at least you have the Ramones to keep you company." She nodded her head.

"Truth. Thank goodness! So, what are you going to wear? It's kind of a big deal, first impressions and all. Sadie had been in the same spot for over an hour. So, this outfit of yours, if it's done wrong, it could ruin any chance you have with Will." I gasped and hit her in the arm again.

"I'm seriously freaking out, and you tell me that!" I got up and walked over to the closet that I shared with Sadie when I was home from college.

"I have the absolute perfect outfit for tonight. At least, I think it is. Tell me what you guys think." I rummaged through the closet, dismissing dress after dress as I went. I became excited the moment I saw the black number before me.

"First off, how do you even have that?" Sadie scoffed at me from across the room. Her eyebrow raised slightly as her lips curved up slowly into a wicked smile. "Secondly, I love it! You could do a smoky cat eye to really make your eyes pop."

Alex jumped off the bed and grabbed the hanger from me. "Um, how on earth are you going to get past Mom with that on?" I put my hand under my chin as if I was thinking, and then waved my hand at Alex like it was no big deal.

"This isn't my first rodeo, sister."

"I approve, black just looks so sultry on your skin. I can't wear that dark of a color without the contrast being too great. Unless it's August and I'm sun-kissed. Maybe pair it with a necklace of some sort to draw the eye? As for Mom, I got just the thing. Put pants on and a loose sweater to make it look like an outfit. She questions our fashion anyway, so it won't be out of place." That could work. It was not Sadie's first time at this. It was the smartest approach to my parental dilemma but unfortunately added to my moral one.

"Agreed." I walked over to our mentioned jewelry box

and ran my fingers through the various glass beads and gold chains before closing the box.

"Ugh." My hair swayed back and forth as I shook my head in disappointment. "What's wrong?" Alex said as she loudly smacked her bubble gum. It was a tick she's had since grade school. Mom used to give her gum to fill her mouth so she could think before she spoke.

"What about the gold heart Dad gave you? Maybe the black beaded necklace?" If only I had something subtle. I hesitated in thought before leaving the room en route to our shared bathroom. Moments later, I returned, dangling a simple black velvet ribbon. Sadie cocked her head and pursed her lips. Confusion furrowed her eyebrows. As I threaded it around my neck, I could see the lights go on with both my sisters.

"Al, can you tie it? Not too tight, though. As it is, I'm having problems breathing." Both Sadie and Alex nodded in unison. Al got up and expertly tied a simple bow around the nape of my neck.

"Bow in the front or the back? The back is better, I think."

Sadie chuckled. "Better for unwrapping!" Alex let out a high-pitched laugh.

"Seriously, guys? Quiet down. Mom will hear you!" I said as I continued to primp.

"Charlie, hurry the hell up already. We're already running late. I told John we'd be there within the hour, and well, we're well past that." I grabbed some makeup and shoved it in my purse. "Bye! Have fun!" Alex said excitedly. Sadie and I shouted back as we rushed out the front door to the car.

As we pushed open the heavy doors of the local bar,

The Uptown, a wave of nerves surged through me. We paused just inside the entrance, and Sadie squeezed my hand. "Are you ready?" I could tell she was as nervous as I was. I didn't know why, though. It was just William, Mark, and our own family. My feelings were irrational and wild. I felt as if I didn't have control of them. Sadie must have sensed my unease as she offered me a smile.

"Don't be nervous, you will be fine. You look great!" I felt calmer having her here.

"You do, too! Mark would be stupid not to realize that." We began to ascend dark, wooden stairs. I took in the odor of stale beer, thick smoke, and body odor and grabbed for my perfume hidden at the bottom of my purse to dab on a little more. I wanted William to remember my scent long after I was gone.

I hurried to catch up to Sadie, who was at the top of the stairs, gesturing for me to move quicker. She was dressed to impress tonight with the hope of catching Mark's attention. Her legs were bronzed and insanely long. The envy of every girl here. Her skin was supple and radiant with youth. Her form-fitted dress revealed her svelte figure, as her long hair cascaded down her back. She rarely wore her hair in any other way. If I had long blond tresses like she did, I would wear my hair down, too. Mark had been her childhood crush. He, too, ran in the same group of boys that William and our cousins were a part of.

As I neared her, she turned quickly.

"Charlie, I see them. Oh, my goodness, I can't. I just can't. I need to go to the bathroom like now. I need to freshen up and get my life together. Are you coming?"

My eyes veered toward where hers were looking, and that's when I saw him. There was this magnetic pull toward him. I caught his eyes right when the music beat picked up. He must have felt eyes on him. My body froze as his eyes fixated on me. The moment was both freeing and intoxicating. His green eyes instantly gave me goosebumps.

Time instantly halted.

The beat, somehow in the background, began to pulsate as my heart added to the rhythm. He offered a slight, upturned smile as he held his pool stick.

Suddenly, he broke his glance as a pool ball jolted in his direction. I took the opportunity to move quickly in the opposite direction toward the bar. My body felt lustful. I was a feeling I knew I should suppress but felt myself giving into. No matter the coldness of the air around me, I felt myself burning from the inside out.

I walked with a purpose toward the bartender, as if on a mission. I needed a steady flow of alcohol to calm my nerves, a stiff drink to help me numb this feeling of intense need. The pounding beat of the music captivated my mind and aroused my skin. My dark tan shimmered with body glitter, capturing the taut lines of each muscle with every strobe of light. The black dress gave me a sensual look. I never wore dresses this short, and am consciously aware of the appeal my legs were giving to each male I passed. Which to me was strange, given that if you were to look closely, you could still see the scars etched on my knees from when I was a kid playing sports.

As I walked past the bar, I could feel eyes upon me. Then I heard the catcalling and derogatory names that followed. The comments slowly gave way to my vulnerabilities.

"Hey, you! Hey, pretty mama, can I get you a drink?" I turned quickly, offering a curt smile.

"I don't need validation from a guy like you. Plus, I can get my own damn drink."

I sauntered past and drummed my fingers along the bar until I caught the bartender's eye. I could hear the guys giving my harasser hell for being put in his place, and a sense of pride surged through my body. My parents always told us that we didn't need a man. We were capable of doing whatever we wanted or needed ourselves. However, I always felt a good man to build a life with would lead to a great one. After all, it had worked for my parents. As the bartender approached, he was shaking what seemed to be a martini.

"What can I get you ladies?" I noticed him staring intently behind me, and then heard Sadie clear her throat.

"A double Patron with lime and salt." His lips gave way to a wry smile as he tipped his head in her direction.

"That I can do, and you?"

As he began to pull out shot glasses, he glanced back up at Sadie, clearly entranced. Sadie adjusted her bra without glancing up and yelled in her dry voice, "Vodka straight with a splash of soda. Throw an orange slice if you have one on hand. If not, make it a cherry."

He arched an eyebrow at her brazenness. I turned around and swatted at her. "Don't do that in public." She looked up, pouting. "Ugh, don't be like Mom. I'm just so nervous."

I laughed. "I can tell. You must have used half a bottle of perfume."

She looked up, panicking. "Is it that bad?" I licked the salt-glazed rim of the shot glass. Then I grabbed the lime and sank my teeth into it. The tangy juice filled my mouth, ridding it of the tequila taste.

"Nah, you're fine. Just kidding, relax!" I turned to grab my other shot and Sadie's drink.

"Going out to battle, ladies?" Smiling, I grabbed my second tequila and downed it. I once again licked the salt from the rim of the shot glass and bit down on the lime. The tangy juice pooled in my mouth, and I was instantly overcome with the sweet taste of tequila.

"I guess you could say that." With that, I tilted my head back and downed the shot, offering a smirk in his direction. As I gave him my card, he waved it away.

"I got this, just let me know if you gals win the war." He winked and flashed a flirtatious smile at Sadie, walking away to the next group of customers across the bar. Sadie, oblivious to the comment, just sipped at her drink. I couldn't help but laugh.

"Seriously, Sadie? You are so absent-minded some-times!" With that, she looked up, genuinely confused.

"What are you talking about?" I gently leaned into her so as not to spill her drink. "Never mind, let's go." I put the glass down and straightened up my body, looking intently in the direction of both Mark and Will.

"Come on!" I said excitedly. I stared directly toward them, unwavering, sensing a change in the air. Perhaps this was a new chapter unfolding in my life. The vibrant beat of the bass and the drums felt like a dance of passion. Walking toward the group, I noticed Will. He looked up instantly, smiling as he shot his ball into a hole. I felt flush and offered a smile.

"Hey! It's been so long!" I said as I greeted John. We embraced, and then I went to hug his brother Paul.

"Yeah, it feels like forever!"

"The Marines really suit you. You look great! Buff like a

life-size He-Man!" He let out a roll of thunderous laughter. I'd not seen John since he had enlisted in the military. The last time he came home was a few months back in the dead of summer. He had come back to grab some things and ended up staying overnight at his dad's. At the time, Sadie and I were watching Paul's daughter, Violet. It was a quick visit, but one I remembered fondly. We all stayed up talking and playing cards. I kissed them both on the cheeks and gave John a long hug.

"J, you have gotten ripped! What kind of boot camp do they have you going through over there? DEFCON 3?" I laughed, and John cracked a smile, rolling his eyes.

"Whatever, we do the same damn thing every day. It's carrying the equipment up the trails that really breaks a sweat and works your muscles. It's exhausting! But I love it! Semper Fi!"

He yelled the last two words, and a few people in the bar yelled back, "HooRah!" John beamed with delight.

A beautiful auburn-haired girl approached John and gave him a sideways hug. She laid her head gently on his shoulder, and he kissed the top of her head. Her hair was the perfect shade of cinnamon, and her skin was so fair it was almost translucent. She reminded me of a fairy. Her blue eyes opened and mirrored the hue of the ocean. The freckles splayed her face like constellations. She was intimidatingly gorgeous. I suddenly felt self-conscious and did my best to push those feelings down.

"Hey, you must be Charlie, John's cousin? Or is it more like his pseudo little sister? I've heard so much about you. He can't stop talking about your entire family. He doesn't shut up! I feel like I know you and your sisters so well already."

I smiled big with true enthusiasm, but also with curiosity. There was an awkward silence for a bit as it finally clicked with her that she had yet to introduce herself. She giggled and reached out a hand for me to shake.

"Oh, my goodness, I'm such a lush. Sorry! I already had like three drinks because I was so nervous to meet everyone. Now, well, I'm a bit hazy. My name is Danielle, but all my friends and family call me Dani. I'm John's fiancée, and we're getting married this coming summer!" She displayed a perfect array of glistening white teeth at the thought of marrying John.

Oh, wow, marriage? So soon? John looked down, flustered, and whispered into her ear. He was calm, but I detected noticeable irritation in his voice. "Dani, we were going to wait to tell everyone at Christmas dinner, remember?" She squinted her face up and peered up at him with apologetic eyes.

"I'm so sorry. Once I said it, I realized what I did." John looked at me, then back at her. He put a finger to her mouth.

"Shh. Let's try to keep it down to just us for now. I'll be sure to let them know this weekend." She winked and kissed John on the cheek. As she did, she pushed up on her toes, reaching to get close enough to give him a swift kiss, and then walked away toward the bathroom. I looked at John, and he shrugged.

"I mean, what am I supposed to do, Charlie? She's perfect for me. I just know she'll get along well with my parents. You guys will love her once you get to know her."

As I was about to respond, Will walked up with a cheeky grin on his face. I felt a fire growing in my chest. He bumped John on the side. "Dude, it's your turn. What the heck? Are we playing or not? You owe me a drink, too; I won the last game and even racked them."

John grabbed his stick and headed toward the table. He called for the waitress. "Another round, please!" I felt a knot in my heart as it was now just Will and me. I turned to face him, soaking up every inch of him. He was flawless–lightly muscular, his sun-tanned skin peaking out from under his cuffed sleeves. I could smell his cologne, deep and earthy, like spice, sandalwood, and oak. His sleeves were half rolled up, forearms showing, his veins on full display. His hands were neat, and his nails were clean and trim.

Then I spotted it, the one piece of metal that changed everything. The gold gleamed as if to say, *Ha, you can't have what you want.* I felt as if someone sucker punched me. I was such an idiot for not noticing it sooner. No matter how hard I tried, I couldn't stop staring at it. That gold band. So simple in its curvature, yet so powerful in its statement. Suddenly, William put his hand on the small of my back to move me out of the way. I shuddered at his touch. It was like electricity shooting down my spine. It's a current so strong that it gave me a chill, a want that I didn't know I had within me. This is a person I could not have. His warmth, his touch against the fabric of my dress, was more than I could handle.

"Charlotte, are you okay? You seem a bit off suddenly. Do you need a drink of water?" I slowly looked up at him and gently shook my head. It was as if I were in a daze. I needed to snap out of it.

"Oh, no, I am sorry. Yeah, I'm okay." I flagged the waiter over and didn't look at William when I asked, "So, how long have you been married?" He was caught off guard by my bluntness and lowered his head. His eyes deliberately avoided mine as I turned to look at him more directly. He took a swig of his beer.

"Oh, um, no, I'm not. That is, I'm not married." He choked out the last bit of his sentence.

"That is, I'm not married yet. I am engaged to be, though." Just like that, I could feel my heart rip open and my pulse quicken.

"This is a promise ring. It's more so for her than it is for me."

I pursed my lips together and squinted my eyes. The blonde waitress walked up to grab the empty glasses around us. I was about to ask for another drink when she winked.

"Let me guess, a tequila shot?" She smiled proudly as I stood my mouth agape.

"How'd you know that?"

As she continued to grab the stray cups lying in disarray around us, she flipped her head around to shout. "It's a party trick! A magician never reveals her secret."

I clapped excitedly. "So cool, love that! Mind making it two with extra lime?" She tipped her head at me as she loaded her tray onto her shoulder. "You've got it, doll." She hurried off as I turned to Will, who met my gaze with a perplexed look on his face.

"Who is the other shot for?" Will asked as he took a sip of his beer.

I let a wry smile flood across my face. If I couldn't have him, at least I could enjoy the time I had. What's the harm in that? I thought naively. "You, of course. A lady never shoots alone in the presence of a gentleman, you know." I let go of a flirtatious giggle in hopes that it would catch his attention.

"So, tell me, why did you feel the need to get married so

young? I'm struggling to understand that decision, I guess. I can't see myself married at my age. Then again, I can't see myself married at your age either." He chuckled nervously and averted his eyes. I could tell I was getting under his skin. As wrong as it felt, I couldn't stop myself. I didn't know how to gain control back.

"Honestly, I get along with her well. She knows everything about me. It's easy. We dated for most of my life. She's all I know," he said, pausing to take another swig. He sounded like he was trying to convince himself. Does he or doesn't he love her? I couldn't tell.

"I don't know what it feels like to be with anyone else." He glanced at me and quickly looked away, then steadied his focus back on me. "I guess I have never had anyone ask me that, and I've never let myself dissect my feelings. I guess I thought it was better than being alone. Looking back, well, it sounds pathetic." He flushed, and I suddenly felt butterflies in my stomach.

"She is steadfast, and to be honest, I guess it transformed into a sort of security blanket for me." He ran his fingers through his thick mass of hair as he averted his eyes from mine. "I've never been asked that question before, especially as bluntly as you put it." He put his hands in his pockets and fidgeted a little bit. I didn't know why, but his anxiety was very appealing to me. His lips were full in the middle, and I couldn't stop staring. He cleared his throat to bring my attention back to the conversation. *Great, how embarrassing. No telling what he thinks about me now. Get yourself together, Charlotte.*

"I think we are meant to have each person in our life for a period. We don't know what the expiration date is for each, but their presence stains our hearts." He stared at me, dumbfounded. He was looking past my exterior now and analyzing my very being.

"Wow, that was beautiful and deep."

Just then, I heard a voice, inaudible to those in the noisy bar surrounding me. *Leave.*

"Will you excuse me?" I rushed out of the bar and down the street to a narrow walkway vacant of people.

I leaned back against the cold wall of the bar, as the music vibrated through the stone, the sting of tequila still lingering on my lips. My breath felt shallow as my heart beat raced.. I could still feel the ghost of Will's hand on my back and the ache that came with it. What was I doing?

God, what *was* I doing?

A flush of heat rose to my face, not from the liquor, but from the sharp sting of regret. I had spent the night chasing a fantasy, playing a role I didn't even recognize myself anymore. I wanted his attention so badly, I let myself inch dangerously close to a line I swore I'd never cross.

I flirted with a man wearing a promise ring. He is taken.

I spoke words that weren't mine—words designed to cut through his defenses, not lift his soul.

This wasn't confidence. This was desperation dressed up in mascara and lace.

Glancing into the bar, the haze of perfume, sweat, and stale beer seemed suffocating. Music thumped, bodies pressed, and laughter echoed, but suddenly, it all felt hollow. I didn't like who I had become tonight. I wasn't proud of the heat in my words or the hunger in my eyes. I felt cheap and dirty, but worst of all, sinful. I wasn't proud of how I made him question what he had already promised someone else.

I felt like a counterfeit version of myself, as if I had let the devil momentarily seize my body, mind, and soul.

Then I caught a glimpse of something in the window of a store across from me. A small gold cross around the mannequin's neck. Simple. Barely noticeable. But it caught the light in just the right way. It flickered like a spark.

A reminder. A whisper.

You are more than this.

My chest tightened. I remembered the rosary tucked deep in my purse, tangled in receipts and Chapstick. I used to pray it on nights when I felt lost. And here I was, lost again, but pretending I was in control.

I closed my eyes.

"God, I need You to pull me out of this. I know what this was. This was not love. It was lust. It was envy. And it was wrong."

I swallowed hard, feeling the weight of conviction press against my ribcage and the alcohol swirl at my head.

"I don't want to be a woman who steals someone else's peace, or their promise. I don't want to become the temptation that someone has to resist. I don't want to be the woman who plants a seed of doubt. I'm no better than the snake that beckoned Eve."

I opened my eyes and stared into my own reflection, smudged eyeliner, glistening sweat, lips parted in disbelief. A girl who was raised better. A girl who still believed she could become whole again despite her many flaws.

The IV drip faded, and suddenly, I was barefoot again,

running toward the sound of waves that once felt like home.

Chapter 12

Charlotte – Awake

J ust then, I was aroused from my chemo-induced daydream by the scent of Alex's expensive perfume. My smile lingered from the memory of Will. The cadenced chemo machine beeped steadily in the background.

I wondered if Alex had just left or was still here. The IV bag was to my right and had been drained completely, along with it, both my mind and body strength. For someone who had just awoken from a deep comatose state, I felt exhausted. It was as if every single part of my body had been physically dragged through the ringer. I began to sit up, but with the IV still pulling at my arm, it was difficult. I reached for my water and took a long sip. I let the liquid cool my throat as it made its way down.

Alex came in and walked toward the chair next to me. She offered an exhausted smile as she sank down onto the pale blue chair. I rarely saw her this disheveled. She blew a stray piece of hair out of her face.

"I am so freaking exhausted. I feel like a deflated

balloon. Work has been insane. Not to mention the jet lag that goes with it. I'm pretty sure I sprained my ankle trying to catch my connecting flight in these damn stilettos." I let out a laugh, and it was met with annoyance.

"I'm so sorry; I don't mean to laugh, but I can't help it. I can just picture the entire scenario in my head. It's like a black and white movie. It's great!" Her face was unmoved by my enthusiasm. I raised my hands, hoping to stave off a snarky response.

"Before you get all upset, just chill a second. Let's talk life choices. Let's begin with your decision to wear four-inch heels while traveling. Then we'll segue into your choice to do so, knowing how close your connecting flights were."

She exaggerated an eye roll and looked just like her teenage self for a moment. "I wouldn't be caught dead in flats at the airport. You never know who you could see. Plus, it's me, and the airport is a hella good place to network."

I dramatically tilted my head backward, making a show of my annoyance. "You could hypothetically trip while sprinting in them, then hit your head and die." She stopped and looked at me, her eyes narrowing. Then we both burst out in a fit of laughter.

"Damn, cancer turned you dark." I gave her a playful sneer as Mariam walked in to unplug the IV.

"Hello, ladies. Let me just wrap everything up here, and then Charlotte, you will be good to go." I inhaled slowly and thought of how good it would feel to be in my own bed.

Later, Alex came back to my house after running home to shower. It was nice of her to make time for me after her long flight from Spain. She must be extremely tired. Earlier,

I had insisted she wait to visit me until tomorrow, but to no avail. Alex has always been stubborn. In this instance, it played in my favor. The kids ran downstairs, bombarding Alex with kisses and hugs.

"Aunt Alex! We missed you!" She soaked up every bit of affection before taking out two carefully wrapped gifts. Molly didn't hesitate. She ripped open her box to find a beautifully handmade doll. Molly immediately hugged it and then Alex. "She is so pretty!" Alex smiled, clearly happy that Molly was so elated.

"She looks just like you. Only you are more beautiful." As Molly twirled around with her new doll, Max opened his to find a traditional matador costume.

"What is this, Aunt Alex?" As she explained, his interest continued to grow. "So do they hurt the bulls?" His eyes filled with worry.

"No, sweet boy. If anything, the fighters are more at risk," she responded as she generously poured a couple of drinks.

"Whoa, Al, I just had chemo. I can't be drinking straight whiskey." As I laughed at the absurdity of the moment, she took both glasses and clinked them together, spilling a bit of bronze liquid onto the floor.

"Great, more for me!" She laughed as she took a sip of one. "Are you going to tell me what is going on, or do I need to guess?" Before she answered, she closed her eyes briefly and breathed in and out. It almost looked like she was doing breathing exercises to relax herself.

"Oh, Charlie, I just can't with him anymore. He says he loves me, and then showers me with everything imaginable: jewelry, extravagant trips, artwork. But every single time she complains, he goes running back. He has his public image to maintain, his teenagers to pacify, and a life that's constantly in the spotlight. The secrecy, the media, the drama. It is absolutely exhausting. I can't keep pretending it doesn't affect me, Charlie. Sometimes, it feels like I'm just another hidden chapter in his complicated political narrative." She looked up and closed her eyes again, leaning her head back on the chair's headrest and rubbing the back of her neck in an attempt to relieve tension. "I need a valium. I need to sleep for a few days."

I stifled a laugh because I knew she was serious. "I don't have a valium, Al, but I can give you some melatonin." We are not, nor have we ever been, huggers in our family. The only one who loved a good embrace was my father. When either of us was wrapped up in any kind of emotional state, it could be awkward. Walking over to her, I placed my hand lightly on her shoulder. I leaned my head onto hers to indicate that I was here for her. She didn't lean in, which I had expected, but rather, she smiled, looking at me with pain-filled eyes.

She dragged herself to the oversized chaise and lay down as if she were a patient, and I shrank back. She drained the first glass as I cuddled up in the corner nook of the couch. I wrapped my cardigan tightly around me and dropped the faux fur across my legs. Cancer made me cold all the time. Chemo made my immune system extremely weak. After my first bout with cancer, I would often feel as if I were on the brink of death. I was pretty sure that to outsiders, I looked sick, too.

The silence in the room was deafening. I cleared my throat.

"So, do I need to pry it out of you, or are you going to

spill it already?" Rolling her thick-lidded eyes, she looked at me.

"He just sent me another damn gift. Like these gifts are going to solve our problem. He called and left a voicemail and said that we needed to talk. He says he will see me soon. I mean, so cryptic." She hit the pillows with her tightly wound fists like a child. "I don't even know what that means."

The best form of therapy for Alex was to let her vent. She wouldn't feel like herself until she relinquished her built-up aggression and sadness.

"So, what did he end up getting you this time?" She gave me a coy smile.

"Not that it's about materialism, but he surprised me with the painting I had curated for him last month. I was so excited when I initially laid eyes on it." I covered myself a bit more tightly. I felt cold and exhausted from today. Then looked at Alex, and I could tell she needed me right now to be my best.

"Yeah, you couldn't stop babbling about it."

She pointed at me enthusiastically. "Exactly, because it's a gem! It's from a painter back in the early 1920s. I fell in utter lust with the way the artist was able to capture the essence of darkness during light. It's effervescent."

I let out a laugh and then covered my mouth quickly. "I'm sorry!" She fixated her eyes on me and was clearly frustrated with my response. "You meant to say you love the color black, which again, is not a color, Al." She looked at me and huffed.

"Char, seriously, that is debatable and beside the point. So, like I was saying, I have this amazing piece of art that would look killer over my dining room table, but I can't even hang it up. I can't believe he thought he could buy me out like that. It's infuriating!" I looked at her, everything clicking into place. The recognition of love presenting itself.

"You love him. I can see it plain as day. It's in your anger and frustration. Oh, my goodness, yeah, you love him! He was trying to do something sweet for you and impress you. It pissed you off because you can't have him in his entirety, and you want to share the picture with him!" She sat there stunned. She started to speak and then stopped.

"First off, I don't love him. I like him. A lot. Okay, well, a lot, a lot. Ugh, you drive me nuts when you do this." I laughed at her statement.

"At what? Pointing out the obvious." She rolled her eyes.

"The unwanted and unneeded obvious. Thanks. It's all so damn complicated. Why does he have to be in the spotlight? Why does he have a conniving wife and interfering offspring? I do like buying things for myself. I don't want to feel owned, but I guess I also like to feel spoiled. That doesn't even make sense when I say it out loud."

She kicked off her stilettos and pulled up her feet. They were bright red and looked painstakingly swollen.

"I'd rather be wanted than needed, too, just like you. But Alex, if you truly love him, you owe it to yourself to be honest—even if the situation itself isn't. At some point, you have to call a spade a spade. Even if he doesn't want to hear it." She took another sip, swirling the whiskey in her mouth before swallowing. I imagined the flavor of the liquor, its intense burning sensation. It made my stomach flip, so I looked away and imagined something else.

"That is not the problem, though. The problem is, I

116

know he loves me. I can feel it. He is a bit obsessive. No, he's possessive. Yeah, that's a better word. What scares me is the idea of him wanting to fully commit. Then what if I decide, after he dumps the family, that I just don't want him anymore? The thrill would be gone, right? I feel like I can't trust myself in these situations." I shrugged at the idea of that being Will. I know what I would have done. I would have gone for Will each time.

"You know, Al, that is not really a problem on his end, then. Especially knowing that he does have a family. It's a messy love affair as I well know. Are you going to tell Sadie?" Alex moaned at that.

"Oh, my gosh, can we just not? She's going to rake me over with questions and judgment. It's BS I can't tolerate right now. It's as if she's Mom when Mom isn't here. I'll tell her once I officially decide what I am going to do."

I sat quietly, my blanket pulled tighter around me. "Al, I know you care about him. I see that. But this whole thing … It's not love if it's lived in hiding. And it's not yours to keep if it was never truly available."

She looked away, jaw clenched. "Don't start with the morality talk, Char. I already know. I feel it every time he leaves."

I leaned in gently, my voice softer now. "I'm not here to judge you. I just don't want to see you keep giving your heart away to someone who's only giving you part of theirs. You deserve someone who chooses you fully. No secrets. No shadows."

Her eyes brimmed with tears, but she didn't let them fall. "It's not that simple."

"I know," I whispered. "But what if the ache you're

117

feeling isn't about missing him? It's about missing your own peace. What if that is God telling you that he isn't for you?"

She stared at me for a long moment. "You really believe I deserve more?"

I smiled sadly. "I know you do."

I stood up and made my way toward the kitchen. Exhaustion was slowly taking over.

"Also, if Sadie asks, I must tell her. I can't lie, Alex. Sorry." She leaned her head back, unresponsive to my comment. "Want some carbs? I can pop some leftover baked ziti into the microwave. Mom made it earlier for me to eat. Perhaps a bowl will help to soak up all the booze you just downed." I needed to get my head focused on something else; sitting and lying, I could start to feel the effects stirring in my body. By day two and three post-chemo, I will be in the fetal position, sick as a dog. "You know what Father Alvarez says?" I offered gently. "I spoke to Father Alvarez once, and he told me that the devil doesn't always show up with horns. Sometimes, it's a good wine list and compliments when you're low, which he manipulates to sway your judgment. Maybe talk to him. If anyone can separate what's real from what's noise, it's him."

I could feel Alex's eyes upon me as I walked to the kitchen.

"Yeah, maybe I should. I don't know." She sauntered over and sat down on the stool. She swiveled back and forth as if she were a kid. Then she laid her head on her folded arms and proceeded to stare at her feet.

Heaviness lingered in the air, but it was late, and we were tired. Maybe food would be a welcome distraction.

Suddenly, she popped her head up.

"You know what, we should order pizza from that

Italian eatery down the street. Didn't you say they have that brick oven and it's to die for? Oh, my goodness, that sounds phenomenal right now. I haven't had a carb in forever. I miss bread. This new diet of mine is killing me."

I picked up my cell phone to begin dialing out. "You mean 'the drink coffee in the morning, salad at lunch, and wine for dinner diet?' Oh, that's not working for you?" I said, dripping with sarcasm.

When I was done ordering our food, I called up to Max and Molly to begin their baths before dinner. They responded in unison. "Okay, Mommy! Can Aunt Alex do bubble time, though?"

I yelled back, "No, next time, Aunt Alex is tired." Then I whispered to Alex, "And buzzed."

Alex chuckled. "So, how are you? How is everything going with Will? Have you talked to the cop guy again?"

I sat at the kitchen table. "You know what's funny is that I get this vibe that Will isn't gone. I don't know. I can't really explain it. I do get weird feelings about all these random things that have been happening lately. It's like a spider web of clues. Not necessarily riddles to figure out, just little easter eggs that are being dropped left and right. I wish I knew what it all meant."

Alex scrunched up her face like she was in deep thought.

"I don't know, Alex. I want to say it could be Will, but then again, there's an underlying threatening vibe that makes it seem like it isn't. I don't know how to explain it. The other day, I woke up to Baxter barking furiously toward the backyard. Like something was there watching us, but I couldn't see out because it was a blanket of night sky. It freaked me the hell out. Not to mention Max and Molly. They had to sleep with me that night."

Alex twirled her hair in her hand mindlessly. "Oh, man, Max is going to have you paying for that for weeks, I bet. Always a scared cat. Sorry, I feel for you. I'm sure it's nothing since in the past, when you guys first got married, he would leave to do a ski trip with his friends and not tell you until he was knee deep in snow. Glad you were able to nip that in the bud; however, he might need a refresher when he gets back."

She smiled, but her eyes gave away a bit of concern. *I appreciate her building my faith up that he is okay. I'm starting to wonder if something really did happen.* "I'm sure he thinks he told you!" I shrugged at the statement. So why leave right after an argument with me then?

Just then, my phone lit up. It was a text from Sadie. *"Wait, Al's back from Spain? Someone spotted her with Sebastian—that shady Spanish politician who's always on the news. Isn't he married? What is she thinking?"* I bit my lip as she scanned the text.

"Here we go." I could visibly see her nostrils flare with anger. A small vein started pulsating in her forehead. "I mean, seriously, this is the kind of crap I can't deal with. I just can't. She wonders why I don't want to tell her things about my life. The judgment is unreal. As it is, I have all these feelings to worry about, and I'm not a natural feelings kind of person! Now I must deal with her and her holier-than-thou crap."

I put a hand on hers. "Let's just take a deep breath. Sadie is under a lot of stress right now with the IVF process and all. She's just trying to focus her mind elsewhere. You can't blame her, Alex. She's also worried. It's her job as the oldest, you know." I offered up a smile.

I loved my sister, and I ached for her pain, but something about the entire process, about life being created in labs and petri dishes, tugged at a part of my soul I hadn't fully understood until now. Was it really wrong to want a child this badly? Or was it the method that needed confronting?

I bit my cuticle, a nervous tic, as I stared at a framed picture of my own children. It kills me that she didn't know this kind of love yet.

But who was I to judge? When I had made a choice years ago, a decision cloaked in selfishness, silence, in sterile halls, under the guise of a culture that called it liberation, and even worse, masked it as feminism. I had aborted my very own child. That truth, to this date and probably until I die, will permeate the very marrow of my bones. I had told no one for fear of shame, ridicule, and judgment. Not from the world but from God. Not Will. Not Sadie. Not Alex. The memory of that small heartbeat stopped by my own hand was the heaviest thing I carried, and the grief was stifled by a world that celebrates it.

"Before I formed you in the womb, I knew you."
Jeremiah 1:5

Those words used to strike like thunder. Now, they sounded like a whisper from a God I had kept at arm's length for years, a God who knows my child. Who knows me. And still, regardless of my many transgressions, He offers unconditional mercy.

Sadie was grasping for life, where I had once chosen

death. And now I could barely tell where compassion ended and conviction began. Maybe God was using this moment to wake me up, not to shame her, but to heal something fractured deep within me.

"Earth to Charlie!" Alex snapped her painted fingers. "Hello, where'd you go? Space out much?"

I shook my head and stood up, offering her a half-smile. "Sorry. Stuck in my head. Well, let's get you fed. Then I am going to bed. I'm shot after today if you can't tell by my blank stares."

Alex looked at me, laughing, then as she stood, walked over and offered a small smile of her own, her eyes cast down sheepishly, "Thanks for always being there. If you're tired, go on to bed. I'll be just fine. I'm just going to crash here tonight."

Chapter 13

Charlotte – Photograph

I dropped my phone, the invasive image burning into my retinas like acid.

It was me. Asleep. In my bed.

The covers bunched at my waist, my hand curled near my face in a position I recognized from every groggy morning. The room in the picture was dark, but moonlight poured through the window, catching just enough light to outline my cheek. It was recent. From last night. I wore the same sleep shirt I'd just tossed into the hamper.

I sank to the floor. My knees hit the carpet, and I didn't feel a thing. Only the white-hot roar of panic flooded my skull.

This wasn't a prank.

Someone had been in my house.

In my room.

Close enough to hear me breathe.

Baxter whined from across the room, ears twitching. He hadn't barked that night. Or maybe he had, and I hadn't heard it over the Ambien fog.

The text had no words. No number.

Just a photo.

My hands shook as I grabbed my phone again, trying to force logic into the moment. I tapped the image. No metadata. No clue. I forwarded it to Cortez and added three words: *"Someone was here."*

Less than five minutes later, he called.

"Don't touch anything," he ordered. "Are the kids home?"

"No. At school."

"Stay on the line with me. I'm ten minutes away."

I wanted to crawl out of my own skin. The house felt smaller. Walls pressing in. Windows too exposed. Every creak of the floorboards upstairs sounded like a footstep.

I walked to the window. The lake looked calm. Empty. But so had the photo.

When Cortez arrived, he brought two more officers. They swept the house. Again.

"No signs of forced entry," one muttered. "Everything's locked."

But I could tell from the tightening of Cortez's jaw that it didn't matter. The image was enough.

He crouched beside me on the couch.

"Charlotte, I need you to go through your day yesterday. Everything."

I did. I recited it like a grocery list. Nothing felt unusual.

"You said you took Ambien?"

"Half a tablet. I can't sleep anymore without it."

He nodded slowly, eyes distant. Thinking.

I added, "There's more. I think it's Baker. I haven't seen him. But I feel him."

Cortez didn't dismiss it.

"I want you and the kids somewhere safe. Family, friend's house. Just for a few nights."

"Sadie and Geoff. They're still here. I can stay with them."

He stood. "And don't be alone. Ever. Not until we figure this out."

When the house emptied again, I sat with the photograph still glowing faintly on my phone screen.

My own face.

Peaceful.

Vulnerable.

Marked.

I delete it. Not because I want to forget, but because I never would.

Not now.

Chapter 14

Will – Conversations

Binoculars aimed at my family's home—it felt invasive, even for Hannah.

I stood behind the curtain, my breath shallow, watching her watch them. She'd set up shop in that rickety shed like it was a surveillance bunker: maps, notebooks, a digital scanner tracking police dispatch. She was calm. Too calm. It was unnerving.

"She moves the blinds every seven minutes," Hannah muttered, not looking up from her notes.

"It's not random. She's scanning. She's scared."

She meant Charlotte.

I swallowed hard. I wanted to tell her to stop. To shut it down. But the sick twist in my gut told me this was bigger than obsession. Hannah believed she was protecting them, us. And in a way, she had.

I might have died if she hadn't pulled me from the river.

"She thinks someone was on the roof last night,"

Hannah said, jotting something down. "It rattled her. Good. Fear keeps her alert."

"That's not good," I snapped. "That's our home. My kids."

She looked up. "Then why aren't you there, Will?"

I turned away. Because I couldn't be. Because if Baker was bold enough to tamper with my car, he was bold enough to do worse. Because if Charlotte knew I was alive, she might come looking. And if she came looking, she'd walk straight into the snare.

Hannah shifted her tone. "I'm not your enemy. I don't want to hurt her. But I'm the only one paying attention. You saw the cameras, the trail cams. Movement at 3:04 a.m., gone by 3:09. Who moves like that? Not a junkie. Not a raccoon. Baker."

I rubbed the back of my neck. I hadn't slept in two days. My ribs still ached from the crash. The worst part? A tiny, terrible part of me believed her.

I sat down, elbows on my knees, staring at the floorboards.

"You ever think about what it cost her?" I asked. "To carry all that weight alone? She never blinked. Not once. Even when she got the diagnosis. Even when she lost her hair, puked after chemo, held the kids at night like she wasn't fading. She just ... kept going."

Hannah was quiet for once.

"She deserves better than this," I whispered.

"Then give it to her," Hannah said, folding the map. "But not dead. Not missing. Plan it. Outthink him. Win."

The binoculars rested between us. I didn't want to look. But I picked them up anyway. Charlotte was on the porch with Baxter. Her face was pale. Strained. Her eyes darted toward the woods.

I lowered the binoculars.

"He was here last night," I said.

Hannah nodded. "Yeah. And he'll come back."

And that was the problem. So, would I.

Chapter 15

Cortez – Clues

Detective Cortez, visibly peeved, sipped a cup of hot coffee as he studied the paperwork set before him. He had become frustrated by the number of inconsistencies that displayed no signs of resolve.

Will Rose had been missing for a while, and nothing was adding up. The crash site where Will had gone over the bridge rail into the water was free of evidence, yet his recovered car showed signs of tampering. There was brake fluid smeared along the guardrail and shards of broken glass scattered oddly far from the impact. On the muddy roadside, there had been what looked to be footprints. Yet, their search had resulted in nothing.

No body. No witnesses. No Will.

I just don't get it. What am I missing?

He scratched his hair and rubbed his fingers over the bridge of his nose. He tried to envision the night of the crash.

What was Will thinking?

He shifted in his leather chair, leaning back as he

scanned the bustling precinct. His eyes rolled over to his partner, Maria, who was on the phone, tapping a pen against her head as she talked a million miles an hour. But Cortez kept his mind locked on the puzzle set before him. It was an uncomfortable itch he couldn't seem to scratch.

His phone buzzed sharply, breaking his concentration. He flipped up all the papers, files, and photographic evidence in search of it. He grabbed it, "Hello, dear," he answered softly, recognizing Martha's number immediately, her smiling face filling the screen.

"Sorry, Ray, I know you're busy," Martha said, her gentle voice noticeably laced with concern. "Have you found anything yet about Will? Charlotte's barely holding it together. I just spoke to her, she's trying so hard to be strong for those sweet babies, but ..."

Cortez took a deep breath, trying to figure out what to say to ease her mind. "I'm doing everything I can, Martha. I truly am, but this case, well, it's complicated. There's someone out there messing with them. So many different potential suspects, yet I can't seem to catch a break. It's so damn infuriating. The only silver lining is that surveillance picked up movement again last night, and Charlotte received an anonymous photo of herself asleep. It might not be anything, but then again, it might just be something."

Martha gasped at that, her breath hitching. Cortez could sense terror in her voice, "Oh gosh, Ray, this is terrifying. Charlotte, she's like family. After our sweet Rosalynn passed away, well, it's as if God placed her in my life at the exact time I needed her. I still can't forget the day she came in asking if I needed help at the library, pregnant nonetheless! Sweet child. She became like a pseudo-daughter to me. I can't imagine something happening to her and those poor kids. Do you think they're safe? Should she even be at home at a time like this? Then, with her health crisis … who would do something like this?"

"A mad person, that's who. I'll make sure they're safe," Cortez said firmly, determination solidifying in his chest. "Listen, Martha, just keep talking to Charlotte, okay? Keep an eye out, let her know we're here. She trusts you. And I promise you, I won't let anything happen to them."

"I know you won't," Martha whispered, her voice thick with emotion. "Just be careful. Whoever this is, they sound dangerous and unstable."

He exhaled deeply, thinking, *More like psychotic.* "I will, Martha. Love you."

"Love you, too, Ray."

As he hung up, Cortez felt the sudden and immense weight of responsibility pressing ever harder. Will is missing. Charlotte is being watched. Baker's threats echo ominously, and both Marla and Hannah hover suspiciously at the edges. The personal stakes were clear, now sharpened by his wife's genuine fear and Charlotte's visible suffering.

He looked down at the chicken scratch on his legal pad, knowing every moment mattered. Cortez wouldn't rest until he had answers.

He wrote down three names.

Baker. Marla. Hannah.

So, which sick son of a gun is it?

Chapter 16

Charlotte – Scans

A s I walked out of the imaging center, the fatigue from the CT scan hit me hard, leaving me drained and unsteady. I had no choice but to drive myself home. The exhaustion felt overwhelming, but there was no one else to rely on. I thought about calling an Uber, but the last thing I wanted was to make small talk with a stranger about what I'd just been through.

I got behind the wheel of my car, and the wind cut through me like a blade, sending a wave of ice through my body. One of the lingering symptoms—both from my first cancer and now again—is that I'm always cold. A constant, bone-deep cold. No matter how many layers I wear, no matter how thick the socks or soft the fleece, the chill has made itself at home inside me.

Despite the early frost building on the side of the road, I decided to take the shortcut through the backroads, knowing very well that the conditions were usually worse during this type of weather. I'm not sure why I did. Maybe I have a death wish.

This morning was one for the books. The air was crisp and cold. Even the trees looked like they were shivering as they swayed back and forth, bare of any leaves. The sun burst through the trees, sending a beautiful glow on the landscape in front of me. Various shades of reds, greens, and browns came together in perfect unison. I wanted to lie down, but not here. It was beautiful, but the winds were what made it unbearable. I longed to be inside my home, curled up by the fire with my kids and Baxter nestled at my feet.

One thing about this season is that it was my favorite time of year. My heart burst each year as Thanksgiving and Christmas approached. This holiday season was tainted, though. Missing the two men who meant the most to me: my father and Will. Engulfed in a cloud of nostalgia. I was mindlessly weaving through the roads when my phone rang. My head elsewhere, I picked up on the fourth ring.

"Char, took you long enough." Somehow, Alex managed to sound both joyful and irritated at the same time.

"Hey, what's up?" My thoughts were still anywhere but the present. I rubbed my eyes, hoping the pressure building within them would be alleviated.

"Are you okay? You sound kind of sad. I don't have much time to chat, but I wanted to check up on you." Alex paused, clearly intending for me to speak.

"Yes, just thinking of Will and Dad. I'll be okay."

She sighed, relief laced in her breath. "Good, well, not good that you are upset about them, but happy that it isn't anything other than that. I wanted to let you know that I'm on my way home. My assignment ended earlier than antici-pated, so I'm boarding a plane this evening. Sadie wants us to grab dinner tomorrow night. She asked me to give you a ring to see if that would be okay."

I thought for a moment, reviewing my calendar in my mind. "I think that should work fine. I'm pretty sure that it does. Where to?" Pressure was building behind my eyes, making them feel oddly heavy. A foggy sensation overtook me. Alex rattled on; however, I couldn't concentrate.

"I don't know, she's thinking Italian. I love me some pasta!" She said it with emphasis on the A, and I could picture her kissing her fingers as she said it.

I abruptly interrupted her. "Al, I don't feel too well. I feel strange suddenly."

Al's voice changed, morphing instantly. "What do you mean? What's wrong? You were fine a second ago. Where are you?" Her rapid questions made me more nervous. My breath quickened, and it was difficult to focus on the road.

"My eyes feel funny. Something feels off, like I must really concentrate to keep my eyes focused on the road ahead. I must focus on them staying put. Alex, I don't like this. What if I'm going blind? Oh, my no, that can't happen. I think I need to go to the ER." Panic rose. Alex began to mirror my emotions. She had never been the calm, take-charge sister. That role had always been destined for me. Right now, I could not seem to harness that sense of control.

"How close are you? Let me call Mom. Wait, I don't want to hang up with you. Let me text Sadie and Mom instead."

I veered off in the direction of the hospital. I think I can make it. I just needed to focus on the road. I had the sensation that my eyes were being magnetically pulled upward. If that happened, I would crash. I silently prayed as I entered the parking lot.

"Al, I'm here. Tell them to meet me here. I love you." I hung up before she could interrupt.

Walking through the emergency entrance, I had a desperate need to sit down and close my eyes. The minute I crossed the threshold, I fell to my knees. My heart was hammering in my chest. I felt as if I was going to have a heart attack, my body numb and tingly. Someone rushed to my side.

"Ma'am, are you okay?" I was startled by the voice, even though I felt someone take my arm and try to help me up. I refused to open my eyes for fear it would be worse.

"Help me, please. I can't see. I mean, I can, but every time I open my eyes, it feels as if they're moving to the back of my head. I don't know how else to explain it. I had chemo this week, and I just came back from having my labs done. Something is terribly wrong. Can you please get a doctor? I'm scared."

The woman gently helped me up and guided me to a wheelchair. "Honey, I'm going to roll you to a room and get you checked in so the doctor can examine you."

I nodded in agreement. I wished that Sadie and Mom would hurry. Mom always knew what to do and say in these situations.

Time passed slowly as I rested on the hospital bed, a warm cloth over my eyes. I heard footsteps approaching. A male voice broke the silence. It was kind and soothing. "Hello, I'm Dr. Chu." I could feel myself weeping through the cloth with relief that I was finally going to get some answers.

"We just administered a medication through your IV to

counteract the one you mentioned receiving during chemo," the doctor said. "In my experience, that particular drug often leads to seizures, which is why I'm surprised it's still commonly used—there are better options available now. Once this new medication takes effect, you'll feel very drowsy and will likely sleep for a few hours. The nurse said your family is on their way. Once they arrive, we'll make sure they know where to find you."

I nodded and could already feel the overwhelming calming effects of the IV. I succumbed to the feelings of ease and allowed my mind to slip away.

The shadows creep up the walls in a dark, ominous way. The dim light paints my father in a sickly glow. In the stillness of this room, his silhouette is prominent as he lies unmoving in the bed. The only sign of life is the faint rise and fall of his chest. His broad mouth is cracked open ever so slightly, struggling with each painful breath. Even from the doorway, I see his stature has shrunk. I can see that the disease has taken his once muscular body and diminished it to practically nothing. He resembles a prisoner of war now. Emaciated, bones devoid of muscle and fatty tissue. If I didn't know he was there, I might not have noticed the figure under the blankets at all. It looks ghastly—reminiscent of a Poe story—where the reader is anxiously awaiting the unmoving body to suddenly rise.

The deafening silence is broken by his sickly moans, followed by a crackling exhalation. His breathing is both raspy and watery at the same time. You can tell something is lodged in his throat, but his state of unconsciousness prevents him from ejecting it. Whatever foreign object is stuck has most likely been there a while, due to the gurgling sounds that are being made.

Growing up, he had always been the shining star in my life. My mother would often catch us on a late Sunday afternoon napping on the La-Z-Boy. He would lie with me as I nuzzled like a small kitten on his chest, my dark brown curls cascading down his arms as our breaths mirrored each other. We just clicked. We always had. My wild, imaginative, impulsive self seemed somehow to captivate him. Perhaps he saw his younger self in me. After all, I had been a product of him. I was the part that had escaped his grasp when he married my mother, defaulting to a life of structure and expectation.

His wooden drumsticks would no longer go whipping through the air to let others feel the music as he had. He would also no longer climb the steps of corporate success due to a lack of time. He valued his family more than all those things. He valued his wife and his three children more than anything. He lived up to the sanctity of marriage as if it were a contract written with his very blood. I had always said if I were to marry, it would be to someone who reflected my father. I had always respected and honored him. I could always be raw in my honesty and tell him anything. Well, almost anything. I have yet to summon up the courage to tell him about my past. I am not brave enough to break his heart like that. Although I knew in the end he would have given me unconditional love, I didn't want my dad's last impression of me to be blood-stained hands. Its blood. My blood. My moment of shame and weakness tainted his legacy.

"You can do this, Charlotte. He needs you." I whisper,

attempting to muster up enough courage to console my father. The intense mental energy required to make my body move is proving difficult. I painfully take a step toward him. I concentrate on the white tile, counting each square as I inch closer. Four. Three. Two. One. As if being pulled by an unknown force. I stop and stare at the almost lifeless man in the bed. The heaviness in the room is unbearable. As if in a dark cloud. Brazenly, I grab his pale, long fingers in my own. His faded paper-like skin, once a deep olive brown, was now a gray pallor. I wrapped my fingers in his, squeezing, but when he fails to squeeze back, my chest fills with pressure. I know he is fading. His hands feel like ice. His fingers were bony and frail. I need to control my composure.

I close my eyes, the eyes that my father used to say were the perfect shade of brown. My father's eyes. I inhale sharply, the air sour and stagnant. I slowly exhale as if I am in yoga class. Then I open my eyes, half hoping that he would be looking back at me. However, he won't ever look at me again. It is harder to breathe as my nasal cavity suppresses the waterfall that I know is inevitable.

Stammering and fighting back tears, I whisper gently, "Dad ..." as they begin to fall. I swipe at them, wiping my face with my sleeve and leaving a smear of beige makeup behind. I lean in close and say, "Dad ..." Tears spill upon his pillow, leaving black ink blots. Tears that were justified for the man he had once been, lying in dark splotches. My father was awe-inspiring and difficult to live up to.

"Dad. Dad, I need you to hear me. Can you just ..." I pause. "Please. Can you just ..." I phrase it as a question. As if he can help himself from the current uncontrollable state that he is in. As if he has a choice not to hear. "Dad, I need you to know that I love you. Do you know that? Did I do a good enough job telling you that I love you? Did you feel that from me? I need you to know that now."

I pause for a moment and suck in a breath of air, willing myself to get through this speech because it could be my last. "You are the best dad. You are the best person. You are the most inspiring and loving person that I will probably ever meet in my life." I close my eyes momentarily, blocking my tears from free-falling. "You know, I don't think anyone will ever love me like you do."

My nose begins to drain clear fluid, each nostril slightly red and flared. My heart feels shattered. A physical, unexplainable ache where a piece had been ripped out. A sadness not for his departure, because for that I am celebratory. I know that he is no longer going to be in excruciating pain. The melancholy is more for the fact that he will not be here to enjoy the lives that he had helped us mold.

My kids will not get to experience the beautiful words that he often spoke in times of need. The always well-thought-out moral of the story kind of talks that seemed to come straight out of the movies. He always had something to say, and it was always intertwined with the right amount of positivity. It had that push of momentum to get you back up and running again. My children wouldn't get to know the type of vigor in his character that I had known and experienced firsthand.

I would look up to see him smiling at me with his big white teeth. His charisma shines through. Death brings forth change. Often, it stirs an inward revolt, an evolution. Things that once were are no longer what they had been. Due to the person putting forth the change. It is that pivotal moment when beautiful things begin to happen, considering those raw moments.

The machines are deafening, filling the air with loud, obnoxious beeps that seem to become louder each moment I linger. The urgency grows with each new sound. *Beep. Beep.* It's a constant reminder of illness. A constant reminder of death approaching. *Beep Beep Beep.* His blood pressure drops to the seventies. Then his heart rate increases to the 150s. *Beep Beep.* His respiratory numbers fluctuate like the stock exchange. None of those numbers are good.

Roller coasters in themselves are good, happy things. This roller coaster is not. Nothing about the heart monitor is registering as well. He coughs, and the numbers quickly change. He stops, and they shift again. It's a constant struggle to understand what his body is trying to communicate. To us. To me. It's almost like playing a guessing game. I suppose that's exactly what the doctors do every day. They must guess. Guess at what the illness could be. Guess at what could potentially be going on inside a person's body. You spend years and years in school to become a doctor, to learn how to make the most educated guesses.

Then the moaning begins. It's agonizing, like hearing someone in absolute desperation, and it pains me to give it no response. I want to leave this wretched place. I hate hospitals. Rarely does anything good happen, except birth. Nothing good to me anyway. I want to run. I want to turn around and tear out of this room. I want to sprint in the opposite direction of this heartache. I don't want to stop for anyone or anything or to even catch my breath. I want to run until I am hit with extreme exhaustion, and that is all I can think about.

I cannot do any of those things, though. I cannot leave this place. I cannot leave him. I'm stuck here in this damn place because he would be stuck if it were me. If it were me lying in that bed sick and dying, he would be unfaltering. If it were me, he would be right by my side, unwavering. He would be desperately tired with under-eye bags reminiscent of mine. He would be clutching a rosary and a bible, no doubt. He would be resilient in mind, body, and spirit. He would do all the things expected and more. So, for that, I must do for him. For those very reasons, I will sit here by his side. I will force myself to sit here despite my own weariness. I will force myself despite my own pain and insecurities. I will let him know I am listening and that I am here.

"Excuse me, Ma'am. Ma'am. Miss? I need to ask if you or your mother has considered all the options." My eyes are open, but I feel as if I am unable to see. I'm caught in a trance, staring unwaveringly at the machine hooked up to my dad. *Beep. Beep. Beep. Beep.* My eyes do not move. They are frozen watching those lines go drastically up, only to dip down just as fast. "Miss." I finally gained control of my body and turned around. I lock eyes with a young woman who appears to be about five years my junior. She is short and stocky, with raven hair pulled into a drastic ponytail. Her face is scattered with an array of different-shaped freckles. She wears no makeup and has a very clear complexion. Dressed in light blue scrubs and her hands lightly draped across her computer keyboard, you can tell she has done this a million times. Talking to people whose loved ones are attached to machines that are struggling to keep them stable and alive. You can tell by her quick dismissal and lack of response to my silence that it is expected. She must ask these types of questions. She must because her job at this cold, clinical hospital requires her to check all the right boxes and leave no stone unturned for fear of a lawsuit.

I did not even hear her come in. She had to have pushed open the heavy wooden door, which scrapes the cold tile floor each time it's touched. I would have heard that, wouldn't I? I am only a few feet away. Am I that out of it? She not only pushed that wooden door in, but she also wheeled in that monstrous computer, which looks as if it predates my birth. She stops and looks at me for a moment before checking my dad's hospital bracelet, then lifts his gown to clean the peg tube, a tube inserted to feed him since he is unable to do so himself. Again, without looking up at me, she says, "The doctor asked me to find out if you or your mother have had the chance to think about plans regarding his continued care. Have you?" I can feel my face scrunch up with frustration at having to deal with this now.

"My mother, sisters, and I have discussed it at length. We're at a loss as to what would be the ideal care for him. In the end, it's my mother's decision as to what she feels is best for my dad, as she is his executor. I believe she's leaning toward a facility as opposed to home. She wants to be there mentally for my father without the pain of having to physically assist with his every need if he were to go home. We understand that hospice is not constant care; however, it's a means to provide some comfort in the end."

I paused to allow her to interject. She smiled and nodded, "Yes, that's very true. We cannot tell the family what the best decision is; we can only give you the updated medical opinion and what the options are at this point. It's up to your family to decide what would be best for your father. He is tentatively scheduled to be discharged tomorrow. We are just awaiting the paperwork from the case worker to move forward and the exact location as to your mother's wishes." She typed something into the computer and then smiled. "Your father must have been quite loved. I have heard there are many people who call for him here. I see you and your mother here rotating daily. It's a hard thing to go through. I know; I lost my parents at a young age. It never fully goes away, you know, that pain. However, it will get a bit easier to handle as the days go by. Take care of yourself." She smiled one last time and wheeled the monitor back toward the hall, lightly shutting the door behind her.

I take my dad's hand. "Dad, I know with every being that you will be okay. You have a one-way ticket to heaven, and your next life is going to be pain-free. Watch over me, the girls, the kids, and Mom. Be my inner voice when I need you." I squeeze his hand and whisper in his ear one last time. "I love you so much. You are and always will be the very best dad." I lay my hand on his cheek and continue to cry.

I closed my eyes, and I am five again. His arms around me on the old recliner, his chest rising and falling like a lullaby I knew by heart. The thump of his heartbeat under my cheek. "My brave girl," he used to whisper. "No matter what." Now, the chest is still–but I still hear his words. They echo louder than any machine in this room. I awoke happy at the thought of my father, but at the same time, I was tinged with melancholy. Engulfed in a blanket of emotion, I began to sob. Dry heaves of ugly, saturated tears. Max popped up from next to me as Molly was sleeping soundly on the other side. He put his sweaty arms around me, cradling me as if I were his child and not his parent.

"Mommy, are you okay? Were you dreaming of Daddy? Aunt Sadie is with Nana outside, talking to the doctor. I hope you feel better." I shook my head as tears poured down my face. Max's own eyes filled with tears, mirroring my own. "It is going to be okay. I promise, Mommy. Don't cry."

My bones hurt from the chemo, and my heart was in shards. My head felt as if it was going to implode. I felt drug-ridden and weak. I wanted to relinquish control sometimes. I wanted to fade away. It was all too much pain to bear. Physically, mentally, spiritually, this is all too much for a mere mortal to bear. I looked at Max's face and then back at Molly's. I wiped my eyes and felt the baldness of my eyelids, raw under my touch. I ran my hands across my smooth head and felt an overwhelming sense of sorrow and feebleness. I wept as I held onto Max with the image of my father's smile imprinted on my mind. He rubbed my back slowly, comforting me. It was times like these that I knew my father was present. It was these times of turmoil and utter desperation that I could sense him. Just as my father's spirit lingered, so does Will's. He wouldn't leave me like this. He wouldn't leave us.

I kissed Max's soft forehead. "I'm okay, sweetie. Just lie back down. Thank you for being so strong for me." I wiped my tears; I took a breath and nestled back between the two of them. I won't allow myself another moment of weakness. I refused the interjection of my personal emotions. I must be resolute for them.

Chapter 17

Charlotte – Red

The morning light cut through the blinds in slanted lines, crisp and indifferent. My body ached, my head still swimming from the mix of meds and memory, but I forced myself up. Routine was supposed to be grounding, they say. So I started small.

I sat at the vanity and reached for Molly's hairbrush, the soft pink one with sparkles along the handle. I ran it absently through my own tangled strands—until the bristles caught. I paused.

There, threaded tightly between the plastic teeth, was a single long strand.

Red. Unmistakably red.

Not Molly's. Not mine.

The world tilted slightly.

I stared at it for a moment too long, willing it to change color. To fade into coincidence. But it didn't.

It was Hannah's shade. The exact hue of memory. The one color I'd spent years burying.

I set the brush down slowly, carefully. The same way

you place something fragile on a ledge—afraid it might fall, or worse, that it already has.

Grabbing the brush and throwing it under the cabinet below my sink, I tried to ignore the findings of earlier. I picked up my phone and reluctantly returned a call from the cancer center to confirm my next round of chemo. I bit my nails like I always had when a situation got the best of me. Before I knew it, I was bleeding from a cuticle. Damn it. I sucked on my finger, tasting the metallic tang of the liquid oozing.

"Hi, um, I was calling to schedule my next round of chemotherapy." There was a brief pause, and then a woman blandly began speaking.

"Name, medical record number, birthday." As she typed on the other end, I could hear the clicking of the keys being pressed. *Click. Click. Click.*

"It's, um, I think 25903, Charlotte Rose. January 1, 1984." Some more clicking commenced.

"A new year's baby, how wonderful." I couldn't tell if this was sarcasm or genuineness, so I just responded with a thank you.

"You are booked for this Thursday. I assume you know the drill. Do I need to give you the instructions again?" I opened my calendar and began pulling up the day and typing the information.

"Um, no thanks. Save your voice, I've got the routine down."

"Suit yourself. Have a good day." Before I could respond, she had already ended the call.

Talk about some below-par customer service. I guess I expected a sing-song voice on the other end. As I stared at the event saved in my phone, the impending stress of the situation mounted. *Crap. I was done. Alex had sat by my side, the nurse had adjusted the drip, and I had pretended it was all fine. But it wasn't. Not really. I had told my family what was coming, but I hadn't shown them. I hadn't let them feel the weight with me. Tonight, at Sadie's, I couldn't keep the mask on anymore. My stomach turned. The memory of the nausea and exhaustion still clung to my skin. Telling my family had been hard, seeing the fear in their faces even harder. But now the weight was different. They knew. They were carrying it with me. And still, the thought of saying it again, of reminding them, felt unbearable."*

Mom must deal with my health issues now after Dad's passing. I can't bear putting all this back on her. It's just unfair. Alex is already flying back and forth for work, and she's in that new romance. She already feels obligated to put everything on hold. I hate this. Geoff and Sadie are doing IVF for the third time. My cancer is not well-timed for anyone, really. I guess you can't time looming death.

I noted the overwhelming emotions that were engulfing my mind. I closed my eyes, concentrated on my breathing, and asked God for peace and positivity. Once done, I grabbed my keys and hopped in my car. Despite my attempt at soothing myself, I could feel my nasal passage expanding and tears bursting through my eyes. Giving in to my emotions, I let my tears of anger and frustration pour down my face. Drops of salty water discolored my shirt.

If Will were here, he would have immediately pulled me into one of his strong embraces. Even when I didn't want a hug, he knew I needed him and would remain near until I caved. When it came to our marriage, he made it easy to lean on him. He would carry my cross as I would carry his. It was something we had learned in marriage counseling before getting married. Will's intuition had always been in tune with my emotional needs. He was always able to read my body language. All those unsaid quirks that made me who I am, Will knew like the back of his hand.

Then "Fix You" by Coldplay began to play over my car speaker, the moment the ignition started. It consoled me as opposed to making me cry harder. It was one of our songs. A song that resonated with both of us. A sign that I needed to get this all taken care of. Letting my moment of weakness go, I wiped my tears. As I drove toward Sadie's house, I sent a family voice text: *Meet me at Sadie's.*

As notifications began to chime, I rolled my eyes.

Sadie: *Are you okay?*

Alex: *What's wrong?*

Sadie: *All of us?*

Mom: *I have kids. They are fine.*

Sadie: *What's up?*

I couldn't help but laugh at my mom's response. She thought everything revolved around my kids, and she wasn't wrong, either. I could feel my sister's angst and pondered what to respond.

"Things are okay. I can't talk to you guys and drive. See you in 30."

Popping gum in my mouth, I unrolled the sunroof to let in some fresh air. The cold breeze hitting my skin jolted my spirits. My mind drifted away to the rhythm of the music. Then, before I could fully relax, another set of dings interrupted the music.

Alex: *Whatever, okay.*

Mom: *See you in a bit.*

Sadie: *Mom is already here, Char.*

Alex: *We can order takeout; I'm starving.*

Mom: *Kids are yelling for Chinese.*

Sadie: *Who wants egg rolls?*

Alex: *Max always eats more than we order. It's annoying because he takes mine.*

Sadie: *I'll order extra just for him then.*

The texts kept going on and on. Back and forth from Sadie to Alex as if they had forgotten that I was on the thread. This is what they do. This is what we all do. We text as if we're talking to one another in person. A series of texts that date back as far as our phone's history will allow. If a stranger read our text threads, they would be able to see the ebbs and flows of our relationships with each other, the emotions embedded within each emoji, and equally, each punctuation mark.

Even before the ability to text, when it was just good old-fashioned email, the banter was always there. It drove Will crazy how many times my phone notifications alerted me. Especially, Sadie. Her texts came through in a million broken messages. That was part of her quirkiness, though. She texted just like she talked. I loved her for it. She was always checking in.

Pulling into Sadie's driveway, I placed my car in park. Her home was stately, framed by box hedges and neat landscaping. I opened my sun-fold, and the prayer card from my father's funeral fell into my lap. For a moment, I stared at it as if it were a grenade. Then I slowly picked it up, holding the thick card stock in my hands. I read the Lord's prayer while envisioning my dad's smiling face.

Dad, I know you're always watching, listening, and are there for all of us. I know you are there. Right now, I could use a special favor.

I stopped as if he could respond, and taking a breath, I exhaled. "I don't know how to tell Mom and the girls that I must go through this whole nightmare again without you there to shelter the blow with your positivity."

Then a memory filled my head of my sisters and me as we used to play church. Alex would pretend to give the homily, Sadie would hand out "communion" mints, and I'd cry for dramatic effect. We were always loud, always fighting over lipstick or snacks. But at night, Dad would sit us down and pray over each of us by name. "You're sisters," he'd say. "Your job is to love each other, even when it's hard." I didn't know then how much I'd need that reminder.

"Thanks for the memory, Dad." I resumed crying and then drew the skin inward on my arm and put pressure between my thumb and pointer. I tended to do this act of self-infliction to prevent emotional breakdowns. It helped to refocus my energy and thoughts elsewhere. It was a mind game. The girls couldn't see me crying, but they could always tell. I faced the air conditioner vent toward me, allowing the blast of cold air to dry my glassy eyes. *Lord, intercede for me and allow me to live by the grace of your words.* I imagined the passion of Christ on the back, placing it back where it belonged.

I reapplied lipstick, scrunching my limp hair before turning off the ignition. As I approached Sadie's house, everyone began to funnel out. Max and Molly raced to me with open arms. Their screams and giggles couldn't help but make me laugh. Max held out a Lego character, newly constructed, while Molly approached with her sticky hands and dirt-stained dress. Her lopsided pigtails were clearly a sign of a well-played day. *One more thing to pre-treat.* I mentally added it to my pile.

Alex, Sadie, and Mom followed behind them. They

approached with less enthusiasm and more hesitancy. "Charlotte, what is the matter? Your text has us all worried. What is going on? Have you heard any news?" My mother's brow furrowed as she crossed her arms, making her look more fragile than usual. I looked at my sisters, making my annoyance known, and both pointed to the other as they began bickering.

"Mommy, Mommy. Look what I made. Isn't it cool? It's a superhero ninja! Do you like it?" Thank goodness for Max's interruption.

I looked at his creation and gave him a big squeeze. "It really is cool, Maxie. I love it!" Molly raised her arms to be picked up for an embrace. She wrapped her legs around me tightly and nestled my neck. She has a petite frame for a five-year-old, and as a result, she is light as a feather, unlike Max.

"Let's go inside. I can answer all the questions once my hunger pains have left. Is the food here yet? I want to beat Max to the egg rolls!" I pointed to him and made a face, and he stuck out his tongue in response. "Not if I beat you first!" Before we knew it, he took off running, laughing as he disappeared inside.

My mom ran after him, yelling, "Max, do not touch the food. Go wash your hands! I am telling you if you touch that food, son …"

As we trailed behind them, my sisters asked simultaneously, "So, what is going on?" I grabbed Molly tighter since she began to slip and pushed her back up my hip. She laid her head on my shoulder, tired from the day.

"Just grab the wine. We'll need it."

Alex groaned loudly. "Ughh. Just tell us now. Why the

secrecy? I already hate this. I can't stand it when people do this. It's like, enough of the theatrics already!"

Ignoring what she said, I placed Molly down, pushing her toward the kitchen. "I hope Geoff didn't drink the 2016 Pinot Noir, it's my favorite. He always has a good stash. Can you sneak a bottle or two, Sadie?" She smirked, running ahead to find the glasses and wine.

I hung up my weathered jacket and bag. As I walked toward the kitchen, I found my mom and sisters crowded around the bar, passing around the cartons of food. The kids were eating at the table, cheerfully joking and giggling. Alex handed me an over-filled glass of wine. Grabbing it, I excessively swallowed and wiped my mouth thirstily. I know I am going to pay heavily for drinking later, but I push that thought from my mind.

Mom gasped, "Charlotte Anne, you better slow down. What would people think?"

I gulped and looked up, ignoring my mom's annoyance. "That she is struggling emotionally and needs liquid courage." Alex flashed a smirk at me.

"Funny, being here with you all reminds me of when we were kids. How we'd sit around this very table with Dad sneaking us extra syrup on pancakes when Mom wasn't looking. How Sadie would lecture us on all her dorky science facts, and Alex would dare me to eat butter straight. Even then, I was the crier," I chuckled, feeling the pressure in my chest rise. "But he'd pray over us. Every night. And now, I swear I still feel him here."

I raised my hands in surrender and stared each of them in their worried eyes, all three inching forward. "I'm just going to say what I need to say, or otherwise I will not be able to say it. It will probably come out all jumbled anyway." I took a breath and did my best to avoid their concerned expressions. "It's back. The cancer. It's back. I've already started treatment as you know, and that first round nearly knocked me flat. It was a jolt of PTSD along with a reflux that my body is just not what it was pre-cancer the first time. I didn't want to burden you with all the ugly details, but I can't hide it anymore. I know I need you. And I'll need you more as this process continues. In fact, I'm still going through emotions. Damn roller coaster. I'm sorry that I had to tell you like this, but I will need your help more now than last time with everything going on. I'm just sorry."

Pools of liquid beads filled my mother's eyes. "Charlotte, you will be perfectly fine. Only God can heal you, and only He can take away life. So, let's just leave it all up to him. Okay? No point in stressing out. We are all here to lift you up. By the grace of God, Will will be found. All will be okay, you just have faith."

It was so interesting how times of intense strain changed my mother completely. She was able to quickly push away her own fear and step into her role as mother with the unconditional duty of putting her family first. Over the years, she's perfected this skill—compartmentalizing her feelings better than anyone I've ever known. She'd lock them away, throw away the key, and arm herself with prayer as if preparing to go to war, displaying no sign of her emotional burden.

Alex's hand trembled as she toyed with her wine glass, her tough exterior cracking for a split second. Her almost unrecognizable and explicit display showed me that it was gut-wrenching for her.

"I'll be alright, Al. I'm not scared, nor am I worried. I'll just need a lot of your sarcasm and, for sure, our good old-fashioned chemo parties."

Sadie chimed in with her most upbeat voice, although I heard a tinge of apprehension. "You've got it! You beat it once, Charlie, and you can beat it again." She instantly turned her back to grab her bottle of water, desperately needing to quench her dry throat.

A confidence I'd never felt overwhelmed me as I looked at the three of the most important people in my life. "Look, I have always had an inner strength and overall awareness. If God wanted me to get cancer again, then I am perfectly fine with His will. In whatever circumstances, God, I know, will have my back. Whatever the situation, good or bad, I am not worried. So, if I successfully make it through, which is the plan, of course, then that's fabulous. If the alternative were to occur, God forbid, I know that firstly, it is His will. Secondly, I know His plan is divine for His reasons and His reasons alone. You guys would be sad, but in the end, you're stronger and more resilient than you know."

I paused, taking notice that each of their faces was stricken with tears, except my mother's, although I saw a subtle shine that had not been there before my monologue. This time, however, I had one hell of an angel guiding me. I had Dad! I smiled at the thought, but the instant I thought of him, an immediate pressure built in my chest, a heaviness I recognized all too well from his passing. The emotional rollercoaster of his lifelong battle with Parkinson's. Then his sudden battle with life and his death itself. My spirit wanted to break. I wanted to give in to the thoughts of negativity that were swimming around because it would be so easy. My resistance was causing a buildup so great it physically hurt me.

"I have my next chemo this week. I'll need all your help in getting M&M where they need to be. I'll be out for the count for an entire week, just like last time post-chemo." Mom was the first to rush in and pull me in close for a hug.

"Okay, Charlotte, I'm here. I'll take off work and get the kids. I'm sure both Sadie and Alex can take turns bringing you and being with you at chemo, just like the last time." I looked at the girls, and both nodded dutifully as if they were back in time, submissive daughters not wanting to disappoint their mother.

"I'm going to go get washed up for dinner, then talk to the kids. They'll certainly have questions afterward. If you guys can just help me out funneling through their emotions, that would help me out a great deal, too. Especially with Max, he gets so emotional sometimes. He still remembers the last time. Then there's Dad, and that was a big loss for him. Now with Will gone, I just don't know. I don't want him to think he will lose me, too. I also don't want to lie to them just in case. You know?"

My sisters eyed each other with a telepathic communication of angst. "Sadie told Alex about Will and the situation. I don't mind taking the kids, Charlotte. You need your strength now more than ever, and these kids need you to be strong and healthy."

I nodded in response, "I know, Mom. I'm sorry you had to hear from Sadie, but I just couldn't muster the courage to tell you all that, and now this. It's all been so much. I have already been to the police station twice since it happened. Now they're saying that they have footage showing that he's alive. So, my question is, why is he not home?"

My mother looked at me with utter certainty. "Charlotte, Will has a good heart, and he is always calculating with every decision that he makes. There's a reason why you're going through this, as well as Will. Rest assured, it will all come out in due time. Like I said, for now, we need to focus on getting healthy." She gave me another hug. I hugged her back more tightly, taking in her light citrus scent. This time, the pressure was greater.

I excused myself, grabbing my wine as I made my way to the guest quarters. The room is calming, with a light blue-gray hue and a trace of lavender in the air. As I closed the bathroom door and clicked the lock, I noticed I was shaking. I could feel my chest swelling and my breath quickening as I held back my tears. I hated crying, especially in front of people. It was a level of intimacy that made me uncomfortable.

As I turned the faucet, my tears mimicked the flow of water. At first, a quiet, understated trickle, but then my tears began to rush down my face with greater intensity. My eyes searched the ceiling for a God that wasn't visible. I dropped to my knees and mouthed a prayer to Him, pleading to be heard. Getting up, I composed myself and splashed my face with cold water. Inhaling deeply, I allowed time to slow the puffiness before rejoining the family.

Will once told me, during the worst round of my first cancer, that maybe I liked the attention. That maybe I was using it. He was angry and afraid, and so was I–but I never forgot it. I never stopped wondering if there was a part of me that believed him. That's when something broke in me.

Chapter 18

Charlotte – Ink

"Max! Molly! Hey guys, can you come over here for a quick minute?" I peeked my head into the kitchen as they yelled at one another about bedtime. "Max and Molly! Did you hear Mommy? Please do me a favor and stop what you're doing. I need to talk to you." Tugging at one another, they reluctantly followed her.

I settled myself on the tufted couch in the sitting room adjacent to the kitchen. It was a bit closed off from everyone, so we had some privacy. I patted the couch, signaling for them to sit.

"What is it, Mom?" Max asked as he scooted next to me. He smiled at me, his eyes sympathetic, and gently placed his arm around me. "Is it Dad? Is he back yet?" His eyes were eager and searching. It broke my heart to tell him no. Molly sat on my lap and mindlessly began playing with my hair.

"Yeah, Mommy, is Daddy back yet? I miss him." I smiled with an incredible force of energy, looking at my

161

children, taking in their innocence. "Daddy will come back soon, but not today. Just keep praying to God, okay? This conversation is not about Daddy, though. It's about Mommy."

I looked at Max, grabbing his chin gently, directing his face toward mine to ensure I gained his fleeting attention. "Max, do you remember when Mommy had cancer?" Cocking his head slightly, he squinted, showing a sliver of his green eyes.

"Not really. I mean, I've seen the pictures and remember a little bit of what happened." He bit down on his lip, trying to recall those moments. "I remember you with no hair. That was scary, and I didn't like it. I wasn't scared of you, though, Mommy." He shook his head in clear disapproval and hints of sadness.

Molly looked at me and didn't let go of my hair as she continued to play with it. "Mommy, you had no hair. That wouldn't be pretty, I think. I like your hair." She stopped and stared at my hair in her hand. "So, you looked like Grandpa?" she questioned with childlike ignorance.

I let out a little laugh at the thought. "No, Molly, I didn't look like Pop because he at least had some hair. Sweet girl, I know you like my hair. And you're right, the last time the medicine made it fall out. It might happen again, but remember, that means the medicine is working hard for me." I held out my finger to emphasize this fact. Bewilderment showed in her big brown eyes, and astonishment was cast upon her face.

"So, when Mommy lost her hair, that was because I had cancer. I know you know what cancer is, Max, because we spoke about it, but Molly doesn't." I turned to Molly with that statement. "Cancer is like a bad bug that takes over a

162

person's body. Those bugs can make you sick. It can slowly eat away at the body. If a doctor doesn't know, then they can't help them get better." I looked at her to understand, but she looked confused and a bit frightened by my words.

"Mommy has to get medicine again, the kind that makes me tired and sick at first but helps me fight the bad bugs. I've only had one round so far, but there are more to come." Max gave me a hug, his arms squeezing me tightly.

"Mommy, don't worry, I will take good care of you."

Molly followed suit and gave me a big hug. "Mommy, I don't want bugs to eat you. Don't worry, though, I will help Max take care of you. I'm sad, though; I will miss your pretty hair." She frowned then, her pouty lips pursed in concern.

I embraced them both cozily. "My sweet babies, thank you for being mine. I love you both very much. Now, what do you say we go finish dinner? Then, maybe Nana will let us all have ice cream because after today, we all deserve something sweet."

They ran away yelling, "Nana! Nana! Mom said we can have ice cream if we finish our food. Nana! We get ice cream!"

I heard her laugh as she attempted to settle them both back down at the dining table. "Hush now, they can hear you kiddos across the world. Let's finish eating our food. Knowing Aunt Sadie, she probably has some tasty treat just waiting for all of us. Maybe Uncle Geoff has his stash of cookies and cream?" They both yelped with excitement and began to shove piles of food in their mouths, snickering as they did.

Walking into the kitchen, I grabbed my glass of wine and drank it down in one gulp as if it were not a fine wine but more so a shot. Sadie walked over, touching me lightly on the shoulder. "You should probably eat something. The idea of you trashed with Mom here doesn't sound like a great idea. Plus, that isn't you. Would you rather talk?" Sadie pushed a plate of food over to me.

"Not particularly." I shook my head, but before I could push it away, she stopped me. "Look, you need all the weight you can get, and you know it. I understand you are under an intense amount of stress, but this right now isn't the best idea. So, if you don't want me to go get your mother, you better start shoving that food in your face like your own children are doing right now."

I rolled my eyes dramatically and brought the plate back toward me like a scorned child. I began to take small bites. "I don't need another mom, geez. But you are right, I am going to pay for drinking later. It's going to hit me especially with this new cocktail of meds."

Sadie pulled up a barstool and took a seat. She whispered in an attempt for the kids not to hear. "Any word on Will?"

Looking down and shaking my head sullenly back and forth, I sucked in a breath. "No. Nothing. I keep getting this strange feeling that I'm being watched. I'm also still getting those weird notes, but some are a bit different than before. Perhaps they're clues of some sort. I can't put it all together. I sound like a crazy person. I know he is alive, though; I feel it in my bones. Perhaps he is watching me, protecting me somehow." I messed with my wedding ring, twirling it round and round.

Sadie put her hand on mine. "You aren't a loony. You are in tune with him, is all. I absolutely can understand the power of your love and connection." I smiled in gratitude at her gesture. "You know, Max and Molly have been seeing stuff outside the house. They mentioned a person watching them from across the lake. They don't seem spooked, though, which is strange. It can't be Will, so it must be someone else, but who?"

As my stress levels visibly rose, Sadie must have sensed it because she came to my aid. "Look, if you need me, I'm here. I don't think Will is gone either. If it helps to say."

I dismissively shrugged. "I'm waiting to be questioned again. They stated that they went to the kids' school, and they questioned the staff and even some of our neighbors. They even rang Will's family and friends, as well. Hopefully, we hear something soon." I looked at her and bit the inside of my mouth hard. I could taste the blood. Smiling wearily, I squeezed her hand. "Look, you need to not stress, as ridiculous a suggestion as that sounds. It's not good for conceiving a baby. I know my situation is not ideal for you, but you also need to try to relax."

She half-smiled in appreciation. "I needed this venting session, thanks." I loved that I had built-in shrinks as sisters. I loved them, and I hated stressing them all out.

"What stress?" Alex looked flushed as she walked over, pink bursts of color riddling her cheeks.

"Al, are you okay?"

Looking frazzled, she grabbed my wine as if it were a fraternity party, then poured another glass and downed it in one gulp. "Yeah, sure, why? I must go to Spain last minute. My job is literally nonstop. Then obviously you just dropped this bad news. I don't even have time to digest it all, to be honest. Then Sadie blabbed about Will earlier." I rolled my eyes at Sadie, knowing that I couldn't be mad at her right now. I needed her. I needed all my family.

"Seriously? I already spoke to Mom. I can only assume Geoff knows now. You haven't told Marla, though, have you? I ask because I haven't spoken to her yet. That's a whole different situation I haven't dealt with. It's all overwhelming." I grabbed the bottle and refilled my glass. I rushed to sip it before it spilled over the top.

Alex laughed. "You can't get pissed at me. If it were me telling you, let's face it, you would have had her on the phone hours ago." I let out a laugh, then we were all laughing. Alex grabbed at my glass and pulled it her way, then downed it. "You don't need this, and you know it." I rolled my eyes but was secretly thankful to her for sparing me hugging the toilet later.

"So, it's okay because you beat me by a few imaginary hours? Oh, okay."

"Alex, on a serious note, I'm okay. Not that this all isn't serious. Right now, I am at least. It's a lot, but the cops are on it. They said that they have footage of him in the office, though, after the craziness. That was a bit frustrating to hear."

Alex cracked her neck, visibly stressed. "Yeah, that is true. You are strong, but remember, you don't have to be around us. You know that, right? Like, we get the amount of pressure with work deadlines and all. Will's business, then the kids, and now your health. We totally understand. You can break, Char; we've got you." I let go of half a smile, fighting back the urge to cry.

"I wonder why he was at the office, though. If he was there after, then why isn't he here now? I don't get it." I met her gaze. Her eyes were red-rimmed and bloodshot, a clear sign she was crying in the other room before she walked in. That's the crappy thing about cancer. It rips apart those who are closest to the patient. It's a traumatic event that has a ripple effect. I hated that about this illness. I needed to distract myself from my thoughts.

"So, Spain, huh? Can you pack me in your bags? Maybe cancer won't follow me to Spain. Plus, I am in desperate need of a trip."

Sadie groaned and looked up at the ceiling. "Ugh, you and me both. This IVF stuff is going to kill me. I am so pissed off all the damn time. I have bruises up and down my stomach. It hurts to even sit or stand. I feel bloated and just gross. This has been a few years too many."

I nibbled at my food again, but I wasn't hungry. "You guys do need a vacation. Too bad you both can't be smuggled away in my suitcase. I don't know how long I will be gone this time. Should only be a couple of days, but I never know when it's going to roll into a longer assignment." Her double lashes fluttered like thick butterflies. I always felt like Alex led such a glamorous lifestyle. Some days I even wondered what it was like to be her. It must be nice to always be jet-setting from one country to the next. Guess grass isn't always greener.

Just then, Mom walked in, her hair falling in her face as she brushed it aside. "Charlotte, the kids are getting sleepy. Did you want me to go home with you or just take off work tomorrow?" My mother has always taken good care of those around her. Naturally, no one does it better than the matriarch. She walked over to me and leaned on the counter directly across from me. A faint whiff of her Chanel wafted toward me. She'd worn it for years, ever since Dad gave it to her for one of her birthdays. "You look very tired. Sleep is important, Charlotte, especially now.

You need to go home and go straight to bed. I can come and make you some tea."

I reached out and touched her hand. It was cold, and her skin was soft under my hand. "Mom, you need a break, not me! Plus, it's not that easy. If only I could go home, sip tea, and sleep away all my problems. It's getting late. I'm going to head out with the kiddos. I will probably take a bath, then go straight to bed myself. No need to come, Mom. I promise to follow your instructions. I will have no problems sleeping tonight."

Turning around, I faced the open door. "Max! Molly! We have to go. You guys have school tomorrow." Immediately, groans ensued.

"I don't want to go, Mama!" Molly's shrill whine echoed through the hall.

"Mom, come on, Uncle Geoff promised that next time I came over that he would play video games with me. He just told Aunt Sadie he was on his way home, too." Max walked in, a pout plastered on his face, giving him an almost cartoonish expression. I looked at them and stifled a laugh.

"We can come back this weekend and you can play with Uncle Geoff, I promise. You guys go get your backpacks and be sure to say goodbye to everyone."

The grumbling persisted as we walked toward the car. I secured the kids in their seats and handed each their water. I gave Mom a tight squeeze before opening my door. As I closed it behind me, she waved, turning to walk away. Alex and Sadie were still talking by the door and waved simultaneously as they turned to walk back inside. That was when I noticed something underneath the windshield wiper. I grabbed it and placed it on my lap as I put the car in reverse. As I headed down the street en route to our home, I stared at the small, paper rectangle with trepidation. There were no markings on the outside of it, just a plain envelope.

I opened it up and slipped out a faded blue paper. Printed in back ink were the words. *Mine.* I gasped. My breath sucked right out of me. Slamming on my brakes, I almost crashed into the truck stopped at the red stop light before me. My head reared back, and my car jerked in place, slowly rocking back and forth at the abrupt stop. I barely missed rear-ending the truck. I rubbed my neck, hoping that I wouldn't have remnants of whiplash.

"Are you guys okay? I didn't mean to do that. Mommy wasn't paying attention."

Max looked at me in the rear-view mirror. "Mommy, when driving a car, you should always pay attention." I rolled my eyes and cracked a smile.

"Thanks, Captain Obvious." He started laughing. Max always found a way to make a bad situation just a little bit better. Unexpectedly, tears began to flood my eyes. I gained an overwhelming sense of fear. It encompassed me.

Who left me the note? Was it Will? Is it me? I'm confused. Why do I have to lose my husband and battle cancer, all while being stalked? This hardly seemed fair. Then again, what in life is ever fair? This wasn't there when I went to Sadie's. At least I don't think it was. It couldn't have been. I tried to remember getting in my car before going to Sadie's and then again when I arrived at her house, but I don't recollect seeing it. I was all over the place emotionally, so I guess anything is possible. Given my string of bad luck, I really shouldn't be shocked. Does that mean that someone placed it on my car after I arrived? I was inside for a little over an hour.

169

Whoever it was, their timing was spot on. They must be following me.

Shivers raced up my spine and tickled my neck. I turned, peering through the car windows. I noticed a few cars behind me, but it could be regular people on their way home. My paranoia was taking over. I felt like I should be medicated.

Who is watching me? Better yet, who is stalking me like prey?

Chapter 19

Charlotte – Confessions

I had passed this church countless times. I'd been baptized here. Received communion here. Cried through my confirmation in these very pews. But I hadn't entered the confessional since college. Not since …

The church was quiet, empty pews stretching like arms toward the altar, offering a peace I desperately needed.

I hadn't planned to come. I hadn't planned anything lately. The day pulled me here, one heavy footstep after the other, like some internal compass was overriding my exhaustion.

I sank into the middle pew and let the silence wrap around me.

Everything hurt. Not just my body, though the fatigue still clung to my bones from chemo, but deeper places. The kind that doctors can't diagnose. The kind that only God can see and heal.

I looked up at the bronze crucifix, analyzing the face of Christ. He is solemn, weathered, yet He watches.

I knelt and pressed my hands together, looking into his

eyes, pleading, "I don't know what to do anymore," I whispered. "I'm trying to hold it together, but I feel like I'm unraveling thread by thread."

I didn't expect an answer. But I've learned over time by immersing myself in deep prayer that it wasn't about hearing but rather about emptying and surrendering to God.

A rustle echoed from the back of the church. I turned.

A man dressed in black vestments with light blond hair was straightening books, row by row. Then his eyes locked with mine, and I noticed the friendly smile. It was Father Alvarez, a friend and our local priest. He walked slowly down the center aisle, his clerical collar crisp and his hands tucked into his sleeves.

"Charlotte," he said gently, taking a seat beside me. "You look like a woman carrying far too much. Do you need to talk?"

"I am, and yes, Father, I do."

He took a seat in the pew in front of me and turned to face me. "What can I do to appease your soul?"

"My husband is missing. My son and daughter are scared. Someone has broken into my home and taken a picture of me while I was sleeping, and I don't know who to trust anymore. My cancer has returned, I'm undergoing chemo, and it's heavy, Father. Much too heavy."

Tears stabbed at my eyes.

He didn't react with shock or pity but with quiet attention.

"And ... I'm tired, Father, from these new rounds of chemo. I'm so exhausted from pretending to be strong for everyone else. My face hurts from pretending to be happy and smiling in front of my kids so they don't see the fear crawling up my spine."

His voice was low. "And in the quiet?"

"That is where I am the absolute worst. That is when I fall apart and am a wreck. I pray, but I don't feel anything. I reach out, but I can't feel His hand. I miss the version of me before all of this. I miss being known, lively, and loved."

Father Alvarez rested his hand over mine. "Well, first off, you are always loved and not just by Our Creator. I think deep down you know that. God doesn't just know the whole of you, Charlotte. He's holding together the broken pieces even when you can't feel it. He is there, but it's not on your time, it's on His."

Father Alvarez's voice softened. "Charlotte, do you remember the woman with the issue of blood? Twelve years she suffered. She was alone and cast aside. But when she reached out even just to touch the edge of Christ's robe, what did He do? He stopped. Not because He didn't know who touched Him, but because He wanted her to know that *He* saw her. He saw her fully and completely, broken and brave."

I swallowed hard.

"She didn't shout. She didn't demand. She just reached, and that was enough. That's faith, Charlotte. Not noise or certainty. Just reaching even in the dark. Faith, hope, and love. Never doubt."

I nodded, blinking away tears. "I keep wondering if all this suffering is part of something bigger. Like maybe it isn't senseless."

He smiled faintly. "That question means your heart is still looking, hoping, and well, God can most certainly work with that."

A long pause stretched between us. The cavity of the church was warm, and the distant voices of the choir could be heard, and it brought comfort just being there.

As I stared at the candles flickering in the corner, I envisioned Max and Molly, "I don't want my kids to see me fall apart."

"Then let them see you lean on something bigger. Let them see that faith doesn't mean pretending things are okay. It means believing you're not alone and having God carry your burden when you can't."

I let his words sink in.

He reached into his pocket and handed me a small card. "Saint Dymphna. Patron saint of those who suffer mental and emotional distress. She knew isolation. But she also knew that healing wasn't always a miracle; it was often a process."

I traced the image on the card with my thumb.

"You don't have to hold the line alone, Charlotte. Come back anytime. You're not just enduring this, you're walking through it with grace, just as He did." He pointed admirably at the cross before us.

I smiled for the first time in days.

As I left the church, the light filtering through the stained glass felt warmer somehow. Not because the storm has passed, but because I know now that I am not walking through this alone. I never was.

Chapter 20

Will – Through Her Eyes

T he morning light filtered in through the high window of the shed, slicing the dim interior with long, pale beams. My head pounded. My back ached. The cot beneath me was barely more than a slab of canvas stretched over a metal frame, and I could feel every support bar.

But it wasn't the physical pain that kept me from resting.

It was her.

Hannah.

She moved like a ghost around the space, always watching, always near. She hadn't changed in the years since I last saw her, not just in appearance, but in presence. Her energy was fractured. She carried herself with sharp precision, like someone who had spent too long on the edge of unraveling and now wore it like armor.

She brought me water. A rag to clean my face. She handed me a bottle of ibuprofen without a word and then stood by the window, eyes scanning the trees.

"You always have a habit of vanishing," I said, my voice hoarse.

Her mouth twitched. Not quite a smile. Not quite anything. "You always had a habit of looking the wrong way."

I didn't reply. My energy was better spent preserving whatever strength I had left.

Outside, birds chirp. A squirrel darted across the clearing. The world, maddeningly normal.

But inside this space, this cocoon of silence and tension, everything just felt wrong. I was dependent on a woman I once loved and have long since feared. A woman who now seemed to know far too much.

"How long have you been here?" I asked.

"Long enough."

I sat up slowly, wincing, the pain amplifying as I moved. "Why are you doing this?"

Hannah turned. her eyes were clear, but something darker lingered beneath. "Because someone had to. You think Charlotte sees it? She doesn't. Not all of it. Not yet."

"Sees what?"

"The setup. The misdirection. The layers of rot beneath your perfect life. You were all being watched long before I showed up. I just happened to notice it first."

My stomach turned. I didn't want her to be right. I didn't want to believe that someone was burrowing into our lives that deeply. But I couldn't deny the signs anymore.

"And you?" I asked. "What are you really doing here, Hannah?"

She paused, then sat down across from me. For the first time, she looked tired. Human.

"I came back because I thought maybe I was wrong

about you," she said quietly. "About everything. But then I saw who else was circling your family, and I couldn't stay away. Not when it's him."

"Baker."

She nodded.

A long silence passed.

"He's not just stalking," she whispered. "He's strategizing and setting traps. Getting into your systems, your home, your heads." She gestured to her head for dramatic effect. "I think he's working with someone on the inside."

My thoughts spiraled.

Hannah stood up again. Her hand rested on the rifle leaning against the wall, a juxtaposing image, one unlike anything I had ever seen from her.

"I need you to trust me," she said. "Just long enough to stop him."

Trust. the word lands like a stone in my gut. But what choice did I have?

Outside, something moved.

We both turned.

The threads were unraveling. and I was starting to see the pattern.

Chapter 21

Marla – Plans in Motion

M arla adjusted her lipstick carefully, her eyes cold and unwavering in the mirror as she rehearsed the lie. What is a lie anyway? A means to an end. I can live with that.

The morning sun filtered through the slats of the blinds as it caught the edge of her silver compact. She snapped it shut. Precision is everything.

What is it that Machiavelli stated, that we need to focus on the consequences rather than dwell on the means used to implement them? Yeah, I believe that is what it was. I reveled in that book back in college. It's what got me through everything.

Every detail has to be seamless. My clothes, my tone, and my alibi. Especially today.

Lawson had started asking questions. His "friendly" hallway conversations had turned into probing, into accusations. He seemed to know something, or at least he insinuated that he did.

Worst of all is that I have to sit here and play the unsuspecting, efficient office manager. The pleasantries themselves are driving me mad. Lawson knows too much. My life is a house of cards. All it takes is one careless word, and everything I have worked for will collapse.

Marla sat at the kitchen table, hands folded as she waited for her 'focus drops' to dissolve under her tongue. They were a gift from a man whose name she refuse to even whisper, of blended nootropics and a hint of something stronger that was untraceable.

She stared at her perfectly manicured nails but noticed one jagged edge. She attempted to even it out but instead ended up ripping the entire nail. Damn it. Marla stared at it unblinkingly. That was when the bitterness hit, then the high lucid tunnel vision that made my world go sharp at the edges.

She took a deep breath, long and drawn. Finally, she could think with clarity. His voice still echoed it her head, the boy was his.

She opened her notebook. A single page, scribbled in meticulous script.

Phase One: Isolation.

> *Charlotte destabilized. Surveillance complete.*
> *Family tension at peak.*

Phase Two: Infiltration.

> *Trust established. Presence normalized.*
> *Blame shifted.*

Phase Three: Collection.

Remove the child. Minimum disruption. Avoid recognition.

She didn't like the word "kidnapping." It sounded so desperate, so chaotic, and so pathetic. What she was doing wasn't theft, it was reallocation. Max didn't belong in that house anymore with Charlotte. Not with a mother unraveling from illness and paranoia. Not with a father who disappears when things get hard. Max wasn't Will's, or so she believed. And if she delivered him, she'd finally prove her worth.

Molly needed structure. She needed safety and certainty. She could provide that for her … and for him.

Marla rose and moved to the closet, extracting the outfit she'd laid out days before. Neutral, timeless, and simply forgettable. The kind you'd see in a crowd and forget by the next block. She folded it neatly into a tote beside a brunette wig, dark, wide sunglasses, and black gloves. The burner phone was charged and ready to go. The route memorized.

Her hands paused over the last item, a small action figure. It wasn't Max's. It never had been, but it would help. Boys his age always reached for a distraction before realizing the danger. It could play into her favor.

In the back of her closet, she clicked open her suitcase. Inside were documents, fake credentials, and a large stash of cash. *This is my safety net. It's amazing what watching criminal shows can do for a person.*

She glanced at her watch. Lawson was scheduled to speak to James this afternoon. When Will went missing, Lawson had magically appeared on the schedule, but by then, Marla knew who he was and what he had been hired for.

She had until then.

Today was the day.

And nothing, no one, was going to stop her.

Chapter 22

Charlotte – Chemo II: The Toll

I remembered the drip of the chemo vividly; each drop felt like a small surrender and a small victory all at once. The infusion room was colder than usual that morning, or maybe it was just me. I sat curled in a blanket Molly had picked out, purple with cartoon stars and her name scrawled in puffy fabric paint across the hem.

Marla rushed in, huffing, tired.

"Really, Marla. I mean it. You've done enough for today."

Marla didn't answer right away. She quietly packed up the empty soup containers, her hands moving with a deliberate precision, almost rehearsed.

"You really don't have to keep doing this," Charlotte said softly.

Marla's smile flickered. "I don't mind. I like helping. I just feel terrible. I have been so MIA, so distracted. Sometimes I don't even know which version of myself to bring around you–the strong one, the optimistic one, or the wreck. Between you being ill and Will being gone … I just feel like I'm failing at all of it." She paused, eyes lingering too long on a photo of Max with Molly framed and placed on the medical side table. "Some people don't realize how lucky they are until they're not anymore."

I cocked my head at that statement. "Sorry?"

The line landed like a cold drop of water down Charlotte's spine. It had been too heavy, too reflective, but she was much too tired to ask what Marla meant.

"Oh, nothing, don't mind me. Just splattering on words that don't make sense." She dismissed it as she shook her head.

"Thanks, Marla," I murmured instead, my eyes feeling heavy with the weight of the drugs.

Marla gave me a final tight smile. "Get some rest." Then she quickly slipped through the door.

The nurse who passed Marla on the way in was new, young, chipper with tight curls and a broad white smile. Her name tag read "Brianna," and she seemed uncertain, her pen tapping impatiently against the clipboard as she reviewed my chart.

"You're here for your second cycle? What were your therapy drugs, do you recall?"

"Yes," I said quietly, swallowing against the raw lining in my throat. "I was told I have more to go. As for what they have me on, I think it's something like Carboplatin and paclitaxel. Not sure if I said that correctly."

She gave a slight grin, "No, that's right. Just checking a few boxes is all. I'll be right back. I am still trying to get the hang of things here at the hospital. I will get this to your regular nurse, Mariam."

The woman across the hall was older. Gracefully thin,

she sported a bright Pucci-inspired headscarf that matched her lipstick perfectly. She granted a small nod of solidarity in my direction before returning to the book in her lap. I recognized the cover, a biblical devotional. I remember my mom having that very same one. It was gifted to her by Martha, Officer Cortez's wife.

I turned toward the window. The sunlight was weak today, barely piercing the clouds. I missed being outside, being a normal human being. And I desperately missed feeling strong.

Back when I first got the call, I thought I'd handle it better the second time. I was wrong. Recurrence hits differently. It doesn't just scare you—it shatters your sense of fairness. I had done everything right. Followed every doctor's recommendation. Changed my diet. Monitored every ache and twinge. And still.

Still.

"How are you feeling today?" a voice interrupted gently. It was Jennifer, the social worker. One of the good ones. Older, warm, no clipboard in hand.

"Tired," I admitted. "But I'm here."

"That counts for something."

She sat beside me. "Mind if I ask you something a little heavier today?"

I nodded.

"When you think about getting through this, what keeps you anchored?"

My throat tightened.

"Max and Molly," I whispered. "And faith. Even when it feels far away."

She nodded like she understood completely.

Kathryn Nichols

"That far-away feeling ... it's normal. God's not offended by our fear."

I didn't have time to respond. A commotion broke out near the entrance.

A person had walked in—brunette, sunglasses, hat, oversized coat. She looked out of place.

Disoriented. Like she didn't belong there.

Then Jennifer's voice sharpened.

"Excuse me, ma'am. Can I help you?"

The woman looked up, startled. Her eyes darted toward me. I froze.

Marla.

I knew her posture. Her walk. The cold flicker in her stare.

"Just looking for someone," Marla said sweetly.

Jennifer stepped closer. "I'm going to have to ask you to wait outside if you're not a patient or family."

For a split second, Marla hesitated. Then she lunged forward toward me.

Chaos exploded.

Jennifer grabbed her arm. Nurses yelled. Chairs tipped. Marla screamed something incoherent as she was pulled back. Nurse Mariam hurried in and hit the emergency button. Security rushed in.

I couldn't breathe.

I couldn't move.

They dragged her out, thrashing. The devotional woman beside me clutched her book to her chest, eyes wide.

My IV beeped. A nurse hurried over to calm me, but the damage was done.

Jennifer knelt beside me, her voice shaking. "She won't come back. I promise."

But I knew better.

There was something in her stare. It was unnerving.

And somewhere deep down, I knew—she hadn't come to scare me.

She had come to hurt me.

Chapter 23

Charlotte – Church Bells

T he wind picked up just as I stepped out of the car. The air was sharp and anxious, pushing against my coat as if trying to keep me from going inside. The sky churned above me, grey clouds swallowing the sun like a promise that would never be kept.

I stood frozen at the steps of St. Gabriel's again. The stained-glass windows glowed faintly with the last of the light, red and gold fragments spilling across the sidewalk. I stared up at the stone arches, the pointed doors, and the gentle sway of the lanterns above them. My fingers trembled against the cold iron handle.

I exhaled, watching the vapor of my breath drift upward like smoke from a dying fire.

Inside, the scent of roses wrapped around me immediately. Not the artificial kind but the sort that lingers from a beloved funeral, reminiscent of the slowly dying bouquets and midnight novenas.

The statues hang their heads in silent prayer, their presence felt.

I moved quietly through the vestibule, past the velvet-lined kneelers and the dark mahogany pews, until I found the chapel alcove.

He was waiting.

Not in a booth but seated in the corner of the quiet side-chapel, where confession was sometimes held during Lent or holy days. Father Alvarez. Gentle in his posture, sharp-eyed.

The moment he spotted me, he nodded and offered a polite smile.

"Charlotte. You've come back."

My lip quivered. I didn't kneel just yet. I stood still, nervous, anxiety riddling my very bones.

"I don't deserve to be here."

"None of us do," he says. "That's why grace was given, not earned. How can I help you today?"

I slowly stepped forward.

"Father, I have to confess. I know it's not the appropriate time, but last time I was here, I should have. I needed to, but I … I just …" With that, he stood and placed his hand upon my shoulder, briefly closing his eyes.

"Come. Let God unburden your heart." He guided me to the confessional on the side of the church where the detailed cherubim look fondly upon the heavens.

I entered the tiny room and knelt before the screen. My eyes closed, my heart heavy.

The silence aches.

"Bless me, Father, for I have sinned… It's been… It's been several years."

He waited in the quiet. A confessor's mercy.

"I killed my baby."

The words hung in the air like ash.

"It wasn't a miscarriage. It wasn't taken from me. I handed it over. I made the appointment. I sat in that waiting room. I signed the papers. I tried to make peace with it. I lied to myself over and over again."

His face did not change.

"I've never told anyone. Not my family. Not even Will."

Father Alvarez didn't move. Didn't flinch. I could barely make out the lowering of his head. As if he knew on some level the weight before I even uttered the words aloud.

He inhaled slowly.

The chapel was so still I could hear the shifting groan of the pew behind me, the creak of old wood remembering older sins. I stared at the flicker of a nearby votive candle, the wax melting in slow, uneven drips. The scent of incense pricked my heart.

"I remember it all," I whispered. "Every single part of that excruciating day. I've tried to bury it … but it buried me."

My chest tightened. The scent shifted, and suddenly, I was not in the chapel anymore.

I was back on that tile floor, back in that sterile white room. Back in that body, back in the conscious mind of the girl who took her child's life.

I cradle myself on the shower floor, holding tightly to my water and tear-drenched legs. My hair is matted to my face, giving me a haunting appearance. The black penny tile surrounding me is stark in contrast to these white subway tile walls. The white feels like a blatant mockery of my feelings. It's a complete contrast of sins. My transgressions bleed slowly from my body, trickling down the drain. The drain allows for a temporary escape. However, the stain will forever be present.

My olive skin is sodden as I sit with my forehead pressed against my knees. I squeeze them to my chest so hard that my head aches. It's a dull, deep-embedded agony, but it goes beyond the physical. The only way I can tell the difference between my tears and the water rushing around me is that one has a bitter, brackish flavor. This intensity cloaks me with a fierce electricity. The shock of what occurred is a current so deep and intense that it feels like nothing I could ever imagine experiencing. This must be my own version of hell.

There is little blood now, for it has been drained out of me. Rather, it has been ripped out of me. The process had been mechanical, humanity left to the wayside. It had felt primitive and savage. Flashbacks play in my head like a twisted horror film being shown against my will. I squeeze my eyes shut, trying to relinquish their images. I pray these haunting visions will go away, but they won't. It's my penance after all. I deserve worse.

Despite my conscious efforts to push out the memories. I still see that red plastic bag with its daunting black, bold lettering stating that the material inside contains hazardous material. The bag was to hold discarded waste. Waste. I cringe at the thought. I had made the decision for it to become waste when it didn't deserve to be. It didn't ask to be given to an adolescent girl who was filled with stupidity, ignorance, and trepidation. It wasn't it at all, but a human life. In the end, the anxiety was what had done it for me. Selfishly, I had placed myself before it. I had dared to play God.

I just couldn't face the blanketed eyes and the judgmental gazes. I couldn't swallow the words of damnation
that I had deserved, but nevertheless, I suck it up and took
it. It came down to a free life versus *its* life. Which one was
worth more? I let the pouch fall to the ground as I hung
from the tree just as Judas had. The weight of my sin burns
a hole in my heart. I had an unattainable remorse. It would
always elude me.

The nurse had asked me three times in a span of an
hour if this procedure was truly something that I wanted.
Something that I had thoroughly thought through in every
aspect. They even sent in a counselor, as if that was who I
wanted to talk to. Deep down inside, I yearned to confide in
my parents. My inner child wanted to be soothed and
comforted. Instead, I had been given this older African
American woman. She seemed innocent enough. I just
can't rack my brain around the fact that she took a job at a
place that kills babies. No matter how you spin it, that's
what it is. That is why I am here.

I swallow as if I am trying to push down a lump of coal.
I had looked back up at the woman who sat before me. She
had the kindest smile paired with eyes that warmed the
soul. Recalling her soft words and directions reminded me
of a siren calling captains to their death. It irritates me now.
How could she have had a love for me, but disregard the life
I had carried? Even her soft presence couldn't negate what
she was distracting me from.

She handed me a tissue, touched my hand gently, and
told me to take my time in answering her intrusive questions. Questions like: Had I been forced into this decision
by another party? Who had brought me in today for this
procedure? Did that party stay or did they leave? Then she

had told me afterward that I would have to wait for about two hours post-procedure so they could ensure that I was okay. I guess they were most worried about our mental state and the potential for PTSD post-extraction.

She had casually stated afterward that I exit the same way that I had come in. The moment she had made the statement, the hard clatter of my heart began to pound in my chest. I had looked up immediately with tears already spilling down my face. They wanted me and the other women here to confidently walk back through the mob that held signs and cast judgmental stones at our feet under the guise of God's will. I had already known it was wrong, but to tie me to the post and light the fire from underneath me had been unbearable.

"I can't. No, I can't. I won't. I can go a different way, maybe the back?" The lady had offered another warm smile, but this time her perfect teeth were framed by her bright red lips. The audacity of her bright smile irritates me. "I am so sorry, Charlotte. I know the people outside have a lot to do with your anxiety, and unfortunately, we cannot do anything about that right now. We can have a care assistant walk you through them. Protect you all the way to your vehicle. They are skilled, and this is the job they are trained to do."

I had held her gaze for what seemed like an eternity. I cast my eyes down. "They are so cruel. They were yelling at me. They called me a murderer. Screaming at me. They followed me from my car all the way inside. How is that okay?" I pause, "I guess it's not okay. I know what I'm doing is not okay. I deserve this and more. But I don't want to be condemned by others when I must already answer to God.

I am uncontrollably sobbing now at the realization that I don't want this. That I am not yet convinced this is what I want. "Charlotte, do you not want to go through with it? It's fine either way." She had looked at me again, empathy in her brown eyes. She had been waiting for a response that I could never give her. "I have to, but I don't want to have to." I had whispered to her in a voice so small she had to lean in to hear. She couldn't know that this decision would haunt me until the day I die.

She had continued to explain the parcels as I had zoned in and out.

"Okay. So, what are we going to do now is walk you to the patient room where the procedure will be completed. You will have a doctor, a nurse, and a care assistant. The care assistant will be with you throughout your stay, so you will have some familiarity there. Your care assistant will be there to hold your hand if you wish while the doctor and nurse complete the procedure. It is a short procedure. It will hurt a bit. I have been told you will feel pinching, cramping, and a dull pain. However, the doctor and nurse will do their best to numb and comfort you. Do you have any questions?"

I had nodded my head back and forth robotically. "No, ma'am." I had felt like I had left my body. Perhaps it was my mind's way of protecting me. She had stood up and taken the file in front of her as she held the door open for me to walk through. There had been a petite blonde woman waiting outside the door. She hands the blonde my file.

"Hi, Charlotte, my name is Monica. I will be your personal care assistant today. I'll be with you through your entire process, just as Sheila explained. I'm going to walk you to the next room, which is around the corner on the right, so you can change into a gown and get comfortable. We will then wait for the doctor and her nurse to come in. If you will just follow me." She gestured to follow her with perfectly manicured hands.

The tan corridor seemed to stretch out farther than it actually was. Perhaps it had been an intentional optical illusion. I had imagined myself as Dorothy in *The Wizard of Oz* when she, the lion, scarecrow, and tin man, had been on their journey to meet the great and powerful Oz. The hallway before me had seemed too narrow. It had a foreboding vibe for the event that lay ahead. Monica had opened the door, and I followed.

It looked like a gynecologist's office, complete with foot stirrups. Monica handed me a clear drawstring bag for my clothes and a faded yellow hospital gown. She then left the room as I stood there in silence. Sheer panic had begun to set in. I looked around the room and noticed the bleached white walls. As I continued to observe my surroundings, everything that lay before me was white. Then my eyes caught sight of a fire engine red trash can. Folded on top were red hazardous bags.

It had been a parallel between the distinct decisions of life versus death, sin versus no sin. That sharp, bloodstained odor had been the epitome of the immorality I was about to commit. I sat down on the medical chair in front of me, its sterile paper covering rustling as my weight distributed upon it. I was shivering out of pure apprehension and fear, the rush of adrenaline surged through me. I began to have small convulsions. The cold air magnified the lack of control my nervous system had, and I attempted to slow my breathing down.

I began to open and close my hands repeatedly, concentrating on the squeezing of my palms. Open. Close. Open. Close. It took everything in me to keep the anxiety attack from completely taking over. My instinct was to start praying the Our Father, like I usually do when I feel overwhelmed—but this time, it didn't feel right. It felt like God wasn't there.

It had been a choice he granted me. I knew with every fiber in my being that I had decided on the wrong path. However, I couldn't bring myself to run. I had been unable to move. I had tried to focus on keeping my body warm with the scratchy blanket that had been given to me. Then, I heard a knock on the wooden door and turned my gaze toward it.

In walked my care assistant, Monica. She was holding a tray filled with a variety of what looked like surgical equipment. I tried not to look, but it had been hard to turn away from the sharp objects on the metal tray. Razor-sharp knives, scissors, shot needles, towels, gauze, and small, tiny glass bottles with tiny writing on them had been neatly arranged. Right behind her was what I assumed was the nurse.

At first glance, she had not seemed friendly, but that swift assumption was quickly changed by the flash of her bright smile. She seemed to be one of those bubbly types of people. Her demeanor didn't seem like the ideal fit for that particular role. But at that point, I was willing to accept help from anyone who could get me through the next hour.

"Charlotte, I'm Nurse Emily. I'll be assisting Dr. Anna in the procedure today. I'm going to walk you through the process, and then we will send in the doctor to begin." I heard the introduction, and then I felt as if I had been pushed under water. I did not hear anything. All I had been able to do was focus on her mouth. She had paper-thin, pursed lips. They had been moving up and down, clearly verbalizing things I needed to hear. I was unable to comprehend anything that she said.

"Charlotte. Are you okay?" I had begun to shake, a mixture of cold, anxiety, and fear. "Will you go grab her a few more warm blankets, Emily? Thanks." Monica grabbed my hand and made me look at her. "Charlotte, you're having a panic attack, and it is perfectly normal given the situation at hand. Rest assured that you will be okay. Let's get you a bit warmer, and that should help calm your nerves a little."

She grabbed the additional blankets from Emily and covered me with them. They had been so warm that they instantly eased the trembling from my body. Emily had begun the IV drip to provide me with medications to assist with relaxation. I had heard a tap at the door, followed by a tall, slender woman with dark brown hair. She had to have just graduated from medical school, as no lines creased her face. She had plump skin and full lips. There was an eagerness in her eyes and a bounce in her step. She had on metal glasses and no trace of makeup besides lip gloss.

"Charlotte, let us get started, shall we?" She smiled as her counterparts had each done prior, and then turned to get scrubbed in. She pulled on latex gloves and took a seat on a rolling chair. She wheeled herself toward the tools and then looked up at me. "Okay, honey, I'm going to have you place your legs in the stirrups on the side now. I will also need you to place your bottom as far down on the table as possible. Almost as if you are going to fall off. Lean back and do your very best to relax. You will feel some tenderness, maybe even a bit of pain and cramping. However, know that it will subside once we have completed the procedure. Let me know if the pain is too unbearable, and we can give you something for that."

She then turned to Emily and nodded as a sign to begin. "Charlotte, your car assistant, Monica, is going to stay by your side to guide you through the entire procedure. I acknowledged her words, but it felt weird. It felt even more deceptive that I was undergoing a medical procedure without my family's knowledge. It felt invasive on so many different levels. Yet I somehow allowed them to continue.

Emily spread my legs farther to the sides so that the doctor had clearer access. She grabbed what looked like one of those game dispensers at the arcade. The ones that you try to grab studded toys from, and she had said it was going to pinch a little. She had then slid the foreign object within me. I shuddered at the intense coldness of the metal. It pinched me as it slowly scratched internally. I flinched. It had begun to hurt even more.

She grabbed a second tool and said something I couldn't understand. Then I began to cramp. It hurt. I grabbed both sides of the reclined chair, my nails biting into the leather. It wasn't what I truly wanted. Then the assistant grabbed my hand. I squeezed her hand as if she were a longtime friend. That moment was so intimate for two strangers.

I had barely opened my eyes when I saw it—the dreaded red bag from earlier. I watched as it was opened, and something was placed inside. Whatever it was, it was heavy enough to weigh the bag down. I shut my eyes quickly, as if that simple act could erase what I'd just witnessed. When I opened them again, I searched the room frantically, eyes darting in every direction, trying to find the bag. But it was gone. And with it—my baby. Where had it gone? It had just been here. What had I done? It took everything in me not to get off the table and go after it—to open the bag, to hold it, to cradle it. But it was too late. I was too late. I had committed a terrible sin. One so great, I believed God could not–should not–forgive me.

I sobbed until the back of my throat burned.

Father Alvarez remained still, reverent, as if he'd heard it a thousand times and still grieved every soul who carried this kind of wound.

He spoke once I had nothing left.

"There is no sin too great for God's mercy. The cross already bore it. You are not what you did. You are His."

I squeezed my hands together.

"But I didn't even fight hard enough. I caved at the first sign of pressure. What kind of person am I?"

"He saw your fear, Charlotte. He sees the child. And He sees you now just as you are. All of you, past and present. And He still says, Come home, His arms wide."

I hung my head then. I had nothing else to give. My voice cracked as I whispered my Act of Contrition.

He made the sign of the cross over me.

"As penance … light a candle for your child. And say their name, even if only in your heart. Give them back to God. He already holds them."

I stayed there long after he left.

When I finally stepped outside, the wind was still strong,

but no longer violent. It moved like a veil being lifted. But even as the wind calmed, I carried the storm within.

I had confessed it all, but part of me still feared whether God could truly forgive a woman who couldn't even forgive herself.

And just as I looked up to the sky, a warmth filled my body, penetrating my soul. An intense emotion of love I had never felt before consumed me entirely. It was then that I knew I had been forgiven.

I looked up and whispered, "Thank you."

I closed my eyes and slipped into a brief haze.

The chapel walls melted, and I was back in that hallway, the one in my recurring nightmare. Empty, echoing. But this time, a rosary lay upon the floor, a light chestnut, still warm to the touch. As I picked it up, I smelled something. Roses. Then I looked up and saw a baby's crib and within it a beautiful baby girl.

She smiled at me, and I knew she was mine.

Chapter 24

Charlotte – Silence That Echos

T he first sign was the silence.

It wasn't the peaceful kind, like early mornings when the house was still sleeping. No, this was the kind of silence that pressed too tightly against your eardrums, like the whole world was holding its breath. The kind that comes before a scream or a betrayal.

I was standing in the kitchen, an untouched cup of coffee cooling in my hand, staring at the spot where Marla always hung her purse. It wasn't there today. It hadn't been there in a while, since this whole thing started.

She doesn't text.

She doesn't call.

She doesn't show.

The last message I'd sent had been read, but not answered.

When I called James, Will's partner, to follow up, he seemed overwhelmed, which is understandable, and stated that she had been up to her neck in work, as well.

Every text I've sent, every call I've made has been met with that deafening silence.

I wanted to believe it was nothing. That she is truly just busy or tired, or perhaps just needed space from the theatrical events that have become my life as of late. But there was a gnawing feeling that kept recurring. It was the same one I had when I found the coffee cup on the porch weeks ago.

Something was wrong. Off.

The doorbell rang. I jumped at the noise and spilled my coffee all over my sweater. The stain instantly started bleeding down my chest.

Damn. I placed the cup in the sink and grabbed a damp rag, dabbing at it incessantly.

If Alex were to have seen this, she would have barreled down with laughter and quipped back, "Reminds me of when we were little and you were always spilling. Quick, Alex, help before Mom comes back." I smiled fondly at the memory, then looked down at my shirt and rolled my eyes.

I opened the door to find Cortez standing on the porch. Again. His expression was grim, and his eyes warranted sadness.

A profound pressure ached in my belly. I began to hold on to the door for stability.

"Is it … Will?" I said meekly.

He rushed to help me straighten up. "Oh no, no, Charlotte. I didn't mean to give you that impression. But we did find something."

He gestured for her to sit down on the front porch swing. So she did, and he sat on the banister just opposite her.

"We found a bag in the woods, way back on your property line. It's actually in conjunction with the vacant land across the way." He pointed in the direction for clarity. "Containing items with Max's name labeled on them."

Charlotte noticed Cortez's knuckles tighten on the railing at his last statement. His voice was clipped. "Not new things. Old things. A sock. A pacifier he must not have used in years. A photo from when he was a toddler." He rubbed his mouth with his hand, visibly disturbed at the items.

"Who would keep those things of my son?"

His grimaced. "We're working on it. But there's something else. There were fingerprints found on the plastic bag. We got a partial … but a strong match."

He paused as if it pained him to say the word aloud, "Marla."

I quickly rose at that statement, and the world suddenly tilted. "No. No, that's not possible. Marla's like family. She … she helps us. She knows Molly and Max. She's like a sister to me. She would never …"

I remembered her holding Max when he was just a baby, swaying gently by the fireplace, humming some tune she said her mother used to sing. It haunted me now, the tenderness. Was it ever real?

Suddenly, Sadie came from behind and placed a hand on my back to steady me. *I had forgotten that she was here.*

Cortez continued, "We think she might be working with someone else, possibly the same person tied to Will's disappearance. Possibly Baker? Maybe this Hannah character?" He paced back and forth. "To be honest, it's, what's the word I am looking for, disordered."

My lungs felt devoid of air. I sat back down on the

porch swing, my hand shaking, coffee sloshing onto the hardwood.

Memories reeled. Marla coming over unannounced. Offering to help with Max's schedule. Suggesting little changes. Rearranging furniture "for safety."

My stomach turned, and the bile made me feel nauseous.

This was not just a betrayal. It was a blatant violation of my trust.

She had been inside our home, entangling herself in our lives. Embedding herself deep in conversations and relationships that surround our daily routine. And I was the idiot who welcomed her.

I hung my head in visible shame.

Later that night, as I sat in Max's room watching him sleep, I tried to understand how I missed it. How I'd let someone so dangerous get so close.

And then the call. I picked up my phone and slowly stepped out into the hall, closing Max's door behind me.

"Charlotte," Cortez said, his voice tight, "we found Lawson dead in his car. There was no clear cause of death, but there were signs of poisoning. It seemed to be quiet, efficient. No fight or struggle of any kind, and um … Marla was the last person to see him."

The name meant nothing to me. I waited, my throat tight.

"He's not one of ours, Charlotte. Private, hired from the outside. He went missing around the same time Will did."

"So, Will hired him?" Confused, I searched my mind for clues of when and why Will would do this.

"We don't know yet. That is one possibility."

I dropped the phone.

Sadie rushed in from the hallway. I couldn't speak. I just shook my head. She picked up the receiver and listened. Her face went pale.

Grief and guilt collided. Lawson had been trying to help us get to the bottom of this. To figure out what happened to Will, and to help Will figure out how to keep us safe. And now he was gone, too, only not gone, dead.

Gone because I trusted the wrong damn person.

Because I didn't or couldn't see the truth.

I curled into myself on the floor, and I made a silent vow that no one else I loved would suffer because of my blindness.

Never again.

Chapter 25

Charlotte – Chemo III: The Silent Hours

"I t's so nice to see your smiling face again, Charlotte. How did the last chemotherapy go? Did you handle it okay? Any side effects?"

I smiled, and before I could reply, she continued. "I see you opted not to wear the wig. From what I understand, they tend to be a bit scratchy. I am glad you feel comfortable here, though. I love the beanie choice. Very trendy."

Mariam smiled warmly at me.

I subconsciously pulled down on my leopard beanie that I strategically wore to cover where my dark, thick eyebrows had once been.

It still made me uneasy. For whatever reason, I just felt vulnerable and raw. *I know my hair doesn't define me, but it sure makes me feel better about myself.*

Mariam is very nice, but often I feel as if she is too happy. Why is that? Is she secretly a serial killer? Instantly, I felt terrible for the thought.

My moods have been a bit all over the place lately. Poison in the veins does that, I guess.

She began the IV meds.

"I am doing good, Mariam, thanks for asking. My main complaint is that I'm starting to get a bit more fatigued as each round continues. This second bout with cancer has proven to be more difficult to keep my strength up. This last session, I was terribly sick. I was nauseated, lightheaded, and cold. In fact, I had double everything on. I can't turn the heat up either because it makes my symptoms worse. I'm not sure if I am getting sick on top of everything, though I know my immune system is all jacked up. It's been awful. It's been one thing after another. I had a full-blown anxiety attack from the medication they gave me to relieve the side effects of chemo. Go figure." I forced a big smile like I had just won the lottery. She looked at me in awe.

"I'm so sorry to hear that, dear. Some of these drugs are terrible. What are you going to do this time for the symptoms from these IV drugs? You know, for the nausea?"

I cocked my head in thought. "Well, I have been researching a few natural methods that people swear by. I will certainly let you know if they end up working."

She crossed her fingers and smiled at me. "That sounds like a plan. I will be praying for you. Like always. I am going to leave you to it now. So let me know if you need me. You know the drill." Smiling brightly, she dimmed the lights. The overcast shadows from the rainy day made the perfect atmosphere for my drug-induced coma-like state to take hold. I slowly slipped into what felt like a strangely familiar dream.

Chapter 26

Charlotte – Wanting More

Out on the beach, the air was crisp. It was a bit chillier than I liked, but there was something about the bitter cold that rejuvenated me. It put my senses on edge. I didn't want to come here. I would have preferred to suffer alone at home while stuffing my face with Ben and Jerry's ice cream and reruns of *Gossip Girl*. That was my kind of pick-me-up. It was Sadie who had refused to let me eat my pain by the spoonful. It was Sadie who had made me get my hair appointment a mere day before we had to fly out for the wedding of Danielle and John. It was Sadie who had picked the beautiful blue crepe dress I was set to wear for the event. It was Sadie who had picked the mansion that was perched on a steep cliff, overlooking the sea. It was she who had strategically picked each of the guest rooms. It was Sadie who would be hosting the pre-rehearsal, rehearsal dinner as a gift to the bride and groom. Geoff comes from a legacy of well-to-do bankers, so when he married Sadie, although a working woman, she had a surplus of funds to use at her discretion. We had all been confused by the suggestion. However, Sadie mentioned that it was intended to dissipate any stray nerves before the impending nuptials.

Since Danielle did not have any siblings, she had asked Sadie, Alex, and me to be her attendants. It had taken us all aback, but John explained that she had always longed to have sisters. So, we had agreed to stand in. It had helped how wonderfully kind, charismatic, and funny she was. She had gone above and beyond for the bridal shower and bachelorette party, and now this. Sadie took her role as matron of honor very seriously. Not only was it to be a family affair, but it was set to be a school reunion, as well.

I had just arrived at the beach. My attire was not ideal, but I had to get my thoughts in order. Instead of being bombarded by a million questions paired with my anxiety, I decided to go straight to the beach. After dropping my bags with the lady at the front desk, I took the path down. When I arrived, the salty sea air filled my lungs. I closed my eyes, and images of him filled my mind. Instead of sugar plums and candy dancing around in my head, I had visions of his face, lips, and eyes. I reminisced about his strong touch and what it felt like to dance with him that last time.

"Charlie! Hey, Charlie! Thank goodness I found you first!" Alex bounded toward me, winded, in high heels. Her makeup was flawless, and her dark mane voluminous. She was wearing a burnt orange wrap around her sweater and fitted jeans. I rarely saw her in casual clothing and with less makeup on, and it reminded me of how strikingly beautiful she was. Before speaking again, she breathed deeply, visibly trying to compose herself. Then she looked me straight in the eyes.

"I really shouldn't be running in this outfit right before

dinner. These pants are too fitted, and these damn heels are too tall, but I had to catch you before you walk in." She took one of her painfully high heels off and rubbed the arch of her foot. "You're going to love this!" I looked at her, my eyebrows raised. This was just like Alex to make a dramatic entrance.

"I was just going for a walk."

She laughed sardonically, "Well, prepare yourself, because he's already here." He came. I tried to call you, but despite my persistence, it wouldn't go through. You might want to walk in the direction of the nearest bathroom and fix ..." She waved her hand up and down. "Fix whatever this is." I frowned at her, rolling my eyes.

"I think it's the cliff this place is built on or something. Maybe the dark clouds forming in the distance. Who the hell knows? Reception just isn't the greatest." I waited for her continued tangent to flow as it typically did. Until she was depleted of her conversation, only then could you get a word in.

"Wait, you are referring to Will? I know he's here. I was forewarned that he was coming with her. He at least had the decency to tell me. He didn't want me to be caught off guard. He dropped me an email last week." Alex stood straight after putting her heel back on. She began to soothe her hair back in place. Then her eyes met mine.

"No, that is just it, Charlotte. He came alone. He said it just wasn't working out with her. He couldn't very well miss this wedding even if he wanted to. The guys would give him so much hell. So, he opted to come. Again, alone!" I laughed at her emphasis on his singleness, her hands gesturing the importance of this fact. She pulled me toward the cobble path, grabbing my hand tightly.

"I think he was looking for you because I caught him checking out every room and crevice. It was as if he were waiting for you to pop up unexpectedly, as if he wanted you to pop up. I mean, he has seriously been looking everywhere but the broom closet." Her boisterous laughter filled the air that surrounded us. The intensity of it got caught in the wind that howled around us.

"You know how he pays attention to everyone when they talk. He gets so fixated on each word. He isn't the best when it comes to multiple people talking to him at once. However, if it's just you, he zeros in on it." I sucked in the ocean air, my jaws tightly clenched. My anxiety was mounting.

"Damn it, Al, I don't know what I'm going to do. I'm not going to be able to stay here knowing he's sleeping somewhere nearby, much less attend this damn wedding knowing he is going to be looking all well … ridiculously amazing. Not to mention the alcohol, music, and dancing. Don't get me started on the ambiance of this place. I mean, need I say more?" I gestured to the skyline, the cotton candy sunset fusing with the horizon in the distance. Clouds loomed dark in the distance, getting ready to cover the sky with a blanket of stars.

"I can't even breathe when I'm around him. I can't function like a normal human. I start acting like a teenager. All I want to do is kiss him. I want to touch him. I want to hug him. I want, no, I need to be with him. Our chemistry is overwhelming. This weekend is going to be a freaking recipe for disaster!" Alex dragged me up the path to the main area. She squeezed my hand.

"Or a recipe for romance?" She said calmly. This was so frustrating.

"I won't last even a single night in this house before I attack him." Alex laughed, then pretended to roar like a tiger. "Rrrrr. Don't pounce now, kitty cat." I shoved her lightly.

"I don't want to scare him away, Alex. An even worse scenario: what if she shows up late? I mean, there is that possibility. It's her friend, too. It wouldn't be like her to miss this." Alex shrugged, offering a smirk.

"You are so grumpy right now! You'd better take a shot if you get one. With that said, do your best to control your damn self, too. It's going to be a long weekend for you both. Ugh, for me and Sadie, too, now that I think of it. Let's be real; you are a mess when you're around him. I didn't sign up to babysit you all weekend, either. I've got to go!" Letting out an exaggerated sigh, she pretended to walk away. She was not even a couple of feet away when she waved her hand for me to follow.

"Come on, sis, it won't be so bad. I promise. After all, you have us, plus this house is oozing opulence. I mean, just wait until you see it all. It's like straight out of a movie! Sadie has this whole weekend planned out so beautifully, too. You would have thought it was her own wedding!" A rumble of laughter filled the air as they walked hand in hand toward the sprawling stairwell. The rocks beat fiercely against the shore in the background. One crashing wave at a time, creating a rhythmic tune. Swish. Roar. Crack. Bang. Swish. Roar. Crack. Bang. Repeating over and over, the waves thrumming an intricately constructed melody. The intensity foreshadowing the night that lies ahead.

Once inside, Alex left me to get ready for dinner. The house was alive with distant chatter. Soft music played throughout the house, the melodies moving through the hallways like a lazy stream. The notes filled every room, every crevice, with their intoxicating sound. Pine and spice filled the air.. The floors were a mix of polished marble and checkered black and white square tiles. Each room was expansive, with elegant wainscoting and trim decorating the walls. The detailed baseboards ribboned beautifully, like that of a wrapped gift.

The wallpaper in each room was delicate yet vibrant, blooming with effervescent hues of blue, yellow, and green. Some rooms were adorned with furniture and draperies in soft, romantic shades of pink, while others embraced a more dramatic flair with deep, brooding plums. Oversized tufted couches invited you to sink in, draped with luxurious fur throws that looked effortlessly placed. Glass tables shimmered beneath grand chandeliers, each room reflecting light in its own opulent way. The mirrors in each room created the sensation of being watched, reminding me of the Hall of Mirrors at Versailles. I imagined that was exactly the effect the interior designer had in mind.

The setting evokes a bygone era, its elegance steeped in history—yet subtle touches of modern charm quietly anchor it in the present. Contemporary trends are thoughtfully woven in: thick hardback books with the names of iconic designers from the worlds of art, fashion, interior design, and architecture are perfectly arranged on table-tops. Sleek lighting fixtures and state-of-the-art technology are seamlessly integrated into each room. A smart home nestled effortlessly within the antique bones of a sleeping giant.

Sadie was busy in the kitchen when I came in, arranging the endless bottles of wine by type on the counter, bright sticky notes distinguishing which was which. She looked up as I approached, impeccably composed, as always. Sadie was anything but a conventional district attorney. In addition to holding a law degree from Columbia, she was strikingly beautiful, exuding a confident charm reminiscent of Elle Woods, minus the pink business suit. Today, she was wearing black suede Louboutin heels, fitted jeans, and an organza blouse revealing a subtle glimpse of a purple bra. Sadie had never been one to shy away from attention; on the contrary, she often sought it out. Yet once in the spotlight, she invariably would find something to occupy herself with—an instinct that gave her an air of modesty, despite initial impressions. Her hair was freshly dyed a warm honey-blonde, and her green eyes seemed especially vivid today.

"Hey, Sadie, are you feeling okay?"

Sadie smiled, shrugging. "Let me guess, my eyes are green? Yeah, Al already told me. Honestly, I think it's because I'm more exhausted than sick. I just have to finish up a few things before I can relax." Shaking her head, she grabbed the next bottle of wine from the box and read the label. "Yes!" I cannot wait to try this Syrah; I hear it is fabulous. It will go wonderfully with the roasted chicken that we're having tonight." As she inspected the bottle, I grabbed her glass and polished off the rest of her wine. "Char, I just poured that! Oh, never mind. This must be a prelude of events to come. I heard Will's here already. I have yet to see him, though. Alex already told me he came alone! Hope you brought your A game." She laughed and then pointed her perfectly manicured finger to the hall on the right of the kitchen. "Your quarters are through that hall to the left. Keep going until you see the stairs at the end. Your room will be the first one up the stairs to the right."

I gave her a long glance. "Do you have a map?"

She put her hand on her hip, resembling our mother. "Just go! I must finish this. You need to hurry, too. I need you to get back here in thirty! Don't be late!"

I waved a hand as I headed for the corridor. A subtle scent of cologne wafted toward me. Not just any cologne, though. His. I instantly became anxious as butterflies began to flutter in my stomach. A faded mist of mahogany and musk hung in the air. I could feel my feet begin to walk faster. If I kept up this pace, I'll start sweating. That's all I needed. I could feel the moistness under my bra and could only imagine what I looked like. I felt like a caged animal trying to get out. As I began to climb the stairs, the scent strengthened. I caught my breath and stopped for a second. *What on earth do I say when I see him?*

"Charlotte, is that you?" I stumbled back, almost losing my balance.

"Ahh!" I nearly jumped out of my skin at the sound of that voice. Of his voice. I turned around slowly. My heart was racing so fast that I felt lightheaded. "William. Oh, hey, ummm … I'm so sorry that I cut you off. It's just that I have too many bags, and I got a bit winded."

He smiled, cocking his head to the side. He walked toward me, grabbing all my bags in one swoop. He nodded. "I didn't mean to catch you off guard. My apologies! How about you lead the way to your room, and I'll follow with your bags."

I turned slowly back around, my heart pounding in my chest. "Thanks so much. You don't have to do that, though. I might not have made it to Sadie's dinner on time, but I would eventually have made it up these damn stairs."

He let out a laugh and then cleared his throat. "Sorry, Charlie! I didn't mean to startle you." My cheeks grew red as my mind flooded with images of us laughing, hugging, and kissing.

"Charlotte. Charlotte. Hey, are you okay?" I looked up, startled at his proximity. He was standing mere inches from me, so close I could see the scar across his eyebrow from where he clipped himself. Willing myself to speak, I brushed the hair out of my face. "Oh, yes. I uh, I'm okay. I'm just tired, that's all. I think I'm a bit out of it at this point." I gestured to the door just past him. "I'm over there, I think. Yeah, that one. Yup, I have number twenty." I was getting flustered more and more as time passed. I felt like a babbling idiot in his presence. What must he think of me?

I pointed to the door as Sadie had earlier instructed, tapped my key at the keypad, and it clicked open. The room was dimly lit with a candle flickering on the side table, a chilled bottle of prosecco and two champagne glasses arranged perfectly beside it. I noticed that the bed covers had been turned down. Sadie sure did think of everything. I smiled to myself at the thought of every detail being painstakingly thought out by my older sister. It was stereo-typical Sadie. She was the only one of us three sisters who had a good dose of OCD coursing through her veins. She once took all her shoes, clothing, and jewelry and decided to color coordinate the entire closet. It was quite the under-taking that would have taken anyone else days. However, it took her a few hours. I often pondered how she and Geoff, who is equally obsessive and detailed, functioned. God must have known they would make a good match. Sadie had picked the ideal profession for her. She ran the DA's office on a bed of strict policies of structure and organization. I bet it drove her employees and coworkers mad. Sadie had done well for herself and had become a local hero. She and Geoff lived on a golf course in the heart of suburbia. She was the quintessential host and had a personal assistant who helped her out with daily activities that she didn't have the spare time to deal with.

Will gently placed her bags in the closet, then turned around and smiled. His dimples and perfect teeth made me clam up again.

"Sadie sure did plan this weekend perfectly. I'm right next door." He smiled shyly as he ran his hands behind the back of his head, physically revealing his anxiety. This display of awkwardness was unlike him. He pointed to the oversized double doors next to the wardrobe. "You see those? Well, that's me. Of course, you need a key to open the doors. Then again, I believe we both have them." Smiling wryly, he cleared his throat and pulled his key out, dangling it in the air. "Well, I'm off to freshen up for dinner and then give my mom a call to see how Rocky is doing." Rocky was the English bulldog that he's had for years.

"Aww, Rocky. Such a cutie. Thank you so much for helping me, Will. I really appreciate it. I don't think I would have been able to muster enough brawn to take my bags up those spiral stairs. I mean, where is the elevator in this place?"

He let out a laugh. "I was told it's strictly for help. Which I do believe includes your sister. Just fib and say you're her assistant!" He winked.

I opened my mouth wide in amazement. "I was actually joking; however, I'm not shocked in the least that there would be an elevator in this place." I flushed as I walked him toward the door. "See you in a few." I secretly harbored the need for a bit of privacy to release the intense amount of heat coming from my chest.

Catching the door with his hand, he stopped me from closing it. "Charlotte." I held the door open slightly, my breath caught in my lungs. "I just want you to know that I'm glad you're here." He pushed the door open a bit more, leaned in, and kissed my cheek. His lips burned like fire on my skin, pulsating at the touch. He lingered a moment before pulling away. It took everything I had not to allow him to engulf me in his embrace. Instead, I smiled shyly.

His hand on my cheek sent a wave through me I wasn't ready for, but I also wasn't his to hold, and he wasn't mine to claim. Whatever we had belonged to the past. I wanted healing, not chaos. I couldn't let a single moment undo all the strength it took to walk away. Even if my heart stammered, I prayed, silently, instinctively, that God would hold me steady. This wasn't love. It was old ache dressed up as longing.

"Of course, me, too. I mean, well, I'm glad you're here, too. We get to finally catch up on things."

I barely heard him as he turned toward his room, a whisper, but it was enough to raise my hopes. "Yeah, we certainly get more than a chance." He closed his door, leaving me alone in the hall staring after him.

I closed the door and fell back against the hard surface, exhaling an exaggerated sigh of relief. I headed straight to the bathroom and audibly gasped. There, in the center of the room, stood an oversized claw tub. Hanging directly above it was an antique chandelier, its crystals casting a breathtaking display of light that danced across the floor.

Perfumed bath salts and lotions were neatly arranged along the edge of the tub, accompanied by a bouquet of roses.

"Thank you, Sadie," I whispered as I began to draw my bath. "Tonight is the night it all begins. I need to get myself together."

By the time I made it downstairs, the atmosphere was sultry. The lights were low, and the music pulsed with a slow, sensual rhythm that seemed to vibrate through me. The rich scent of poultry had made its way upstairs, stirring my hunger.

I'd chosen a black, thin-strapped dress that hugged my figure in all the right places. The buttery fabric parted at the hip, and a vintage brooch—once my grandmother's— glinted at my décolletage, drawing the eye with its golden sparkle. I wore my hair in a tousled side bun, the easiest style to manage on short notice. A nude cat eye gave me just enough false confidence to hope William might notice me. My skin still carried a sun-kissed glow from my recent trip to Cabo with Alex.

I entered the dining room to find it vacant, but the doors that led to the patio were wide open, exposing a grand view of the vast Pacific Ocean. The salty breeze captured strands of my hair as they danced in the wind. An elegantly lit table had been laid, filled with grand candelabras, fruit trays, cakes, cheese, and drinks that presented a beautiful display. I gasped at the view set before me as I ventured farther out onto the patio, the lighting dim, casting a wonderful golden glow. I could barely make out the outline of the ocean in the far distance. Sadie has outdone herself. I'm sure she knows that.

The music and environment invigorated me, giving me a sensual sense of recklessness that I hadn't experienced in a while. I felt possessed by the pulsating beat of the music. Perhaps my mood was a direct reflection of my earlier encounter with Will. The rhythm was drawing me in, luring me to a freedom unlike anything I had ever felt.

Entranced by the scenery, I almost forgot that there were others around me. "I should have known you would look anything but spot on tonight. Smart girl." I turned around, already smiling, to find my younger sister smirking with two flutes of champagne in hand. Alex looked radiant, her hair cascading down her back in perfect waves. She was wearing a one-shoulder red dress, its slit providing a peek at her perfectly toned legs. She was killing it in every department. Her fashion was a direct representation of her personality, and I loved that her assertiveness was displayed so beautifully.

"I must be. Don't pretend like you don't know why. I had no choice but to bring my A game and nothing less." A Cheshire cat smile adorned my face. She twirled her finger, gesturing for me to follow suit and show off my entire ensemble. As if she were the master of my marionette. I spun and gave a curtsey per her instructions. She clapped with enthusiasm as her champagne spilled onto the floor. "Whoops!" She giggled as she handed me a glass. "You earned this." We clinked our glasses together in laughter, and the trumpet-like ding resonated in my heart and echoed through my body.

"Well played. Here's to a night of second chances and long dances!" We both loved to construct literary pieces. It had always been one of our favorite things to do as kids. We were modern-day March sisters. She was my Amy, and I, her Jo. We laughed again, taking long sips of our bubbles. The fizz tickled my tongue. Alex gave me another once-over and nodded her head in approval once again. "I have to say, I especially like what you did with Grandma's broach. It draws attention perfectly yet discreetly. However, it also sets off the dress. Both a smart call and a classy touch."

For whatever reason, if anyone else were to compliment me, it would fall on deaf ears. However, when Alex noticed, I gained a boost of confidence. She continued, "Your tan has kept its shade. I'm shocked. That also gives the outfit a sensual look. I think it will go over nicely. I just saw him. He was talking to one of John's buddies by the stairwell."

Just then, Sadie walked in as if on a mission. She had changed from the outfit she was wearing earlier to a sequined dress. It had an open back that provided a glimpse of her silhouette underneath. Her mane was straight and polished, and her diamond earrings looked like mini chandeliers hanging from her ears. I caught her beaming with pride at the success of the menu and the delighted guests before her. She grabbed her champagne and a fork and tapped lightly on the flute to gain everyone's attention.

"Hello, beautiful people. If you could please make your way to your table. Everyone's names are written on place settings. So, please find your seats so dinner can be served." Alex and I found our place cards and were pleased to be in proximity to one another, but also close to the bride and groom. Sadie and Geoff took their seats, and Alex and I took ours. Alex kicked me under the table and let out a cunning laugh.

"Ouch. Damn it, Alex!" I whispered loud enough for her to know it hurt, yet soft enough so that her ears could register it. Will brushed up behind me, gliding his hand on my neck as he took his seat. His touch was unexpected, and it sent immediate chills down my spine. My nerves intensified, as if I wasn't nervous enough that Sadie had put me right next to him.

As if her ears were burning, Sadie quickly turned and whispered something to Alex, a puzzled expression on her face. I looked at her and mouthed, 'What?' She immediately glared at Alex, who opted to play dumb. Sadie hit Alex's arm. "Ow! Sadie, damn it. That hurt."

Sadie hissed back at Alex, "You moved him. You messed with my table setting! Things were the way they were for a reason. It was carefully curated based on everything from religion to politics."

Al let out a laugh, "Calm down, lady, it will be fine. No one knows or even cares but you." Sadie huffed, and Geoff nonchalantly handed Sadie a glass of wine. Then he pulled her to him and gave her a kissed her on her neck. That kiss must have magical powers because it noticeably calmed her down. She turned and sparked up chatter among the guests seated directly across from them.

While Alex was distracted, talking with an old friend from school, I bravely turned to Will. "Hey," I said nervously. *Why do I feel like I am back in high school?*

"Hey, cool that we got to sit next to each other. What are the chances?" He smirked. "It gives us time to catch up again. So, tell me, Charlotte, what have you been up to since the last time we spoke?"

I sat straighter in my chair and composed myself. I began to tell him about my last few years post-college and talked about the additional course work I completed and my recent trip to gain research for a book I was writing,

"So, traveling, huh? Where were you last?"

My eyes lit up. "I was so excited because I was able to

go to Czechoslovakia. You see, I got to know an older couple while at a coffee shop in Paris. They were originally from Czech. We got to chatting, and then they invited me to visit them. So, believe it or not, I took them up on it."

He sat stunned, staring at me. I smiled widely, just reminiscing about my days on their farm. "It was breathtaking. The scenery, the whimsy of it all. Mostly, their magical stories were filled with heartache, love, and dreams. I learned so much about their lives as well as the country itself."

I couldn't tell if he was captivated by me or by my story. He caught my eye and then laughed nervously. I immediately stopped talking. "What? What's so funny? Oh, my goodness, am I talking too much? I am, aren't I? Ugh, I hate when I do that."

He let out another laugh, took a sip of his wine, and touched my hand gently. "Oh, how I missed your tangents." I felt my face flush red and then dropped my head down to disguise it.

"I was just laughing at the idea that you went to Paris alone, much less befriended an unknown couple and then ended up staying at their farm in an entirely different country! I mean, only you. Only you, Charlotte, would even fathom doing that." He said it with a fondness and admiration that filled my heart.

"Opportunities or situations that produce fear make a person grow. So, if I can conquer my fears, then perhaps I can conquer my aspirations, right?"

He nodded.

"And you, William, what have you been up to since the last time we spoke? It's been a while." I saw him brace himself. His posture tensed.

"Well, honestly, inner growth has been a journey for me, as well. I've been working steadily for a big company in Washington. Big tech firm that I have come to love. It's taken me some time to figure out what I want in life. I mean not only professionally but personally, as well. You know?" At the last phrase, he turned. "I think I know, but one can never fully tell. Life is always changing. Something unexpected can happen at any time."

Just then, we were interrupted by the tapping of glass. Ding. Ding. Ding.

"Might I get everyone's attention? Attention please, I have an announcement." We all turned to face Sadie. She was standing at her seat; everyone's eyes were focused on her. She was gleaming brightly. Then she put down the glass.

"Thank you so much for being here for the rehearsal of our sweet love birds. It is truly a pleasure to have you all here today to mark their special occasion." Sadie went on to introduce the bride and groom, and they both gave speeches. Will excused himself and got up to leave once he finished eating. I talked to Alex for the remainder of dinner, anticipating Will's return, but he never came back.

As Alex excused herself, I began to think about the things that Will had been saying earlier. He was everything I had always wanted. He was perfect in my eyes. I'd always been cautious and intense in all my actions. Everything had always been purposeful, even when I had intentions of being reckless. I tended to get lost in my impulsiveness. There had always been a magnetic pull, a rush of blood pumping so fast to my heart that it leaves me lightheaded.

Everyone had gone back to the beach house to drink and continue the celebration. We were having a great time, caught up in the intoxicating energy of the matrimony that was about to take place.

"Headed for a midnight stroll, you want to join?" I allowed myself to smile. I looked at everyone, and they nodded their heads; each began to take off their shoes in anticipation of the cold sand. I scanned the crowd, except one person was still missing. "Where's Will?"

Sadie glided by quickly. "I'm going to go to the bathroom. Don't leave just yet. I think Will is in his room."

"I'll go get him." I ran off as soon as I said the words. I grabbed my heels and smeared lip gloss on my lips as I headed inside. Walking toward the kitchen, I opened a wine bottle and filled my glass to the brim. I took a long sip and topped it off again. At this point, I felt like I needed a bit of liquid courage. I had an energy about me, an internal fire that had been ignited and that wouldn't go out with a mere blow.

I picked up my glass and headed up the stairs to Will's room. I popped into my room and tossed my shoes onto the floor. I quickly went to the bathroom and made sure I still looked presentable. Then I gave a light tap on the door that joined our rooms together.

"Will, it's me. Charlie." I could hear the springs on the bed shift slightly, followed by shuffling just outside the door. A key entered the keyhole, and the door pulled open. I could tell he seemed a bit frazzled at my appearance.

"Charlotte, what's up?" I walked into his room and sat on his bed, where I noticed an open book on communication. He also had a glass of wine on his bedside table.

"Doing some light reading?" He sat next to me as he grabbed the book and placed it on the nightstand.

"Yeah, I'm trying to get ready for a presentation at

work. You can never be too prepared, you know?" He looked nervous and rubbed his shoulder. I think his apprehension made me want him even more. Maybe it was the idea that I made him so jittery. It could also be the alcohol coursing through my veins. He smiled widely, flashing his perfect white teeth, and sat up straighter. We were now eye to eye. His light green eyes blazed into my soul. It took everything I had to keep my composure.

"So, a bunch of us are going down to take a walk on the beach. I wanted to come get you before we headed out. Everyone is waiting downstairs." I smiled, grabbed his hand playfully, and pulled him to his feet. He was startled by my brazenness and visibly moved away from me, but didn't release my hand from his. It sat warm in mine. I could feel myself frown, but bravely moved forward.

"You must come. It is beautiful outside right now. The sun just set, and the moon is big and bright. It's like something out of a movie. You must come with us. You must." I began to move toward the door, but he pulled away again. His hands were a bit clammy, undoubtedly from the anxiety and endorphins coursing through his veins. He turned away from me.

"Charlie, I don't think that's a great idea. You know. You and I." He paused as I turned to face him. In a colder voice than I intended, I questioned his reservation.

"Oh, really. Why not?"

He sighed and looked down at his hands.

"We both know there is this tension between us. We cannot go to the beach because something will happen. I'm not sure if either of us is ready for that." He paused before continuing. "Hannah and I. Hannah and I are complicated. There's a history between us. I can't just leave her. I can't just one day be with her, and the other day be with you. It doesn't work like that. I'm not that type of person."

Pressure rose in my chest, and I felt more let down than anything. I needed to leave before my emotions got the better of me. I turned to walk toward the door.

"Nor am I. You can't give mixed signals either. It's your loss." I heard him calling out to me, but I didn't relent, walking back down the stairs and out onto the patio. I guess everyone had already headed to the beach because there was no one left but me.

I walked toward the balcony overlooking the beach and saw lights. The guests were enjoying the evening, the distant sounds of laughter floating through the wind. Then I felt it, a warm hand on my shoulder, the current so forceful that it caused me to ache inside. I didn't have to turn around to know it was Will. He kissed my neck and whispered, "I know with every fiber that you are what I want, Charlotte. You are intoxicating to me. You light up every single nerve within me. You are pure electricity. I can't have you right now because I know once I get a taste, I won't be able to think about anyone else. I won't be able to concentrate on anything but you. Your ridiculously big doe eyes and the way they sparkle when you look at me. Your tan and the way it glistens in the sun. That perfect, maddening pout that always looks as if you just bit your lips. Then there's your gorgeous, flowing hair. You are invigorating, and I know you want me, too. I can feel it because I want … no, I need you, too."

I remained staring at everyone laughing and carrying on in the distance, but my focus was on his breath. His hot breath was making every single hair on my neck stick up. It was shooting vibrations to every body part. I felt as if I couldn't move; I was struck with nervous anticipation.

"We just can't right now. I have to figure out what I need to do. It's not fair to you or Hannah." I cocked my neck slightly, exposing it even more to him. It was not a play to entice him, but I could tell it did because I heard him exhale. He grazed my neck with his fingers as they brushed back the stray hairs. Then he kissed me gently.

"I'm sorry, Charlotte. You deserve a man who can be one hundred percent committed. Once I'm committed, I will be yours forever. I promise."

The song playing in the background gave way to a heavier, methodical beat. I noticed that I did not feel him behind me anymore and turned around. He was gone. I took a deep breath, and tears started to pour down my face. I didn't know why I was crying. Maybe it was defeat. Maybe it was a feeling of pain for a love I knew I must wait to understand. Maybe it was because he might not even come back to me. I didn't know. A sadness loomed, veiling itself over me.

That was when I felt it, an unsettling sensation of eyes upon me. I turned to see a distant figure staring at me.

Chapter 27

Charlotte – Reflection

I woke up to both Sadie and Alex calling for me. "Charlotte, hey, wake up! Mom wants you on Face-Time." I slowly opened my eyes and saw my sisters staring at me, one on each side of my chair. Alex was holding her phone and pushed the screen toward my face. I shoved it away groggily, and she pushed it closer. I attempted to swat at her.

"Alex, can you be more annoying?"

Alex smirked, "Do you really want me to answer that?"

"Say hi, it's mom." I pulled my head back and grabbed the phone from her. "Al, that's too close to my face. My head hurts, and I feel foggy."

Alex wrinkled her face. "Whoops, sorry."

I squinted to try and focus on my mom on the screen.

"Charlotte, are you okay? Were you asleep? Did you sleep the whole session? Have you seen the doctor? What did they say?" It was typical for my mother to ask me a million questions before I'd even had a chance to process one, much less answer them all.

I forced a smile and said, "Hey, Mom. I'm okay. Just tired." I knew that if I did not do my best to answer all her questions, she would continue to berate me until I did. It was always best to just play the game.

"I just have a slight headache. Nothing too bad. I slept most of the session. This stage of chemo always seems to knock me out completely. It takes everything out of me, you know?"

Sadie and Alex were having a side conversation and started to laugh because Alex was now annoying Sadie. Typical little sister. We were all close, but we still had our little tiffs.

"Charlotte, what about the doctors? What did they say?"

I looked back at the screen, "Oh, sorry, Mom. Yeah, as for that, well, I haven't seen the doctor yet. Usually, she makes her way around toward the end of my session, so it honestly shouldn't be too much longer."

I touched my right arm where they had me hooked up to the infusion. "My arm is so sore this round. I feel like there is scar tissue building up there now, and I bruise so easily these days."

I winced in pain as I attempted to show her. She brought the camera closer to her face, and I couldn't help but laugh.

Alex snapped her fingers to get my attention and waved at me to wrap it up. Then she pointed to her own arm and made a painful face. Sadie started laughing.

"Why is your sister laughing? Are you girls making fun of me?"

I shook my head in the negative and managed a soft smile..

"Well, anyway, you need to rest. I'll make you some fresh ginger tea once you are home. You'll be okay, you just wait and see."

"Thanks, Mom, but Alex is telling me to wrap it up because her arm hurts and you're talking too much."

Alex softly hit the arm that wasn't hooked up to the machine and turned the phone to face her, "Mom, she's lying, I wasn't doing that."

She glared playfully at me. "Honestly, Alex, I don't know what I'm going to do with you. Well, bye, my girls. I will see you at Charlotte's house. I'm going to grab Max and Molly from school and then start dinner."

In unison, as if we were cued on to it, all three of us replied, "Okay, Mom, we love you. See you later!"

Alex hung up as we all started to laugh.

Chapter 28

Charlotte - Shadows at the Lake

T he kitchen still smelled like the chicken Sadie had roasted earlier, but the warmth of the food had done nothing to thaw the knot in my chest. Geoff was putting Molly and Max to bed while Sadie sat across from me at the table, thumbing through the mail I had let pile up for weeks. Her brow furrowed as she reached for a pink envelope that stood out among the white.

"From the insurance company," she said, tapping it. "Want me to open it?"

"Go ahead," I replied. My voice came out hoarse.

I had barely spoken since the police left. My nerves were frayed raw, Baxter hadn't moved from the door all night, and Max had asked three times if he could sleep in my bed again. Of course, I will let him. *If I am scared and anxious, surely he can sense it, too.*

Sadie slid the letter from the envelope, her eyes scanning.

"It's about Will," she said slowly. "Policy status updated to ... tentative claim. Pending investigation."

My blood turned to ice. "Why would there be a claim?"

Sadie didn't look up. "They must assume he's dead." The moment she blurted out the words, her eyes flew up to mine. She dropped the envelope and rushed to my side.

"Oh my gosh, Charlie. I'm so sorry. I didn't … I wasn't … oh gosh, I am just sorry. My stupid mouth got the best of me, is all."

Why would she say that? I tried to push the feelings of anger and pain aside. I knew deep down she didn't mean it, but it still stung. It hurt because, what if it's true?

I gripped the edge of the table, knuckles turning white, my teeth grinding a bit as I spat out the words, "They think he's dead because he hasn't been found. Not because of any proof."

"I know," Sadie said quickly, softly. "He just hasn't been found. He will be, though."

I pushed up from the table, heart pounding. "Will isn't dead. He can't be. My gut tells me he is out there, somewhere." *Wouldn't I know if he wasn't? Don't people feel their soulmate die? Aren't there studies on that?*

But the silence was becoming unbearable. And the idea that others were already preparing for the worst made me want to scream.

Geoff came down the stairs swiftly, holding Molly's unicorn plushie. "She wanted you to have this tonight," he said.

I took it, holding it against my chest. "Thanks."

Sadie stood. "We should all sleep in shifts. You go up first. I'll stay up for a few hours, then Geoff will take over."

"You think he'll come back?" I asked.

Sadie hesitated. "If it were me, I wouldn't come back. I'd run. Especially if I knew someone was watching."

That hit hard. But I nodded.

Upstairs, I lay in bed, Molly's unicorn tucked beside me, Max curled on the far side with his feet pressed to my back. I stared at the ceiling.

Then the phone buzzed. An unknown number.

My hand trembled as I answered. "Hello?"

No answer. Just static.

Then a whisper in a robotic voice: "Don't trust the one who knows your favorite flowers."

My breath caught.

Click.

The line went dead.

I sat upright, heart hammering. *My favorite flowers? No one knows that. No one, that is, except Marla.*

My phone buzzed again. A new message.

"Bringing by a fresh batch of chocolate chip cookies. I'll leave them by the door so as not to disrupt. Praying. — Martha"

Chapter 29

Molly – Taken

I had been exhausted lately and was trying my best to get myself back into normal shape. I couldn't seem to find my energy, though. I walked every day to build my stamina, but some days were easier than others.

I was sprawled on the oversized couch in the den, a fur blanket over my legs and a fuzzy beanie on my head. I felt like a poster child for a fashionable cancer ad minus the healthy pallor of my skin. That had been my steady routine since chemo began. I typically moved from my bedroom to the living room couch to the porch swing. The small change in scenery seemed to help me recover. The fight against cancer was just as much a mental fight as it was a physical one.

My family had been taking turns bringing food and helping me with the kids. I was very fortunate to have them here. However, they were no substitute for Will. It was very different having them versus him. There was a vacancy in my heart that idled in a state of perpetual agony. I did my best to keep moving. Prayer helped me the most. Some days were easier than others. Some days I was angry at God, raising my fists to the sky in utter protest. Other days, I fell to my knees, pleading in desperate sorrow.

I replayed her voicemail that I received earlier that day, pressing the phone tight against my ear.

"Hey, Charlotte, it's Marla. I…uh, I just wanted to say James… I'm sure James has everything in order at the office. He always does. You don't need to worry about that. I've been… unwell, honestly. The hospital—I wasn't myself that day. I'm sorry if I frightened you. I didn't mean to. I haven't been around, I know, and that's on me. I've just needed time…because of you…"

Her tone sharpened, bitter, before abruptly softening.

"Well… not because of you. I mean, um… I just needed time. That's all."

Another pause. A nervous laugh. Then her voice sped up, words spilling like she needed to outrun the silence.

"Anyway. I hope you're resting. Really resting. Everything's fine, it's all being taken care of. Just focus on yourself, okay?"

And then, faint and muffled under the static, a man's voice cut through: "Who are you calling?"

The line went dead.

I hadn't heard from the kids in a while. I really need to check on them. I got up slowly and started to make my way around the house. Molly usually loved to make playhouses in the most unusual spots. I could usually find a paper trail leading to her. I looked under my desk, behind the couch, and in the laundry room. "Molly! Molly, can you come here?" I called as I walked up the stairs. I had to stop every few steps because it not only took the wind out of me, but it also made me dizzy.

I got to her room and was greeted by glitter, scissors, and stickers strewn across the floor in complete disarray. I looked around the room, confused. I checked her bathroom just to be safe. I decided to go find Max. I was sure he knew where she was hiding out. She might even be with him.

I walked to his room, and he was lying on his stomach in the middle of what looked to be a Lego avalanche. It was an explosion of every color and size. "Molly is missing, Max. Do you know where she went? I can't find her anywhere. Were you guys outside playing on the playground or playing hide and seek?"

Max shook his head, his brown hair swinging back and forth. "No, Mom. We were playing fetch with Baxter, but then I got thirsty and decided to come in for water. When I went back outside, she was gone. So, I came inside to see if I could find her. I looked in her room but had no luck. I can't find Baxter, either. I think he's with her."

Panic began to rise within me. "Max, why didn't you come and find me?"

He looked up at me. "You looked tired, Mom. I didn't want to bother you."

As sweet as his words were, they were equally frustrating. Something was wrong. I could feel it at my core. The dog was missing, and so was Molly. My sweet Molly. Where

243

was she? What if she went near the lake and fell in? She knew better than that, though. She knew never to go near it. I walked downstairs and texted my sisters. Then I told Max to put on his boots and jacket. I grabbed a backpack and threw in a flashlight, just in case. Last minute, I grabbed a switchblade and a couple of bottles of water and dumped them in, too. "Max, let's go. Now."

For someone who just had chemo a few days earlier, it was funny how a sense of urgency can make you feel invincible. Adrenaline pumped through my veins, making me feel as if I had just had a pot of coffee. I would rather die than have anything happen to my children. I would be damned if I went to bed not knowing Molly and Max were curled up right next to me.

I opened the side door that led directly to the handmade trail spiraling toward the lake, and I closed it behind us. Will had constructed it with river rock until you hit the lake. Then, as it goes around toward the woods, it turns into a dirt path. The sun would be going down in a few hours. My nerves were shot. I felt my body waver. I tried to push my fears away and focused on the task at hand.

My head was beginning to pound as it often did after chemo. I tended to get headaches that could turn into full-blown migraines. I couldn't afford to think about myself, though. "Molly! Molly! Where are you? Molly!" I started to scream for her.

Then Max followed suit. "Molls! Molly, where are you? Molly!" We kept walking hand in hand, kicking up the dirt as we went. My eyes scanned everywhere for a clue. Then suddenly, I heard a faint bark in the distance. Max looked at me, his eyes wide. He heard it, too. "Mom! I think it's Baxter!" His eyes filled with excitement.

"Baxter boy! Baxter, come here! Baxter!" I screamed loudly, hoping he heard his name.

Baxter would not stop barking.

The sound was frantic, almost human in its urgency. Charlotte stumbled along the trail with Max close behind, her fingers white-knuckled around the flashlight, the beam bouncing wildly over trees and underbrush as she followed the blur of fur crashing ahead.

"Molly!" she cried into the woods.

The trees swallowed her voice.

Max was right beside her, his breath puffing in quick bursts. "She might be at the treehouse," he said.

Charlotte nodded, though her legs were trembling. The chemo had drained her. Her bones ached. Her skin felt too tight. But the adrenaline numbed everything except the terrifying need to find her daughter.

They pushed through branches, thorns grabbing at her sleeves like fingers. Baxter's barks turned sharp and excited. They created a blanket of leaves and moss. The smell of pine penetrated my senses. If I weren't in a panic, I would want to linger and take in the scenery. My senses were on full overload, my eyes constantly surveying the landscape. No one or nothing was visible. There was no trace of Molly or Baxter. Knowing there were a fair number of dangerous animals in these woods, my anxiety rose. I should have packed my gun, but I had to scatter to run and get it from the safe in our bedroom.

Then, "Mom!" Max shouted, pointing. As I turned in the direction, I saw a red flash in the distance. Whoever it was, they were moving fast.

"Molly! Is that you? Molly! Stop!" Max started to yell. "Baxter, come here, boy! Molly! Molly! Where are you?"

The figure didn't hesitate at our calls. They kept sinking deeper into the woods until eventually they were out of view.

We ran, tripping over the long grass and cracked ground below us. "Max, be careful not to step on a rock and twist your ankle."

I wonder who that could have been. They were too far, and it was too dark to distinguish any features. Much too tall to be Molly. Max was huffing and puffing, trying to keep up with me. His brow was creased, and his hair was damp with sweat. "Molly! Where are you?" He yelled. Then we both stopped as we heard the incessant barking. Simultaneously. We both chanted his name as we followed the sound. The barking grew closer. We picked up our pace.

We came upon Baxter barking at a tree. He disregarded our presence as he jumped at the stump over and over. There was a sense of urgency to his bark.

There.

The small silhouette curled at the top of the treehouse ladder. Molly.

As I got close, Molly stood, her mouth taped; tears wet her face. I told Max very calmly to stay with Baxter. I examined the wooden ladder before I ascended. I felt light-headed and stopped midway to catch my breath. In my head, I prayed. *Please, Lord, let me be able to get my kids safely home. Give me the strength to keep my kids safe.*

The closer I got to Molly, the louder her muffled cries were. Her body was so small, and there was a heartbreaking vulnerability to her. At the sight of her tears, my own eyes prickled. I fought them off so as not to scare her. When I got to the top, I whispered, "Shh." I was unsure as to who was around and if there were eyes upon us. I looked down to check on Max. He was sitting with Baxter by his side, his eyes fixated on us.

"Molly, baby, it's okay–it's Mommy. We're here now," she called gently.

My little girl didn't move. She just cried.

Molly didn't resist. She sagged into my chest, small and quiet.

I descended with her cradled tightly. My foot slipped once, sending a jolt through my leg, but I tightened my grip and kept going.

Max met us at the bottom, tears on his cheeks. He kissed his sister's forehead and held onto my arm as we started back through the woods.

The world tilted. My knees buckled again. My body couldn't do this much longer. Darkness bled in at the edges of my vision. The world spun.

Then an arm looped under my own.

"I've got you," a light and gentle voice said.

I couldn't focus. I blinked up.

A flash of bright red hair. Familiar. A blur.

Hannah.

Together, we carried the children, Max holding Molly's legs while Hannah supported me.

When we finally reached the back porch, I collapsed onto the steps, the ground cool and hard beneath me.

Everything faded to black.

I awoke in bed.

Soft light poured through the windows. The hum of cartoons from the living room buzzed low and comforting. I could hear Max laughing. Molly babbling.

My limbs felt like sandbags. My throat was dry.

I turned my head slowly.

Memory flickered, the weight of a hand on my shoulder. The scrape of boots. Red hair against moonlight.

I closed my eyes.

I didn't know what Hannah's role in all of this was. Not yet.

But she knew this: my children were safe.

Chapter 30

Hannah – Desperation

The water scalded Hannah's skin, but she didn't move.

She stood in the shower, forehead pressed to the cool tile, hot rivulets cascading down her back. Her arms wrapped around her stomach like she was attempting to hold herself together. She wasn't crying at first, not really. Her breathing was labored, though, letting the steam choke out everything she couldn't say.

Then it came.

A silent sob. Then another. Until she collapsed to her knees, the spray drenching her tangled red curls, her body shaking beneath the weight of all the things she couldn't undo.

Hannah had helped Charlotte and carried her half-conscious body through the woods. She had wrapped her arms around that little girl as if she were hers. But she wasn't. None of this was hers.

Not the kids. Not the house. Not Will.

And yet ... she wanted them to be. She desperately needed them to be.

Hannah loved Molly. It was like staring at herself as a little girl filled with innocence and promise. *Gosh, I love her so much, and Max is such an awe-inspiring boy.*

It wasn't rational, she knew that. It was real. Something about that child pierced straight through the numbness that had wrapped around her for years.

And Will ...

She pressed her fist to her mouth, her lips touching her skin, a yearning for that touch to be his.

Will was here, sleeping just in the other room, lounging across a bed, breathing and alive.

Her hands itched for something to do, something beyond watching him sleep like he belonged to her again.

"I saved you," Hannah whispered into the silence. "So now maybe ... you'll stay."

But he didn't belong to her either. He never would. No matter how long she had imagined it, no matter how often she had pictured them as a family, it would always be just a fantasy.

And Marla ...

Hannah choked.

Marla had gone too far.

Seeing Molly huddled and afraid, Charlotte barely clinging to consciousness, it changed something in Hannah. It was like a switch flipped, and now she didn't know where she stood. She was at a loss between utter guilt and frantic longing. Between protector and perpetrator.

She gripped the tile, her knuckles going white. Everything was unraveling so fast.

Then there was a soft knock that broke the silence.

She froze.

"Hannah?" Will's voice, muffled but unmistakable.

Her chest instantly tightened.

"You okay?" he asked again, a note of concern threading through the door.

She didn't answer; instead, a long pause filled the void.

"I heard you crying."

Hannah cursed under her breath and shut off the water. The quiet was louder than the spray.

With shaking hands, she reached for the towel and wrapped it around herself. Her hair clung wetly to her neck.

When Hannah opened the door, Will stepped back slightly. His eyes scanned her face, searching.

Hannah knew she probably looked like a ghost, with her pale skin and red eyes.

"What happened?" he asked.

Her voice caught. "I can't ... I don't know how to say it. Don't worry about it. I'm fine," she said dismissively. Part of her struggled with her wanting him to walk away, while another desperately wished he would pull her in.

"Try," he gently commanded.

Hannah looked at him, her eyes pleading, and then he softly smiled. "I can try."

She told him everything, and it was hard at first. She explained how she came across Molly, about Charlotte collapsing, about carrying them both through the trees like some silent, invisible savior. But also about feeling her heart crack in half while doing it. A feeling and sensation that she just couldn't understand.

Then Hannah told him how she had a radical change of heart, how, when she pictured the kids, she didn't want to give it up. Not any of it. The illusion was powerful, impactful.

He went rigid.

She could see it in his eyes, the shift, the betrayal, the primal fear and need to protect.

He took a step back, his jaw tight, making her heart pound harder.

"You should have told me sooner."

"I know."

"You kept me from them. From knowing. From helping."

"I didn't want to lose you."

He let out a bitter laugh. "You never had me, Hannah."

She could feel her face instantaneously crumple.

He turned away and grabbed the edge of the kitchen counter, a plate shattering against the floor. She flinched, waiting for the violence that never came.

Memories of her dad flooded Hannah's mind, and the desperate need to run took hold, but she didn't move an inch.

He stood over the shards, chest heaving, hands clenched.

She didn't speak, and she kept her head down. She just stood still, dripping onto the tile, as if that would somehow ground her.

Then he finally looked up, his expression unreadable. "Hannah, I just wish sometimes that you would see what God is trying to do in your life instead of trying to pick up all the damn pieces yourself."

God? What does He have to do with any of this? she thought, annoyed at the idea that her very humanity was tied to her vulnerable confession.

"He gives you a chance to feel something real, and you twist it!" He ran his hands anxiously through his thick hair. "It's crap like this that you do that always frustrates me. Whenever someone tries to help, it's your immediate instinct to just run. I can't with you right now. I need air."

Will began to turn and limp away, leaving her alone. It was a feeling Hannah didn't like. It was all-encompassing; it was suffocating. She hesitated and then reached out. "Wait!"

Steam still clung to the walls when Hannah stepped into the doorway, hair damp and shirt plastered to her skin. Her arms wrapped around herself like she was trying to hold her body together. For a long moment, she just stared at him.

"I am sorry. I just … I know I have issues to work on, but please just listen. Let me explain."

Will stopped, his shoulders slumped. He let out a sigh and slowly turned his head back toward her. Listening.

Her voice low, shaky. "I can't breathe in here. Let's go outside. Give me a minute."

Will hesitated. The last thing he wanted was to give her more space to get close. But there was a hollowness in her eyes that unnerved him. He waited for her to appear back into the hallway and then pushed himself off the wall and followed her through the narrow hallway, through the kitchen, and out the back door.

The night air was sharp against his skin, cutting through the haze. Hannah exhaled like she had been holding her breath for hours. She busied herself at the porch table, pulling a deck of cards from the counter and setting it down between them. A bottle of whisky appeared next, two glasses clinking together.

"Gin rummy or blackjack," she asked, trying for light-ness, though her hands trembled as she shuffled.

Will arched a brow, a flicker of sardonic humor crossing his face. "Does it matter? You always cheat."

"Only when I know I'm going to lose," she said with a smile that didn't reach her eyes. They played in silence, the cards snapping against the wood. Every few turns, she took a long swallow from her glass, her laughter breaking into sighs, until finally, she set the cards down with shaking hands.

"Do you remember a truck stop years ago?" Her voice had gone small, childlike.

Will looked up, growing. "A truck stop?"

She nodded, eyes fixed on the worn wood of the table. "I was just a kid. My dad had me with him on one of his trips. He left me sitting in a booth at the diner while he went off with some woman he'd just met. Didn't even look back to see if I even sat down."

Will's face hardened, his jaw tightening.

"One of the workers came over. At first, he was nice. Then he wasn't. He forced me ..." Her words broke, caught. "I, um ... I panicked. I didn't ..." Her throat closing around the memory. "I thought I'd never get away, but then I did and um, he went back to his job like normal. Left me broken, scared, bruised, with a platter of pancakes in front of me." Her eyes narrowed, and her voice hard-ened. "As if the stupid pancakes would erase a damn thing."

Will's cards slipped from his hands. He leaned in, voice rough. Her eyes pooling. "Hannah ..."

She cut him off, her voice now desperate, like it had been waiting years to be spoken. "And then you were there.

You sat across from me like it was the most normal thing in the world. You gave me that stupid little toy car out of your pocket. You didn't even know me, but you gave me hope. You were kind when no one else was."

Will blinked, the memory flickering faintly at the edges of his mind. "That was you?"

Her eyes brimmed, her whole body trembling. "From that day on, I couldn't forget you. Not your face, not your voice. You were the only person who made me feel safe when everything else was broken."

The porch was hushed but for the buzz of cicadas.

She reached across the table, her hand shaking as it brushed his. "I've loved you since that night, Will. I thought … maybe someday …" Her voice faltered, swallowed by the night.

Will shook his head anguish shadowing his features. "Hannah …"

Before he could pull away, she leaned in and pressed her lips to his. The kiss was soft, desperate, years of unspoken need poured into a single act. For a moment, Will froze.

Then, faintly from inside, a song drifted through the open window—Coldplay. "Fix You." Charlotte's song.

Reality crashed down. Will broke away, breath ragged. "I can't," he whispered.

Her face crumpled, raw and exposed. "You'll always choose her."

Will turned from her, fists clenched tight at his sides. "I already did."

Hannah stood for a second and then sank to the floor like a puddle of water.

I am alone again, just like always. Except this time, pride made the choice.

Chapter 31

Charlotte - The Breaking Point

The room was dim, filled with the soft breath of curtains lifting gently in the morning air.

Charlotte blinked awake, confusion swirling before memory clicked into place. Her arms ached. Her legs throbbed. The remnants of last night clung like cobwebs. She sat up slowly. The world felt muffled, like she was underwater. But then she heard it–laughter. Max's laugh, light and free. Molly's high-pitched babble chasing after it.

She eased herself out of bed. Her body felt foreign, hollowed out, and bruised. Every step toward the hallway was slow and careful.

The house smelled like toast and sunshine. The hum of cartoons buzzed low from the living room. She paused by the staircase, steadying herself against the wall.

Max's voice drifted out.

"Dear God," he whispered.

Charlotte froze.

She followed the sound and stopped outside Max's

partially open bedroom door. He was kneeling by his bed, hands clasped tight, eyes squeezed shut.

"Thank you for keeping Molly safe," he said. "I was so scared, but you were there. I know it. I felt you."

A pause. A sniffle.

"And please help Mom not to die. She's tired a lot. And she cries in the bathroom sometimes. Please make her strong. Like she used to be."

Charlotte pressed a fist to her mouth.

"And please ... bring Dad home. I don't know where he is, but I think he's in trouble. I think you know that already."

He shifted, his voice trembling.

"And about Hannah ... please help her. She's really sad, even if she smiles sometimes. She looks like an angel, but I think she's hurting real bad inside. Can you send someone to sit with her? So she's not alone?"

Charlotte blinked hard, tears clouding her vision.

"And God ... if Baker is my dad... can you make him stop being scary? I don't want to be scared of him. I don't want him to hurt anybody anymore. Not Mom. Not Will. Not anyone."

He stayed still a moment longer, then slowly climbed back into bed.

Charlotte stepped away before he saw her, one hand against her heart.

Her son had asked for nothing for himself.

Just healing.

For all of them.

Interlude I: The Quiet Fog

I don't remember when the fog set in. Only that it never left.

It drapes over everything–morning emails, bedtime stories, the weight of a grocery bag. I move through my life with precision, but no color. As if someone else has folded themselves into my skin and taken the reins.

There are days I don't remember driving home. Times I watch myself smile in conversations like I'm behind glass. I tell myself it's stress. Fatigue. Hormones.

But sometimes I wake with the faint smell of something I cannot recall. A half-memory of a dropper. A name I shouldn't know. A note I can't explain.

He calls it clarity. Says it helps people like me focus. Let go. Says the world has too many sharp edges and he's just trying to round them out.

He never says what's in it. I don't ask. Maybe I don't want to know. Maybe I already do.

He's good at finding cracks in people. Quiet ones.

Lonely ones. He doesn't need violence to bend them—just need. Just trust. Just a whisper that they matter.

And I … I want to feel needed.

Even now, I'm not sure what's real. The dreams linger too long. Some days, I see Charlotte's face in every reflection. Other days, I feel nothing at all.

I used to be someone. I was kind. I was steady. I was loved.

But the fog doesn't care who you were. Only who you become inside it.

Chapter 32

Cortez – Silent Pursuit

Detective Cortez slammed the door of his cruiser, the early morning mist curling around his boots like smoke. The lakefront community was quiet, deceptively so. He'd been at this job long enough to know that danger rarely screamed. It whispered. And this place was whispering in a language only his gut could understand.

He walked up the path to the Rose house, nodding at the uniform stationed on the porch.

Charlotte had refused protective custody, but she'd accepted overnight watch. Cortez didn't blame her. No woman should go through what she had, let alone by herself, with two kids. Not with three suspects still out there.

Baker seemed to be the worst of them all. That name set his jaw tight. With a background like his, it was enough to set the watchdogs after him.

He pulled out his notepad as he stepped inside. Charlotte sat on the edge of the couch, pale but upright, her eyes shadowed. Max and Molly were in the other room with the dog, Baxter, who had taken to guarding the hallway like a soldier.

"Morning," Cortez said.

"Morning," Charlotte replied hoarsely.

He sat across from her. "I need to go over the events again. I know it's hard. But every detail matters. Especially with Lawson dead."

Her jaw trembled, but she nodded. "I know I said I didn't know Lawson, but I didn't know him because he didn't state his name in the voicemail he had left me. I guess for safety purposes but ... he was trying to help me. He knew something was wrong. He left a voicemail the day he died ... said he thought he was being followed and if Will was home. Why would he ask if Will were home? It doesn't make any sense." Her eyes were glassy, worn, and bloodshot.

Cortez made a note. That voicemail still hadn't been recovered.

"Did he mention who might've been following him?"

Charlotte hesitated. "He mentioned Marla once. Offhand. Said she was asking odd questions at work, lingering around the visitor logs. But he also said he kept seeing a figure visibly taller lurking in shadows, and another time, a vehicle was following at a distance during the night."

Cortez tapped his pen against the page. "That aligns with what I've got. We've traced movements through security footage for all three. Marla has access to records she shouldn't have through Will's company."

"Do you really think Marla could be capable of harming my family? We have always been good friends. I know recently she has been off, but something tells me there is something with her, that she is going through that hasn't come to service."

He leaned forward. "It rarely ever does, Charlotte. We believe someone's been pulling her strings. Baker's name keeps circling back in ways that don't make sense."

Charlotte's eyes widened. "So this ... this wasn't just her?"

"We believe she was manipulated. Maybe even drugged. We found residue in her desk drawer. Something called 'Clarity Drops.' Experimental. Off-market. Psychotropic with memory suppression properties."

Charlotte closed her eyes, her body sagging slightly.

"She almost killed me," Charlotte whispered, as if saying it aloud made it real. "In the hospital. During chemo. If Mariam hadn't walked in when she did..."

Cortez's pen stilled. "Mariam said Marla used a disguise. That she had a wig, glasses, hat."

"Yes," Charlotte said. "And she snapped. Screamed like a switch flipped. Then she was gone."

"And that's when the trail goes cold," Cortez muttered. "She called and left that voicemail, though."

Charlotte couldn't help but interrupt, "Were you able to recognize that voice?"

He paused, thinking. "We believe it could be Baker, but we have no way of confirming that information. Just speculation at this point."

He stood. "We're getting closer. She's spiraling. But that makes her more dangerous. So be cautious; don't pick up her call. Let's keep picking up the crumbs."

He looked toward the hallway where Max's voice rose in laughter.

"We'll keep someone on the house. I want you to call me if anything, anything feels off. Even a shadow."

Charlotte nodded. "I will."

"Cortez, what about Hannah? Any news?"

"You know, she's always just out of reach. It's like she knows we're watching, and she moves just outside the frame. Strangest thing."

Charlotte hovered at the door as Cortez stepped outside. She thought about Hannah and a vague memory of her helping. She didn't know why, but she couldn't bring herself to tell Cortez. Something held her back. He looked across the lake. Mist curled over the surface like breath.

"If you find her ... let me know. I don't think she will ever forgive me for Will."

He turned around slowly and looked at Charlotte. Wisdom creased his eyes. "You can't lose what was never fully yours."

With that, Charlotte allowed a tiny smile to form across her worn face. "Thanks. Have a good night. Tell Martha that I said hello."

He tipped his hat, "Will do."

He was missing something. A thread. But it was unraveling fast. And he intended to follow it to the end.

Even if it led him straight into the dark.

After leaving the Rose house, Cortez pulled out his phone. He hesitated, then tapped Martha's name.

"She's safe for now," he said softly. "But it's worse than we thought."

Her voice broke on the other end. "Just keep her safe, Ray. Please. She's been through enough."

"I will," he promised, his jaw set. "She's hanging in.

Barely. Looks like hell warmed over. But she smiled when I mentioned you."

"I miss her," Martha whispered. "Tell her I'll drop off some lemon loaf. Maybe a few books for the kids."

"I will. And Martha?"

"Yes?"

"Thank you for loving her like she was one of ours."

After leaving the Rose house, Cortez drove straight to the precinct. He couldn't shake Charlotte's voice, her fear, so he decided to rally for a few more hours.

He queued up the hospital surveillance footage again. He hadn't had time to review it fully before.

He analyzed the grainy footage. That was when he saw the intensity of Marla's cold gaze. The quick flick of her hand near Charlotte's IV.

When he got home later that night, Martha was sitting in the dark, a rosary in her hands, her eyes closed in prayer on her favorite chair. When she heard the door shut, she looked up.

"She almost died," Cortez says quietly. "Marla nearly killed her. I saw the footage." He shook his head in disbelief.

Martha's eyes brimmed. "I knew something was wrong with that woman. What do we do now?"

"We send our best to hunt her down. And we end it."

That's when he remembered the voicemail from Marla's husband. He pulled it up and played it.

"Hey, Detective. I don't know if this matters, but ... Marla's been acting kind of off lately. Talking to herself. Which doesn't seem too weird, I know, but I walked by our room the other night, and she was having a full-on conversation with someone who wasn't there; she wasn't on the phone either. She referred to the name, Hannah. Said she knew secrets only Hannah would know. When I asked her if she was okay, she looked at me blankly, you know, like someone from that old movie *The Stepford Wives*. She was smiling, robotic, frozen. She said, 'Of course, honey. Why ever would you think otherwise?' Then she just kept scribbling in this notebook like nothing happened. It honestly, really freaked me out. There are a few other instances that are really making me nervous. If you can give me a call, I would appreciate it. Um … but not on this line. If you don't mind calling my work phone, VirtuEx. Appreciate you. Bye."

Cortez exhaled sharply, dragging a hand down his face.

This doesn't sound like just psychosis anymore.

And if Hannah's name was in Marla's mouth … then whatever threads we think are separate are now twisted together.

Interlude II: Charlotte's Memory

I used to think I was good at reading people. That I could feel a lie vibrate beneath someone's smile. But I somehow missed this in her. I missed all of it.

There had been signs, now that I trace them backward, the late-night calls she brushed off, the shadow in her voice when she laughed too brightly. How she hovered too long at our door, how her hugs started lasting too long. I thought it was love. Maybe it was, once. But something else had taken root.

Polite to a fault, she had always been tightly wound, like a clock ticking louder than necessary, especially whenever David's name came up, or when certain college memories slipped too close to the surface. I didn't question it then, not the stiffness in her tone or the way she dodged certain subjects. But now I wonder if she'd been bracing for the truth to return all along. Polite to a fault, sharp in the right circles, almost invisible in others.

But I had seen her once, before the mask thickened. Before the silence felt rehearsed.

I don't know if she ever admitted it to herself. That the man she built her life with was one of them that night. Not Baker, but someone else in that room. Someone who had stayed silent while it all happened. Complacent in the act. Yet now, he wears a new name, a new job, a clean face. He seems changed, but I have problems trusting someone who never attests for their sins.

But silence has a scent, and Marla breathed it every day. Maybe she convinced herself it is normal. Maybe that's how she survived.

Now I think about those lunches we shared, the way she watched my kids as if memorizing them. The day she gifted Max a sweater, then forgot she had already given it weeks earlier. The way her voice cracked when she talked about fairness. About consequences.

And I remember one moment, clearest of all. A twitch. A strange pause when I mentioned a name I hadn't spoken in years. Her face didn't move, but her knuckles whitened against her teacup.

I remembered thinking, even back then, how Marla had this uncanny ability to show up at the exact right moment. After breakups. After hard news. After the miscarriage that I barely spoke of. She'd bring tea, light a candle, and just sit. It felt kind, but also ... curated. Like she knew when to step in almost too well. And yet, I never asked how she knew. I never wanted to ruin the comfort.

I see it now. The unraveling had already begun.

And maybe ... maybe she was already gone.

What I didn't realize then, what took me until much later to piece together, was that Marla had married one of the very men who hurt her, David. One of the frat boys from that awful night. Not the worst of them, not Baker, but another who stood by and did nothing while it all happened. He had rebranded himself, built a clean life, but his silence was its own kind of violence. And Marla? She never escaped that dynamic. It replayed in their marriage. Quietly. Powerfully. And she stayed.

Until it all bled out, years of buried pain seeping into every corner of her life until she couldn't keep it hidden anymore.

But the worst part? There were moments, small, fleeting ones—when I wondered if everything in her perfect life had been built on someone else's choices. A silence she guarded like a secret too dangerous to speak aloud.

It makes sense now, the panic in her eyes when someone mentioned paternity tests. The overreaction when I joked about family resemblance. Her love wasn't fake.

But it was warped. Twisted by shame and dependency.

And she never got out.

Chapter 33

Will – The House of Watching Eyes

As he walked toward his house under the ocean of stars, Will's feet crunched with each step. The light rain from earlier had caused ice to build like tiny glass roads upon the grass. Moisture filled the air. This was usually his favorite season–the cold evenings spent on the back porch with the warmth of a roaring fire and Charlotte in his arms. If he concentrated hard, he could still smell her sweet scent.

Will couldn't believe that everyone bought that he was missing or dead. He thought by now someone would have caught on, possibly tracked down Hannah or himself. He wondered if what he did was considered a crime. *Surely not, I don't know who cut the brakes. Have the cops figured it all out by now? Surely Charlie knows. She must. If she doesn't yet know that I'm alive, she'll be the one to figure it out. My money is on her. She can sniff out a lie from a mile away. I always joked that she should have been a detective. She's probably been on my scent like a hound since I left.*

Will hated the way he left and how that evening played

out. For everything to go smoothly, he had to create the illusion of foul play. The fight escalated quickly. Channeling his anger toward Baker had helped portray his emotions as raw and real. Will just hope she bought it. He just couldn't fathom his family being in danger. Baker had taken this charade too far. He was off the rails. A psycho maniac.

Hannah had always been one to contend with. But Baker? He was a damn wild card.

Hannah would never hurt a fly. Her heart could be bleeding on the table before she would take a swing. She had obsessions like any other. Her background had left a mental scar that went beyond mending. But she would never harness her pain and manipulate it into something dark and vengeful.

Will had started noticing strange happenings more and more frequently. Then one day, he saw him lurking around town. Will had been walking and spotted him across the street. Not a care in the world, just standing there staring, but when he'd turned back, Baker had gone. Will thought he had imagined it.

Will felt like he was the co-star in Baker's twisted movie, and Charlotte was his star. He hated the guy for making them constantly watch their backs. He had seen how unraveled Charlotte had become, knowing that he'd been creeping around. Will tried to remain composed and present a cool front. Then the damn letter arrived, and that did it. It was the nail in the coffin. The grimy paper with oil and dirt penetrating its folds. The smell of urine tinged Will's nose as he brought it in closer to inspect. In the middle of the rancid, folded card was a single item: a perfect ringlet from sweet Molly's golden-brown head. To add fuel to the fire, the creep added a picture of her innocently sleeping in her room. In their house of all damn places, while Will and Charlotte had been downstairs. The actual nerve of this cocky bastard.

That note was why Will was in this falsified new reality. It made him sick. Anger fueled him each time he opened the note. He carried it in his pocket as a reminder of why he was here and what he needed to do to protect his family. That note was why Will hired a detective. It was how he'd pin this son of a gun once and for all. He had no clue, however, that his brakes would be cut, and he didn't know he would be rescued like a damn damsel in distress by his scorned and somewhat psychotic ex. Now that—well, that was a surprise.

Will knew the cops were going to drag their feet on this case. Just like in every situation. There had always been a lack of support among our officers here. It was to our own detriment. Perhaps being presumed missing or even dead would create a buzz, but he wouldn't hold his breath. From what he'd read, nothing had yet been found. Other than his vehicle.

Will knew it was best to get out of Hannah's house. He didn't feel as if he could trust her one hundred percent. Her intentions had yet to become clear. She did save him, so he had to give credit where credit was due, and she did warn him about Baker, as well.

But this was his family. No one was going to hurt them. They were Will's priority. Not Baker. Not Hannah. Only them. Over his dead body would anyone harm them. Charlotte was incredible. She'd figure this out eventually. She loved a good puzzle. And with the stakes involving her family, Will knew nothing would get past her. She would not lose hope. He took solace in that. It was what he knew to be true and what kept him going.

His plan of manipulating Baker by staging his own death went awry. Will knew it wasn't a bulletproof plan from the beginning—maybe even foolish. But he needed time. He needed Baker to believe he was out of the picture. Will left crumbs for Charlotte. He needed her to know he was still alive, still fighting. He just hoped she'd follow the trail.

And now? Now he walked. Alone. In the dark.

Will pushed himself, body trembling with effort. He took one step, then another, toward the thought of home. Toward Charlotte, toward vengeance. But the world tilted, and the porch light flared behind him. A shadow lingered there. He wasn't free yet. Not from this place and not from her. Something telling him it was not the right time. But he had to see Charlotte, even if it was for a moment. He trudged onward, eyes at his back.

Chapter 34

Marla - A Dangerous Bargain

They were asking her questions. She heard them, distantly, like a muffled sound through water.

"What did he give you, Marla?"

She blinked slowly.

"He called it clarity. Just a few drops—only when I got too loud."

"Who? Who gave you the drops?"

She looked at her lap. Then up at the two-way mirror.

"Baker."

The officers glanced at each other from behind the glass. Marla could feel them calculating.

Her legs swung slightly beneath the metal chair, child-like and detached. The cold from the room had found her skin, but she didn't flinch. Didn't wrap her arms around herself for warmth. She just stared ahead, unblinking.

Her hands were raw from the nervous pulling of her cuticles. Tiny flecks of blood dotted her nails like confetti.

"I didn't mean to hurt her. Charlotte. I just needed ... I needed to see. To know if she was part of it."

"Part of what, Marla?" The voice was measured, gentle. Still too far away.

She looked down at her lap again. Her hands twitched. "He said they were all liars. That they were laughing behind the curtains. Whispering about me. Even when I couldn't hear them ... I could feel it."

The light overhead buzzed. Or maybe it was inside her head. It was getting hard to tell the difference lately.

"And Molly? Did you take Molly?"

Marla tilted her head. "She was innocent. A little light in their lives, and I wasn't going to hurt her. I just wanted them to know what he felt. I wanted them to know how something you made could be missed."

"You were found outside the school grounds with a bottle of something in your purse. Do you remember that?"

Marla's eyebrows knitted together. Her voice dropped to a whisper.

"He said the drops were good. That they would help me remember. But they make everything hazy. I can't tell what's now and what already happened."

A silence stretched.

Then she looked straight at the glass again. Her voice was eerily calm.

"But I remember everything ... unless he put something in the tea again. He does that when I get too loud."

The glass didn't respond. But she smiled anyway, as if Baker were right behind it, watching. Waiting.

She whispered, almost fondly, "He always said I was his favorite project."

"Unfortunately, we don't have much to hold her with. I just feel like now we have more questions than before.

Gaps," Cortez said to the officer once the door was shut. "We need to figure out her past to figure out the future."

The other officer nodded in agreement.

Chapter 35

Charlotte - Shattered Calm

T he sun filtered through the curtains like a whispered promise, brushing its warmth across the quilt covering my legs. It had been days since everything happened–since Molly was found, since I collapsed, and since Marla vanished into whatever dark corner she'd crawled from. But time still felt fragile, like the thin edge of a soap bubble, threatening to pop with the slightest touch.

I hadn't told the kids everything. Not yet. Only that Mommy had gotten very tired and needed rest. Max hadn't pried, but his eyes held questions that he was too gentle to ask. Molly clung to her stuffed unicorn like it was the only thing anchoring her to this world. Will hovered like a shadow, guilty and grieving, unsure where he belonged.

I sat quietly in the sunlit kitchen, wrapping my fingers around the chipped ceramic mug filled with tea. I'd always thought healing came like a sunrise–sudden, bright, and overwhelming. But it wasn't like that. It came like light through lace: uneven, quiet, and threaded with pain.

Father Alvarez said something to me during one of our talks that I kept coming back to.

"Grace is not the absence of pain, Charlotte. It's the presence of God in the middle of it." I didn't fully understand it until now.

I looked out the window at the lake, calm and vast, mirroring the morning sky. So much had happened by its banks. So many memories, some I wanted to keep, some I wished I could erase.

But I hadn't been alone.

God had been there. In the dark. In the pain. In the search. In the moment I collapsed. And in the moment Hannah helped me stand again. Even she, in all her brokenness, had played a part in saving what I hold most dear.

I heard soft footsteps behind me. Molly. Her tiny hand slid into mine. She said nothing, just leaned her head against my shoulder.

And that was grace.

Not perfection. Not resolution.

But presence.

And presence, I was learning, was everything.

I closed my eyes and whispered a prayer. Not with fancy words. Just with a tired, grateful heart.

Thank you for not letting go.

Thank you for the morning.

Thank you for grace, still holding us together.

Chapter 36

Charlotte - Fractures

M orning slipped in like a thief, sliding into the cracks of my fragile bubble and stealing the warmth the sun left behind. I sat upright in bed, groggy, every muscle aching with the kind of exhaustion chemo leaves behind, like silt in the blood.

My hand searched the space beside me where Will should be.

It was cold, empty. A feeling I have grown accustomed to, of course.

I knew better, but hope still reached anyway, the way a hand reaches for a light switch in a dark room it already knows is broken.

For a moment, I clung to last night's feeling, that sense that he'd been there. The weight on the mattress, the whisper of someone moving in the hall. I still question: *Was that him?* I tell myself it was real, then immediately scold myself for attempting to believe it. Some mornings, the meds blur the edges between dream and memory so well that they pass as fact. It often leaves me skeptical of my own mind's reality. Maybe last night was one of those. But how could I be sure?

Through the window, fog swallows the woods in slow, curling breaths, clinging to the trunks like damp wool. The scent of sodden earth penetrated my senses. From the hallway come the kids, muffled in laughter, a plastic toy clacking against tile, Baxter's uneven sigh. The sounds of life tug me toward the day, a reminder that I have life yet to live.

I swung my legs over the side of the bed and stood carefully. The ache from yesterday's fall, Molly going limp in my arms, my knees finding the ground before my hands, life sparking under my skin.

"Okay," I tell my body, "we're doing this." One step at a time, I make my way down.

Max was sitting cross-legged, with Baxter sprawled like a furry comma beside him as they built a skyline of cardboard edges. On the couch, Molly was lying nestled in blankets, cheeks pink from her fever, but breathing steadily. Relief loosened my shoulders in a rush that left me lightheaded. "I know I am supposed to be careful and not be around her because she is sick, but she is my child. How can I not comfort her in moments like these?"

"I'm going to take a quick shower," I said, and Max nodded without looking up, the concentration of an eight-year-old stitched across his face.

The bathroom door clicked shut behind me. I turned the lock, stripped carefully, and caught my reflection with the corner of my eye. The mirror had no mercy. Peach fuzz was no longer visible and oddly yearned for. Purple half-moons cratered under my eyes. My skin pigmentation was gone, and the color of pale paper was left in its place. I forced myself to look anyway. I had come to detest my reflection. But I attempted daily to look into my exhausted eyes. Perhaps if I could bear the rest of it.

The water came out hot. Steam rose fast, fogging the glass, softening every hard edge until the room blurred to an outline. I pressed my forehead against the tile. The heat made my bruised knees throb, then ease. Tears surprised me, hot, salty, and immediate.

"God," I whispered into the hiss, my eyes gravitating upward. "I can't be everything for everyone and still stand up. I love my children. But I feel like I'm dissolving. I need help."

The steam thickened. It moved strangely, almost pulsating, shifting in little tides, but I couldn't quite time the water. My fingers slid along the wall, seeking the grout's grit; the tile felt … too soft for a blink, like velvet. I closed my eyes, counted to five, and then opened them. The room wavered and then steadied.

Something creaked.

I turned toward the vanity. The mirror was no longer foggy; it was fractured into a spiderweb of fine cracks that weren't there a moment ago. In the broken panes stood Will, whole and close, his eyes carrying that familiar mix of sorrow and kindness I know as well as my own name.

"Charlotte?" he said, voice low, careful, as if the sound itself might break me.

My breath caught in my throat. "Will?"

He stepped inside the halo of steam. His clothes looked dry. They registered as an off note, the way a wrong key sounded in a song you knew by heart, and then it passed because everything in me wanted to reach for him.

"I'm here," he whispered. "I had to come back."

Something in me, logic, pride, whatever thin thread still tried to save me from myself, asked the obvious question: *How?* It broke easily under the weight of my longing.

I went to him. His skin felt warm, the way memory insists it is. When his mouth touched mine, it began tentatively, then grew hungry, as if both of us remembered the language and were relieved not to have forgotten.

"I miss you," I said against his shoulder, my voice smaller than I meant it to be. "I think I am losing myself."

"You're not lost," he breathed in my ear. "You're still mine."

We moved with the urgency of people who had already survived too much, clumsy with relief, greedy for contact, unpracticed at gentleness because gentleness felt like a luxury we could not afford. Clothes became a scattering of fabric that I didn't even watch fall. I closed my eyes and let my body carry the remembering.

A slip of doubt threaded through then. The steam didn't bead on his hair. When he said my name, it echoed, not in the room, but deep within *me* as if the sound never left my chest. I didn't stop. I couldn't. I don't want to.

And then, like a curtain being pulled, the fog thickened all at once. The room tilted. His face blurred at the edges, then from the center, dissolving.

My eyes snapped open.

The shower was running, steady as a metronome. The water drumming on the tile. The mirror across from me was whole. It was uncracked, perfectly ordinary, the same old streak in the corner where the glass never seems to dry right. The towel bunched under my hand. The only warmth on my skin was from the steam.

No Will.

For a long second, I didn't move. My heart thudded in my throat, my ears, and in the base of my skull. Then the cold came, first to my shoulders, then everywhere at once, followed by the ache behind my ribs that grief always seemed to find.

I straightened up, my body protesting. The room steadied around me, square and real and painfully merciless. I shut off the water. The sudden quiet made the rest of the house sound louder: the soft click of plastic toys, Baxter's tail thumps, Molly's cough. Life relentlessly reminded me of its voice.

A hallucination, then. That was what it was. The meds, Molly's fever, the night sans sleep. My rational mind spread the pieces out neatly, a puzzle I couldn't seem to complete even if I wanted to. The other part of me, the one that still listened for his key at the door, slid a piece out of place and kept it close.

I wrapped the towel tighter and pressed my palms to my eyes until light pooled under the lids. When I dropped my hands, my fingers trembled. Shame arrived in a familiar double wave: first for wanting what I want, then for not being able to hold the wanting without breaking open.

I stood in slow, practical motions and unlocked the door. In the hallway, the air felt cooler, cleaner. I did what people do when they refuse to trust a single explanation: I timidly checked. Our bedroom, empty. The hall closet, the smell of cedar balls and coats, yet nothing else. The back door, bolted. I tried the handle anyway. It was locked.

My heart sank.

On the way back to the living room, I stopped by the kitchen window. Fog pressed against the glass like a breath.

285

Beyond it, the trees stood layered in pale gray, quiet as if holding a secret.

"He's not here," I told the ghost in the glass reflection, and then, because faith is sometimes a whisper spoken to the smallest, truest part of yourself, I added softly, "But God is."

Max looked up when I came in. "You okay, Mom? You look sad."

"I'm okay," I answered, and it was partially true. "How's the Lego city coming?" I nodded toward his creation.

"Falling down," he said gravely, I managed a smile.

Molly stirred and blinked at me, her little hand pushing the blanket up to her chin. I went to her, putting a mask upon my face first as a precaution, and gently touched her warm forehead, breathing in the damp-sweet smell of sleep, illness, and childhood. The ache inside me shifted, not smaller, but anchoring itself to something I could now name.

In the bathroom, I wanted a miracle that looked like a person, like Will. Out here, the miracle looked like two small lives and a dog who couldn't seem to ever stay off the couch.

I poured water, found the thermometer, and texted the pediatrician's office to check for Molly's dosing. Routine built itself around me. It might not be pretty, but it was my life right now, and I needed to lean into it.

And still, because longing doesn't vanish on command, I brushed my thumb over the faint red line across my shoulder where the towel cut and wondered at the precise weight of his hand in my dream. I told myself it was only my mind offering comfort in a language it knew I could answer. I told myself a lot of things that were probably true.

Underneath all of it, a smaller truth hummed: it felt real. Maybe that was the cruelest part, or maybe it was the proof that I was still fighting, against fear, pain, for the right to keep loving the people who needed me.

I tucked the blanket under Molly's feet, straightened, and breathed. The day waited, fog and all. This time, my perspective had changed.

"Breakfast?" I asked, and Max cheered, which meant he wanted one thing: chicken strips and waffles. Baxter thumped his tail like an amen, knowing very well he would get a strip of his own.

As I moved toward the kitchen, I carried both realities with me, the one with the bolted door and the one with the vision. I didn't know which one won today. I only knew I had work to do.

Chapter 37

Cortez – The Diary

D etective Cortez slammed the car door with more force than intended. His knuckles whitened around the steering wheel as he stared down the dim stretch of road leading toward the lake.

He was running out of time.

The pieces weren't aligning the way they should. The brake failure. The missing husband. The hospital incident that no one wanted to talk about. And now Marla Kennedy, a woman who slipped in and out of view, always conveniently absent when questions pressed too close. A woman whose husband even has questions. Her name kept surfacing, tied to Charlotte, to Will, to the office. The more Cortez looked at the board, the more it felt like every string eventually looped back to her.

Cortez flipped open his notepad, eyes narrowing at the sketches and scribbled names. Lawson. Hannah. Charlotte. Baker. Marla.

Too many overlapping threads. Too many lies.

The scent of stale coffee clung to the interior of the

cruiser. It was past midnight, but adrenaline trumped exhaustion. He glanced again at the photo sent to him. The social worker had finally filed a report after being prodded by a hospital administrator who'd reviewed security footage of a woman in disguise. Charlotte had nearly died that day, Cortez was sure of it now. Someone had tried to inject her IV with something lethal.

And the woman in the video? Marla Kennedy.

She had slipped in during Charlotte's chemo, dressed like a cancer patient herself. A wig. Sunglasses. A scarf wrapped around her neck. It would have been genius if it wasn't so damn evil. And for what?

Cortez rubbed the back of his neck, the weight of the case pressing in. Every instinct told him it was personal. Not random. This wasn't about money. It wasn't even jealousy in the traditional sense. This was about control. Obsession and maybe even power. A game.

The streetlights flickered overhead as he turned the ignition. He'd be meeting Father Alvarez in the morning. Apparently, Charlotte had confided in the priest during a breakdown. Cortez respected the confidentiality of the collar, but he also knew when a soul was crying out, priests had a way of pointing to the truth without betraying the sanctity of confession.

And then there was the boy's prayer. Max.

Cortez had listened to the recording Charlotte had taken. The child's prayer was raw and unfiltered, fearful but anchored in something deeper.

"If Baker is really my dad ... can you make him stop being scary? If Daddy isn't my daddy, please make sure he knows I still love him."

Those words haunted him. They were heavier than

anything Cortez had read in all the statements. And they told him more than any witness could.

He couldn't let this spiral any further. He couldn't wait for more bodies.

Just before he was about to leave, his phone buzzed and he noticed that he had a new email. He clicked on the message.

To: detective.cortez@crescentpd.gov
From: david.w.kennedy@usmc.mil
Subject: Findings
Attachment: IMG_4375.jpg

Detective Cortez,
Apologies if this isn't the right way to go about it, and I don't want to cross any lines. However, something's been off for a while with my wife, Marla, and today I found something by accident while cleaning out our home office.
I wasn't looking for anything. Her journal had slipped behind the drawers, and I was just trying to retrieve it and place it back. I didn't even realize what I was reading at first, but the entry on the open page stopped me cold. I've attached a photo of it.
I'm not making accusations. I just … I didn't know any of this. And now I don't know what's real.
Maybe you'll know what to do with it.
Please don't let her know it came from me. Not yet.
- David

Cortez clicked on the attachment and then enlarged it on his phone. The photo was of a note, blue ballpoint printed handwriting covering the page.

[Journal Entry - Year: College, Senior Year]

I kept telling myself it didn't mean anything. That I probably had too much to drink, and maybe someone had spiked my drink, and things just got out of hand. That's it. I am making mountains out of mole hills.

But the problem is that I wasn't drunk, and I remember every single painstaking second.

The small room, the open window that faced the train tracks, the queen-sized bed. The sound of that stupid song on repeat and the way the walls smelled like mildew, sweat, and an array of colognes.

I had said no.

I know I said no.

I didn't just say no during, I had said no repeatedly before. It had been my mantra. I repeated it over and over again.

Hadn't I?

I remember their faces, each and every one. I can recall their voices. The way they kept laughing and mocking the situation as if it were all one big joke. Only, I wasn't laughing ... I was crying.

I didn't tell anyone, not a teacher, not a soul at that party, no one.

I went to class the next morning and pretended nothing happened, even as I passed the group of them sitting in the quarry lined up against the library wall. As I had passed them, a few even grotesquely acted everything out. I had fixated my eyes upon the sidewalk, refusing to allow my eyes to bear witness to such debauchery.

I made an appointment with the campus counseling center that week. I've seen the same therapist on and off ever since.

Back then, she gave me strategies. Breathing techniques. Focus rituals. She said I was brave. I needed to hear her voice, her accolades, her validation.

Maybe I was brave, or maybe it was just a lot of crap she spins to all her clients.

Lately ... I don't feel whole. I feel scattered. Like pieces of me come and go without permission. A million little shards of glass upon the floor.

I'll say something and then wonder if it was really me who said it. I'll feel calm one minute *and like I'm drowning the next. My highs are high, and my lows are rock bottom.*

It's getting harder to pretend I am okay, though. I have to be extra polished as if on cue.

And the worst part? I'm afraid that if I stop pretending, everything will break.

Including me.

Cortez hit the gas, gravel crunching beneath the tires.

He read the journal entry three times, the words swimming in front of him. It wasn't just what it said, Marla's fear, her trauma night in college and what it was implying. Her husband had been there.

Something tugged at his memory.

Weeks earlier, his partner had tossed him a link to an old yearbook archive, half-joking that Cortez might find more dirt online than in the station's databases. He hadn't thought much of it at the time, clicking through black-and-white composites of frat houses and bad haircuts. But now, the image came back sharp: a fraternity spread, young men lined up on a porch, their arms slung across one another with drunken pride.

There, staring out from the grainy photograph, David Kennedy. And beside him, unmistakable even decades younger, was this Baker character.

The recollection rattled Cortez. What the hell were the two of them doing side by side?

Cortez's gut twisted.

This wasn't just college drinking buddies. This looked like allegiance, the kind you don't walk away from.

Who is this guy, and what is his game in all of this?

He would find Marla. And maybe she could shed more light on this entry and her husband. He didn't trust him. This feels strategic.

He would track down Baker. He would bring Will Rose home, and he would make damn sure Charlotte and her children stayed alive.

This case wasn't just tangled anymore.

It was unraveling fast.

Chapter 38

Will - The Watcher's Trap

The sun had long disappeared behind the horizon by the time Will made it back to the outskirts of town. His legs burned, his ribs ached, and every breath tasted like metal. The weight of what he left behind pressed against him with every step, but it was nothing compared to the fire in his chest when his house came into view through the trees. His house. His family.

He crouched low, moving along the perimeter of the property. Lights flickered inside. It looked normal, too normal. My instincts screamed that something wasn't right.

Then he saw her.

Hannah stood just beyond the tree line, near the side of the garage. Her red hair was unmistakable even in the darkness. She was watching the house with an unreadable expression, arms crossed tightly across her chest.

Will stepped out of the shadows.

"Hannah," his voice cracked from cold and fatigue.

She turned, startled. Then relief washed over her face, followed quickly by something else.

Regret? Anger? Maybe both.

"Will," she whispered. "I knew you would try to come here. I had to beat you to it."

"This is my family, damn it. You don't tell me what I can and cannot do."

They stood in silence for a moment, breathing the same frozen air.

"They're inside," she said finally. "Charlotte. The kids. They're safe."

"Because of you? Or despite you?"

Her eyes flashed. "I didn't come here to hurt anyone. I came because of Marla."

That name tightened Will's spine. "What do you know?"

"She's been playing us all. She knew you were alive. She's been tracking Charlotte. Watching her. Manipulating everything behind the scenes."

"You keep saying that but why now? Why show up again after everything?"

Her voice shook. "Because I saw her. With Molly. I followed them. I tried to stop her. But she, she was like someone else. Cold. Detached. Not even human."

Rage sparked behind his ribs. "Where is she now?"

"I don't know. But you need to be careful. Charlotte ... she needs you to be strong. Not confused. Not broken."

He stared at Hannah, unsure whether he hated her, pitied her, or something far more dangerous. She had saved me. She had betrayed me. And now, she was the one warning me. His head was spinning, filled with an array of possibilities for her actions.

"If you really want to help," he said, stepping past her

toward the house, "then stay away. From me, and from my family."

She didn't respond and just stood there under the winter moonlight, alone and shaking, while Will walked toward the place he never should have left.

Charlotte. Molly. Max.

It was time to face the wreckage he caused.

And rebuild whatever he could before it was too late.

Chapter 39

Charlotte - Pieces of Me

I woke to the rhythmic sound of the ceiling fan spinning above me. My skin was damp, and the sheets were tangled around my legs. For a moment, I didn't know where I was.

Then it hit me.

Like a bad dream being replayed over in my head. The woods, the barking, the figure that had been looming, Molly. My heart dropped.

A dull ache radiated from my hips and shoulders, a stubborn reminder of how far I had pushed myself. But beneath it all was something I hadn't felt in what seemed like weeks.

Relief.

I sat up slowly, ignoring the stiffness in my joints. Sunlight filtered through the gauzy curtains, casting golden stripes across the floor. The sound of muffled laughter carried from down the hall.

Molly.

I swung my legs over the edge of the bed and pushed

myself up. My robe hung from the hook on the door, and I wrapped it tightly around my frame before heading toward the sound of life.

Max was kneeling in the living room, building a fort with couch cushions and blankets. Baxter barked as Molly danced in circles with a spoon in one hand and a tiara on her head.

It was chaos. Beautiful, sacred chaos.

Max looked up and saw me. "Mom!"

His cry was a balm to my spirit. He barreled into me, wrapping his arms tightly around my waist.

"Hey, buddy," I whispered, kissing the top of his head. "Everything okay?"

He nodded. "Molly had a bad dream last night."

I cocked my head in interest. "Okay, what about?"

He hesitated before responding, "About, um, Hannah and the woods again."

The memory came rushing back. Her red hair. The way she'd appeared out of nowhere and helped me carry Molly back. The way I collapsed in the snow. Her hands, steady but trembling.

I looked toward the kitchen, half-expecting to see Hannah.

"You okay, Molly?" I asked carefully as to not upset her.

With a nod she smiled. "Yeah, Mommy."

My throat tightened. I didn't want to talk about her anymore, about my world falling down. She saved me, again. There was somehow a heaviness in her wake, a tangle of grief.

I walked into the kitchen to find a note resting against the salt shaker.

"Keep going, Charlotte. He still chooses you."

Tears stung my eyes as I traced the words with my fingertips. The penmanship was slanted, rushed. "This means he is still alive. Will. Oh, thank God."

Behind me, Max and Molly erupted into giggles.

I let the note fall to the counter.

Then I breathed, fully, deeply, for the first time in a long time.

The storm hadn't passed, not entirely. But I was still standing. And that, for now, was enough.

Chapter 40

Charlotte - The Knock at Midnight

I always hated folding laundry, but I had no choice. Piles of clothing strewn across our beautiful home didn't sit well with me. Cancer or no cancer, I still must run my household. My mother and sisters could only help so much. Alex took the kids tonight, so I had a chance to play catch-up on all the chores. Grabbing Molly's frilly dresses and Max's graphic t-shirts, I began to walk upstairs. I looked out the windows on the stair flat and saw the last flicker of sun die behind the foliage in the distance.

I finished hanging Molly's clothing and had grabbed Max's when a piece of paper fell out of his pocket. It was slightly torn, and the writing had bled some. I could barely make out the words. "Max. You are mine." I stared at the writing, the circuits in my brain working overtime in an attempt to decipher the message. When it hit me, I felt faint as if all the oxygen had been sucked out of the room. My fist tightened around the paper, secretly wishing, almost willing, it to be his neck. The neck of the only person who could have written this.

As I turned to leave Molly's room, I stopped at the sound of the front door. The door creaked open. Our main double doors were antique and heavy-framed. I had begged Will to let me buy and restore them. It had been a labor of love in the end. The oak doors set off our exterior perfectly. The only thing that I hadn't been able to fix was the heavy screech they made each time they swung open or closed. There was not enough oil I could soothe on the old bones of the door to make them stop moaning. I guess the weight of the doors is too heavy. The only plus side was that we could hear them open from anywhere in the house. It acts as a sort of alarm.

I was not expecting the kids back. They were still with Alex at her house. It wasn't Sadie because she had Pilates scheduled for this evening, just as she did every week. She didn't miss a class even if she was under the weather. She claimed it was her one saving grace to a clear mental state. She had been especially excited about today's class because there was going to be a guest instructor. Some local influencer was going to teach. She had been raving about it for weeks. Mom had a book club with her sisters tonight, so it was not her either. Then who could it possibly be that had a key?

As I stood in the same spot, my ears perked up at another noise. This time it was a dull, heavy thud. It immediately sent sparks flying up my spine. I flicked the lamp off and slowly stepped behind my daughter's favorite hiding spot. I crouched carefully behind Molly's dollhouse. I remember when we gave it to her. She had been so happy that she had started screaming hysterically. The walls in her room were a muted pink, and the wallpaper on the ceiling had an enlarged floral print. It also contained an oversized window with a custom seat filled with fluffy white fur pillows and a variety of her favorite stuffed animals. Each animal was strategically placed in order of the colors of the rainbow, and by the looks of it, they must have recently attended one of Molly's tea parties. Molly had a few obsessive-compulsive ticks, and organizing was certainly one of them.

Another door squeaked as if it had just been closed. I froze. That noise was so much closer now. I felt like my pulse was vibrating. Every inch of me was ice cold. What was I supposed to do? In this house, I knew every shuffle and every shift of body weight. I knew that the cabinet in the kitchen by the sink gets stuck, even though it was a recently built home. I knew that there was a floorboard that squeaks loudly toward the back of our home. It's like the house is whispering to me secrets that only I know. Whoever had just closed that door was most likely standing directly below me. I dared not move. I willed myself to breathe slowly and silently, even as it quickens. Was it her? Was it him? My relentless stalker. Their letters. Their unnerving gifts. Will I finally meet the unwanted sender?

As I closed my eyes, my iWatch flickered, and I felt a thrill of relief escape. I wasn't sure if it would reach my phone, which was located downstairs on the table in the foyer. I slowly moved my hand from underneath my leg, where it was resting in an awkward position. I tapped the screen and watched as it came alive. I clicked on the text icon and began tapping out a message to my sisters: *SOS. Someone in house. Call cops. Log into cameras. Keep kids. Don't tell them. I'm ok. XO*

Then I switched off the volume on my iWatch to ensure that it didn't give my location away. I looked up at the ceiling, and the darkness seemed to engulf me. I closed my eyes and hoped to God they would leave. I rolled my neck and released a bit of tension that had weighed on me. Then I heard the shuffling of feet in the hall outside Molly's bedroom. I immediately held my breath. Fight or flight, which would prevail? In any scenario, I would think flight, but as it was my stalker, part of me wanted to meet them face-to-face.

The door groaned open, grudgingly, almost foreboding as leaden steps entered the room. Pressure built in my chest, and I realized that I was still holding my breath. My chest felt as if it were on fire. I opened my mouth and exhaled slowly. A familiar fragrance of wood, pine, and musk filled my senses. That smell. I inhaled, and a flash instantly thrust me back toward an image of myself and Will intertwined with one another. I could almost feel the moisture of his sweat on my body. I could feel the raw lust we'd shared flood back. That very same fragrance. Excitement took over with the idea that it could very well be him. I had been dreaming of this moment for what seemed like forever. His aromatic scent almost lured me out of hiding. My body remained still, though. My eyes were tightly shut.

A presence loomed before me. My reflexes took over, and my eyes snapped open. Before I could analyze who was in front of me, I got a whiff of peppermint breath. Tears prickled my eyes. My heart once again pounded, but not for the reason that it had been before. Now it pounded with a vigor so intense it made my eyes water. Trumpets sounded as every emotion glided over me. I gently moved my quivering hands forward, longing to touch the face studying me. I ran my fingers lightly across the rough skin. Hair tickled my fingers.

I traced the hollows beneath their eyes and the straight line of their nose. My fingers slid into a mop of dense hair before I could stop their curious search. Almost instinctively, I moved to the neck, feeling for a familiar imperfection. And there it was—the irregularity—and my heart jolted. A small smile crept across my face, and for a moment, every worry slipped away. As I opened my eyes, the outline of a man began to take shape before me.

"Will?" Darkness shadowed his face as my eyes adjusted. I focused on a mass of scruff that now covered his youthful appearance, giving him an aged and vacant look. His glistening eyes mirrored my own, both filled with tears of joy and remorse.

Before I could speak, he took hold of me, his hands caressing my face. His mouth closed over mine, electricity reverberating our needs and wants in unison. We longed to become one. He pulled me down, breathing me in like air. He removed my beanie and whispered through tears, "I love you, Charlie; I love you so damn much. I'm so sorry. I can't begin to tell you how much I love you and how much I've missed you." He kissed my head gently as his tears washed over me. My body seemed to float in a state of transcendence, peace encompassing me.

He kissed my shoulders, my back, and neck, and trailed my stomach with soft lips. He traced my body with purpose and meaning, imprinting my flesh upon his lips, eternally engraving each inch on his mind. I pulled him toward me, my nails embedding themselves into his back, longing for him to never leave me again. He ripped at my shirt and I at his. We moved rhythmically and in complete unison. I aggressively nipped at his neck, then shifted back to kissing and biting. He didn't flinch, didn't move away. Instead, he

309

moved closer. Grabbing at him, I pushed him down to the floor. By that point, nothing could stop us. Ecstasy consumed us, our ragged breaths coming in quick, shallow spurts that slowly regulated as our passion was quenched.

As we lay side by side on the wooden floor, our clothing splayed around us, my breathing finally calmed enough to speak. I turned my face to his. The moon illuminated his silhouette, and my brain etched it into memory. "Where did you go? Why did you go? I just, I don't understand what I did." As Will stared at the ceiling in silence, I looked up to face the array of tiny plastic stars glowing above me. Molly had insisted I put each flower up by hand to create a garden.

Will took my hand and squeezed it tightly. As if whispering a secret, he moved his mouth slowly, and I leaned in closer to hear. "I had originally planned the whole thing, well, the disappearance at least. Then things went terribly wrong. The accident was caused by his hand, not mine. I did not plan that part, I swear. He stopped talking, his fist clutching my hand. Frustration overtook him. I let him process and soothed his chest with my other hand.

"I know I don't make any sense. I sound like a fucking lunatic. Listen, though, it was the only way to ensure you all had a chance. He's out of his mind. He doesn't care if you are sick again. He couldn't care less." My body tensed at the mention of the only "he" that it could possibly be. It must be Baker he's referring to. Will turned to face me. He rested his head on his hand as he propped himself up. I could see tears glistening in his eyes, ready to drop at any moment. "Why didn't you tell me your cancer had come back? I found out by watching you from afar. It was my own personal hell. My heart broke every single time I saw you. Every time you appeared to be in a weaker state than before. I couldn't let another second go by and not be here. I don't know if it's safe. It probably isn't since he's still out there somewhere. I don't know anything other than how much I love you and our kids."

He kissed my forehead gently but with great intensity, and then we slowly dressed, his tears blending with my own. He stared at me with profound pain deep within his eyes. "We may fight, but that never takes away the love that I have for you. Everything we bicker about is minor and not worth a moment in my life without you. You are the only one, Charlotte. The only one who could ever make me catch my breath. The only one I want to go on with forever. In sickness and in health. I am in this to the end with you."

Chapter 41

Charlotte - Buried Secrets

A sound shattered the moment. A noise so loud, my ears rang as if an alarm had gone off mere inches from us.

What's going on? I turned to look and get my bearings.

Through the windows, the moonlight shone luminously, and I could see the horror on Will's face. It morphed into sheer terror and pain. A loud cry tore through the silence, and I realized that it was Will. A dull thud followed as he collapsed to the floor.

"Will!"

Falling to his side, I put my trembling hands over the wound in his shoulder to stem the bleeding. The blood gushed past my fingers as if nothing was barricading the way. I forced more pressure on the wound, but realized I was beginning to feel lightheaded myself.

Panicking, I quickly surveyed the room, but I didn't see anything. My eyes frantically scanned the perimeter for the piece of the puzzle that didn't belong. Even though I couldn't see it, I could feel a heavy, ominous presence. I instinctively knew who it was. Anger swelled inside me, my fatigue lifting if only for a moment.

"Baker," I hissed. "Why? Why! Damn it!" My voice increased to a raging scream.

I glanced at Will and then in the direction where I sensed the energy. I looked down and touched my watch, thankful that my body hid the use of my hands. I dialed 911 and then lowered the volume before it rang so the dispatcher could hear everything that was going on, hoping it would give them enough time to track my call. I noticed the mirror opposite the room cast a shadow as it slowly edged through the doorway. It was a man, a man with a gun in his hand.

He was wearing a checkered flannel shirt unbuttoned over a plain white undershirt. It was untucked and paired with a dark pair of jeans and dirty street shoes. His hair appeared to be dark and tousled in complete disarray, much like I felt. He then stepped into the moonlight, his facial features on full display.

He turned around with an eerily calm manner, his demeanor calculated as his eyes connected with mine. A sinister smile spread across his face, then snapped to anger, his face morphing into vehement disgust.

"You didn't even tell me he was mine. You picked this bastard to be his dad over me. Him?" He let out a sinister laugh. "Really, Charlotte? He doesn't even love you. Not like I did, anyway. You tried to replace me with a lesser version and buried me in silence. But Max … he looks like me, you can't pretend that he doesn't." He ran his hand through his hair. "I'm sure that just drives you wild." He let out a bellowing laugh then raised his finger to his lips as he silently and mockingly mouthed, Oops. "That was kind of mean, wasn't it? Especially since ol' Willie probably has no clue." He glanced in Will's direction before continuing, "I sincerely apologize, but you'd be pissed off, too, if your kid was taken away from you."

He walked over to where Will was wincing in agony and crouched down. I kept the pressure on his wound and jeered, "Get away from him."

He playfully trailed the gun along Will's head. "You know, you are nothing to him. Why do you think he left? It was me who always loved you. I was always there waiting in the wings for a chance for you to just see me. A chance for you to want me back. However, you never did. Did you? You were always so damn busy with your new perfect life. This family of yours. Did I even cross your mind? How you screwed up my life?"

He raised the gun toward me, and I stared straight down the barrel. Then he turned it back toward the temple of his head. He cocked an eyebrow and then threateningly pointed it back at me. He then began to pace like a rabid animal.

"You know, it's quite amusing, really. This whole time, you thought it was her. Didn't you? You know that little ex of his, but it wasn't her. It was me. Why would you even think it was her? I mean, are you that obsessed with him that you couldn't even see what was right in front of you the whole time? I left you clues everywhere. I even left him breadcrumbs, for crying out loud. I'm like the damn witch from *Hansel & Gretel*, but you two are too daft to put it all together."

He pointed the gun at Will, letting the silver metal linger a bit too long in his direction. Perspiration dampened my brow; this situation was perilous. My eyes darted to Will; his eyes were clenched shut as he clutched his wound. His shirt was stained a bright crimson red, just like my hands.

"What are you talking about? You're making no sense, Baker." Despite parts of what he was referencing, I was starting to piece it together. He shook his head with disappointment.

I looked down to check on Will's wound. He was still bleeding, despite the pressure I was applying. I made a split decision and took my sweater off to wrap it around Will's shoulder like a tourniquet. I pulled the knot tightly; blood quickly spread throughout the white cotton fabric, each thread quickly absorbing the thick liquid. I looked up at Baker and squinted my eyes in tormented concentration. I could tell he was focused on my lace bra instead of my face. "Hey, eyes up here," I growled.

He smiled coyly. "Sorry, it's been a while. The bald head doesn't even bother me as much as I thought it would. Perhaps it's growing on me. You're giving off G.I. Jane vibes." He winked at me, and I cringed in disgust.

"I repulse you that much? Really? Screw you, Charlotte, and your high-and-mighty crap."

Then it clicked together, like a door closing shut. Cocking my head to the side, I said, "The wooden box outside my window, that was you? The rattle, that, too?"

He chortled and walked closer to sit on the bed. "One of many," he said, seeming to enjoy this new banter. He grinned at my recognition of each past gift as if all this were just a game to him.

"… and the beer in the bathroom. That was you, too? The bird in a cage outside my house with a bow on it. You again?"

He nodded his head at the first but shook his head no in clear confusion at the second. "Hmmm, no, that one, sweetheart, was not me."

He flashed me a coy smile. "There is a person downstairs hurt. Who could that be?"

My head was spinning. "What the absolute hell, Baker? Did you hurt Marla? Is she okay? What do you want from me? I'm married with two children. I just finished my second round of chemo. What could I possibly give you? I barely have the energy to go about my day, much less entertain your bullshit."

He laughed as if we were two old friends just catching up. "Marla? Ha. Marla is not your friend. She never liked you. If anything, she loathed you for everything you possess. What is so damn hilarious is that you all think I'm the loose cannon in this scenario. Now, she is off her rocker. She peeled her car up your driveway, and as soon as she opened the door, I was ready for her. She didn't see me coming. I don't know who the gun in her hand was for, though. If I had to guess, it was for you. So, for that, you are welcome. She was tired of waiting in the wings, I guess. I couldn't have her screw everything up either. Anyway, all I came for is him. I want him. I don't even really want you anymore. I just want what's mine. Have you ever stopped to think that perhaps you getting cancer was a bit of karma for being a bad person?"

He pointed to a picture of Max and Molly on her nightstand. Max's toothy smile was framed perfectly for the camera, as his arm was wrapped around his little sister. I

317

stopped and looked at his calculated stare and then back at Will before my eyes filled with an image of Max. My sweet, innocent, perfect boy.

"You want our Max? You have lost your damn mind," I growled in fury.

As Baker yelled, his saliva spewed out of his mouth, landing on my face. Repulsed, I wiped it off. "He's mine! You lied to me, damn it. You are still lying to me. You have told so many lies over the years to yourself. You don't even know what the truth is anymore. That boy is mine, and this asshole is raising him as if he were his own. That is complete horse shit. I am not leaving until he is with me. That is my kid. Do you understand me?"

He began pacing again, waving the revolver loosely around as if it were a toy prop in his hand. I lay my body strategically, shielding Will. "I have always loved you, but then you pull this. You are garbage, you know that. What kind of mother takes her kid away from his dad? Don't think that I didn't notice just how much Max looks like me. I'm not a moron. You just think I am." His voice was vibrating now in anger. I wasn't sure what he was capable of, but he is not taking Max. Over my dead body.

"I'm tired of you not respecting me. Our entire relationship was a joke to you. You had no issues whoring yourself out to this asshole. I don't want him anywhere near my son. He's a bad example." The irony was not lost on me. In the past, I would have recoiled at his manipulative abuse, cowering at his verbal assaults. However, now I felt only pity for him and was fueled by it.

"I am so tired of this. Why didn't you tell me? I had and still have the right to know. I went through stages when I thought it was in his best interest to be with you. That I couldn't have possibly deserved him in my life, but then I come by and see all my stolen moments. Max playing baseball or playing tag with him. I want him back."

I was overtaken with an immense sense of guilt mixed with rage. I controlled myself and my need to attack him.

"I still have damn rights. What the hell does he even have that I don't?"

He swerved the gun in our direction again, this time firing a bullet, which went straight through Molly's dollhouse, sending shards flying everywhere.

"Leave her alone, Baker. It's me you want, but leave Charlotte out of this." Will raised up on one elbow and then fell back down.

"Don't move, hon, please, you'll just make it worse," I whispered.

Baker was erratic, growing more and more unpredictable with every second that passed. He tousled his hair, rubbing his hands up and down his arms, displaying what seemed to be old and new track marks. I stared back at him, perplexed, not recognizing the man I once cared for.

He exhaled and looked right past me to where Will lay, then violently kicked him in the stomach. Shrieking, I placed my entire body over him. Will groaned in agony. Baker was trying hard to control his panting.

"When you left me, I was broken into pieces. You didn't tell me why you just got up and left. That was it. It tore me up from the inside out. I couldn't function or think about anything else. You wouldn't even return my calls. I had already lost my family, and you knew that. Then, I couldn't find steady work because I wasn't in the right mindset.

Enter Max, well, that was like pulling my heart out and stomping on it."

I stared at him, lost and in shock. I knew the events were being contorted into his script right now, but it hit me deep down. Baker was always the king of twisting a scenario to make others believe its truth; it happened daily with me in our relationship. He had a way of going from mad to composed to furious again, making my head spin with every personality switch.

"Baker, that was years ago. You assaulted me that night. I will never forgive you for that. Did that even ever cross your mind? You know why I left your house while you were in the bathroom. You can't be that narcissistic. I couldn't stop crying while you were shoving yourself inside me. You made me feel worthless. You manipulated me then, and you are manipulating me now. The only difference is that now I know my worth. I found my voice. I will be damned if you touch me again or take my kids."

He watched me now, eerily still, darkness filling his cold eyes. I knew I needed to stop talking, but I couldn't. Words were spilling out of me like vomit.

"What on earth have you been doing for all this time, anyway? He is not your kid, you sociopath. Max is not yours. Max is Will's! Yes, I was pregnant. Yes, that baby was yours because you forced yourself on me. I had an abortion, dammit, because of that night. At the time, I couldn't take the idea of you being inside me. I selfishly picked myself over a sweet, innocent baby. I couldn't get past having a constant living reminder of that night, of you. A baby made from abuse and physical assault is not what I envisioned for my firstborn. That wouldn't have been fair for them either. Now, that is a scar I must hold for the rest of my life. The murder of my child is on my hands, and I must take that to my deathbed. That is on me. I will fall on my knees every damn night and pray for my redemption. I don't deserve this beautiful life I have now, that we can agree on. For whatever reason, God still thinks I am worth a damn, and he gave me a second chance. I am going to take it. I regret not being stronger in that moment, but that doesn't change the fact that my Max is not, nor will he ever be, yours. I have the medical records to prove it. When Will and I started messing around, I ended up pregnant with his baby not long after. I can see how it would seem that way to you, though. Max was born earlier than I anticipated; he was a preemie. Not that I owe you an explanation."

As I yelled at Baker, who was blankly staring out the window, I continued to place pressure on Will's wound. He seemed to be slowly fading in and out of consciousness. I had longed to scream my past transgressions that had been tattooed on my soul, and I never thought I would ever breathe a word outside a confessional. I was no longer owned by my sins.

My words were soaking through him. I could tell he was trying to assimilate whether it was fact or fiction. His voice was low at first, as if trying to convince himself of the lies he had been telling himself over the years.

"That's bullshit, Charlotte, and you know it. I know because I have been following you consistently for years. If I couldn't have you, I was going to make damn sure I was there when he screwed up so I could pick up the pieces."

I looked up at him more brazen than I felt. Hate radiated from my eyes. "Pick up the pieces? Are you kidding? You're the one who broke me into pieces. With every slap, every push, every kick to the rib. I never forgot, nor will I ever."

He recoiled at that last statement, turning his head as he clenched his jaw. "Oh, how you always love to play the victim. Certainly, one for the dramatics. You wanted it that night. So, don't pretend like you didn't. You came over in that tiny skirt, flaunting yourself in my face after you had the audacity to break it off over the phone. You consented. If you didn't want to be there, you wouldn't have even come. So, don't pull the assault card on me, honey. I understand I wasn't the best boyfriend, but you were no angel. You made it hard as hell to be a good man. I had to remind you of that every day. Who knows who else you would have whored yourself out to if it wasn't for me?"

I reached for one of Molly's dolls and chucked it straight at his face. Sometimes physical actions respond with no foresight. "How dare you!"

He stomped over to me, reeled back, and punched me in the face before I could duck away. I lost my balance, and as I attempted to stand, he pushed me with so much intensity that, before I knew it, I was flying backward. Intense pain pulsated from the back of my head. My vision blurred.

"As I was saying, I always had, and apparently still must, keep you in check. Nothing has changed." I could hear him chuckling, but it sounded muffled. I was lightheaded and dizzy from the hit, but I slowly scooted myself back toward Will. Baker was acting strangely, like a rabid dog. His eyes were wild, with a fever to them, and spittle dripped down his mouth. I had never seen this side of him. It was frightening.

"Oh, shake it off already, Charlotte. If you hadn't

thrown a doll at me," he sneered, clutching the doll like a rag, "I wouldn't have snapped."

I wanted to punch him, and my head was pounding. Despite my attempts to hide it, I was visibly shaken. I needed to change tactics. Perhaps if I appealed to his softer side, I could work around this psychotic episode.

"I didn't want to be around you. I didn't want to see you. I couldn't, you couldn't possibly understand that. When the baby was taken, part of me died with it. My love and fear of you stopped instantly, as well. Call it grief, call it depression … call it whatever you damn well want to call it. I had to put that chapter to bed for me to move on with my life. I had to compartmentalize. Then I married Will and had Max out of unadulterated love. My life changed at that point; I had a second chance to right a wrong. That scared little girl I had once been is forever gone. I will do anything to protect my family. They matter more to me than myself."

At that moment, sirens blared in the distance. I bit my lip in anticipation, and a metallic taste filled my mouth. Blood. "Damn it," I muttered audibly.

In a low voice, Baker spoke as if it were not to anyone but himself. "You must know this wasn't what I intended. I played it out a million times, and this scenario wasn't one of them." Baker moved toward me, shoulders sagging a bit. My body immediately pushed back in a flight-or-fight reaction. He stopped dead in his tracks. His features quickly turned cold again. His emotions gave me whiplash.

"I just wanted to see if you were okay. You know, to help, to explain, to connect with you. Shit. You'd rather be hurt or die than let me get close to you again, right?"

At that moment, Will groaned. I leaned into his ear, whispering. "Hold on, babe, just hold on, okay? Love you,

Will." My head ached from crying, and my hands were numb from applying pressure to Will's wound.

"You still choose him, don't you? Even after everything with her. He never stopped loving her, you know?"

My eyes shot up as I looked at him. I was more annoyed than anything. He moved to sit on the edge of my daughter's bed. He was so close to me that I could smell the rancid sweat coming off him. The odor of booze soured my stomach. He must have downed heavy amounts of alcohol before having the audacity to walk in. The odor was reminiscent of every college bar street. It was an alcohol meets vomit meets piss scent. I wanted to hurl at the stench of it.

"Baker, of course, he never stopped loving her. They were together for such a long time. There is history there. She is a human, as is he. He is allowed to have a heart and empathy for the girl who will forever be his first love. You can't erase history. I don't blame him for that. He is a good man. He is everything you weren't and couldn't be. He is everything you will never be. I don't blame you, though. I blame myself. What I am sorry about is that I didn't have the courage to stand up for myself. What I am sorry for is that I wasn't woman enough to stand up for my own damn child. I couldn't disassociate myself from you, from the incident, the trauma of it all. I will forever be sorry I wasn't mature enough to deal with my own emotions. We were just kids, and we were about to have a damn kid ourselves. I didn't know how to deal with any of it. Those are my crosses to bear. Yours, well, yours are about to be much bigger."

I looked toward the window, referring to the police parked out front. I looked back at him, but he didn't follow my gaze. He was completely lost in thought. Everything around him clicked, but he stood still. He was struggling with his emotions. He was a complex person. His adrenaline must have been running at an all-time high because beads of sweat were rolling down his hairline. It was as if he had just finished a marathon.

He had changed in so many ways. His face was weathered by sun and time. Flecks of white were sprinkled like soft snow through his hair. A deep scar cut above his left eye, and a faded tattoo peeked from beneath his shirt. There was a time when Baker was the cleanest-cut person I knew, looking like he'd leapt straight out of a Gap ad. It was never that I didn't love him.

Back then, he was everything a college boyfriend was supposed to be: charismatic, smart, the life of the party. He drew people in like air. Being around him felt like inhaling something wild and electric, like heroin, and I was the addict. But there was always another side to him. One that snuck in quietly when no one else was watching. In those still moments, his vulnerability would catch you off guard. He swung between uncertainty and fierce recklessness, just like today. Dr. Jekyll and Mr. Hyde. Every emotion magnified by alcohol and drugs. The masks he wore were invisible to most, but I saw them. I lived behind the curtain.

When I was pregnant, I used to think about him. About the darkness that would suddenly descend over his face. A shadow that could linger for days, even weeks. The thought of raising a child in that volatility terrified me. The physical abuse was bad enough, but it was the silence after each argument that gutted me. His coldness. It left me alone for days. A single disagreement could crumble me. I'd find myself curled on the floor, too numb to cry. It was wild how the body remembers. Even now, mine recoils like it's reliving it all over again.

"Baker, leave here. I won't tell anyone you were here. Just go. You can run out of the back door and into the woods where no one will find you. The trees are dense and vast. Go and start over. Let us be, please," I pleaded, and the desperation and sadness took me by surprise.

He stood up from the bed and walked to the window where the moon shone its light upon his features. If I looked close enough, his eyes looked wet. The sirens blared outside, just feet away. I heard doors slamming shut. Just then, my phone rang downstairs. It echoed through the hall. My wrist vibrated with the incoming call.

He shook his head slowly and raised the gun, placing it just under his chin. Click. The gun cocked. His hand had the slightest tremor.

His gaze flickered to the photo of Max and Molly again. "You think I'd walk away after all that?" His voice dipped, colder now. "No. This time, I get to choose how the story ends, and I am not leaving without my son. So don't move, Charlotte. Don't even think about it. You want to tell Max you killed his dad, well, that will be on you."

I closed my eyes because if he pulled the trigger, I didn't want to see it. He ran his hands through his hair, lightly tugging at it. "I didn't know how to cope, either. You remember I had just lost my mom months prior. I had been spiraling when this guy entered the picture. Then shit hit the damn fan. I couldn't deal with losing you, too. I started self-medicating. When that didn't work, well, I settled for numbing the pain. My old roomie, Dylan, had leftover Oxy–before I knew it, I was a full-blown addict. When the flow stopped, I looked for other ways to silence the voices and mellow my mind. I'd snort, shoot up, swallow whatever I could get my hands on. All because of this asshole right here. Then you married him shotgun style, and my mind lost it. How the hell is he any better?"

He gave a slight smirk. "People are easier to control than you'd think. A little fear. A little chemistry. I've tested it … on a few … unsuspecting types. Mixed doses, watched the shifts happen. Voila. It works. Man, does it work."

He spontaneously started kicking Will. His eyes were wild with rage. "Stop! Stop it, Baker!"

He turned around, grabbing at his hair again as the gun dangled from his hand. He was sweating more profusely. His pupils were dilated, his movements jerky and spasmodic. He turned, locking eyes with me, and his facial expression softened. Just like that, he instantly morphed into a different person right before my eyes. Regardless of his dual personality, I had to stand my ground. I took a breath and harnessed myself.

"For starters, Will never laid a finger on me. He doesn't belittle me, nor has he ever physically accosted me." If only I could figure out his triggers.

He whispered, almost inaudibly. "I am sorry, Charlotte. I don't know how to fix this; I don't know how to fix me. My head is always spinning. I can't live in this world where my mind doesn't work. Where everything that is mine is taken away from me or just gone. I refuse to live in a place with padded walls and constant medication. I can't live in a world where my son doesn't get to know me, and I, him. I have nothing. I have no one. Not even you. Not even him. Instead, he has you." He gestured to Will again, instantly fuming again.

I laid my body on top of Will's chest to shield him as

best as possible. The bleeding had seemed to slow. Baker continued to rant, completely unaware of the blood penetrating the light pink rug on the floor.

"The cops are just going to kill me or take me in. Then what? I rot? I get executed or whatever they do now to prisoners. That's it?"

He shook his head again and again. Then he turned to look over at me. "You see, I can't let that happen. I've wasted what little life I have on you. Just thinking about little ol' you. Spent hours watching you with him. Watching him steal away all those moments that were supposed to have been mine. This was supposed to be all mine. My life!" He raised his arms and spun around, signaling the house and everything in it. He stopped turning and began kicking Will again, completely unaware that he was kicking me at the same time. Every blow, I braced myself, but I would rather it be me than Will.

"All because of you, you bastard. You are the reason she's not with me any longer. You are the reason my life is absolute shit."

My body reeled in pain. My words tumbling out were incoherent, my voice cracking with every syllable. My face was wet with tears–hot, salty, and endless. "Stop, Baker! Stop, you are killing him."

Not thinking about my own actions, I ran directly at Baker with full force. He turned in my direction just as I was about to run into him, and he hurled me toward the door. I flew into the hallway and hit my head on something hard. I felt an immediate sense of pain. My eyes blurred, and dizziness overcame me. I felt as if I was going to fade away completely. Everything around me was spinning in different directions. My eyes were heavy. I blinked in an attempt to stay awake. I wanted to yell for help, but I couldn't seem to make the words form.

Suddenly, I saw a person emerge near Max's room and heard Baker speaking. "Shit, what have I done?" Then I saw long red hair cascading around a face that seemed recognizable. The picture before me frayed at the edges. They put their finger to their lips and mouthed the words, "Shhh." Then a loud bang—and my eyes went black.

Chapter 42

Charlotte - Ashes of Silence

I opened my eyes to a blur of white. When I was able to gain focus, I took in my surroundings. The room was beige, but the lighting gave it a slightly blue haze. A melody of machines ticked away in the background, and I spotted a nurse outside my door. As I looked around the room, I stopped at my sisters' sad faces deep in conversation with one another. They sat by the side of my bed. I didn't remember getting to a hospital.

My head was pounding as I attempted to move. *Great, where else am I injured?* I stretched my legs, arms, and neck, making a mental checklist of each body part, attempting to assess the damage. With worried looks plastered on their faces, Sadie and Alex noticed me stirring. They immediately stood and crowded around my bedside.

I stirred in the hospital bed, blinking slowly as the light above cast pale shadows on the walls. My mouth felt like sandpaper, my limbs too heavy to lift. I tried to speak but only managed a rasp.

A hand touched me gently but grounded. It was Sadie.

"You're awake," Sadie breathed, relief melting across her face.

Alex leaned over the opposite side of the bed, arms crossed but eyes rimmed in red. "You had us terrified. You collapsed in the hallway. Alex found you."

"I wouldn't use the word collapsed, Sadie." Alex chimed in. Sadie shot her a look.

I licked my cracked, dry lips. "Where ...?"

"Hospital," Sadie said, placing a cup of ice chips to her lips. "You've been out for a while. Chemo exhaustion, perhaps panic over the Will situation, and your blood pressure tanked. It's been a lot, Char."

I nodded faintly, then glanced down at my arm. The IV drip. The oxygen sensor. The fragile throb in my temple. Reality.

After a few beats of silence, Alex cleared her throat.

"There's something I've been meaning to ask," she said carefully. "You had mentioned a while back ... that Baker had insinuated in the past that Max might be his."

Sadie flinched but didn't interrupt our bold sister.

I caught my breath. Then I closed my eyes and let the truth settle between us like a stone dropped in water.

"No. Max is Will's. I've always known. Even when the timing was close. Even when everything else was chaos ... I never doubted who his father was. Not in my bones."

Alex nodded slowly, her jaw tight. "Good. Because Baker doesn't get to rewrite that story."

Sadie leaned forward. "We just needed to hear you say it."

My voice cracked. "I couldn't afford to doubt myself. If I did, I'd fall apart. And if I fell apart ... who would pick up the pieces?"

"We would," Sadie said firmly.

Alex nodded. "Every time. Every damn time."

My throat worked around a sob that never fully formed. My gaze drifted to the small bouquet on the table beside me, a few white carnations in a mason jar, already wilting at the edges.

"He always loved carnations," I whispered.

"Dad," Sadie said simplistically.

I let loose a small smile of remembrance, and a tiny tear trickled down the corner of my eye. "I still feel him. Like he never left."

"It's okay, Charlie, it's okay. Just relax. Alex, go grab some ice water and the doctor, please." Sadie was right by my side, looking at me, while she gently squeezed my hand. "You're okay, you just had a bit of a head injury, along with some minor bruising."

I attempted to talk as I settled back down on my pillow. My head felt as if it had its own pulse. "Is Will okay? Did Baker ..." I couldn't bring myself to finish the last sentence.

Sadie nodded her head with a small smile. "He's fine, be lost a lot of blood. He's in the ICU right now, but he is going to be okay. In fact, we've been alternating going from your room to his in shifts. His parents are with him right now, and his sister is on her way. I will let him know you're finally awake. Mom is with the kids. She was here forever, but we could tell she was tired, so we switched with her. The kids know you're in the hospital, but don't worry—we chose our words carefully. They're excited that their daddy is back and that you both will be home soon. You had us scared there for a moment. We weren't sure if you were in a coma or what."

I smiled with relief at the news that Will was okay.

However, as I moved, pain surged. I brought my hand to the side of my head, wincing as I touched the gauze that covered my injury. Triggered by the pain, trepidation coated my next question. "Baker?" I whispered, my voice almost inaudible.

Sadie looked down, shaking her head in a definitive manner. "No. He didn't make it. He was shot. Right after he threw you. You hit your head on the railing, and shortly after, he was shot."

She sensed my confusion and responded by sitting up a bit straighter to clearly explain what had happened. "Right after you hit your head, you were knocked out. Apparently, someone was in your house listening to the entire situation. That was the person who shot him after you blacked out."

I looked at her, studying her facial features. "Red hair. They had big hair. Hannah?"

She nodded. "Yes, it was Hannah. So you do remember? You remember seeing her? The police have her in custody at the station. They say she is going to be charged with murder. She refuses to get a lawyer. I'm in the process of trying to get one of my friends on her case. Not sure she'll accept it. She'll need someone to post bail, though."

I pondered all of it. She continued talking as I thought about it. "The officer over Will's case has been trying hard to get the doctor to allow you to be questioned. Ruthless, I tell you. Vultures circling the prey."

I attempted a smile, but my lips were too cracked. "Great. I'm the meat on the side of the road."

Sadie shrugged, grabbing a Chapstick from her purse. "Pretty much." She gently applied the cherry balm to my lips. The relief was instant. "I'm sure he will try again in a few hours. He keeps pacing around outside. Don't you still talk to his wife? I forget her name. He refuses to leave, though. He told me he needs to know you're okay. Wife's orders. I can't tell if he's worried or anxious to barrage you with questions. It's just a matter of time before he comes in—either here or at home."

Just then, Alex walked in with a doctor. Sadie moved out of the way so he could examine me more closely.

"Charlotte, my name is Dr. Fulton. I'm the chief of neurology here. I'd like to run an MRI just to make sure nothing is happening inside your brain. Would you be okay with that?"

I nodded. The nurse unplugged the various monitors and wheeled the bed out of the room, her long red fingernails clicking on the metal bed rails. She paused before exiting. "She'll be right back, ladies, promise. Give us about an hour. Go grab a snack and walk around outside."

Sadie and Alex looked at me, unsure, and said in unison, "We'll be right here when you get back. Promise."

I nodded as I was quickly wheeled away.

When I got back to my room, I found that Sadie had left. As the nurse was leaving, Alex returned. "Hey, how are you feeling? You seem more alert than earlier. Want me to ask the nurse if we can order you some food?"

As if on cue, my stomach growled, and I realized that I was ravenous. My hands reached for my stomach as if the mere pressure would make the pains go away. I nodded eagerly, "Yes, that would be great. Thanks, Al."

Alex stepped out and called for the nurse to bring a

menu. Then she walked toward my bed. "I bet this is all overwhelming for you."

I looked at her with blatant stupidity across my face. "Uh, yeah. I don't know what on earth Hannah was doing there. I can barely wrap my head around Baker showing up randomly. I mean, I guess I always thought about the possibility of something happening. However, that was fueled by all the thriller and horror movies that we watch. I guess anything was possible in his mental state."

"You never truly know a person and their motives, do you? I didn't want to tell you this, but did you hear about Marla?" Alex sat on the bed and took a sip of my water, then put it back down. "Sorry, I was parched and ran out of water. I would have grabbed some, but they wheeled you in right when I was about to go."

I waved her off. We were blood after all.

"What I meant was, did you have any clues that could have led us to this drama? Any indications that this crazy psycho ex and your very own stalkers were going to work their way in to your life, then make a total mess of it? You must have had, well, I don't know, a hint of some sort?" Her eyes searched mine.

"No, I had a feeling I was being stalked by Baker for years, although it was never serious enough to do anything about it. I didn't know about Hannah until it was too late. Weird things happened so often that it became sort of normal in a screwed-up way. It's messed up, I know that. It was all so harmless at first. Small things, like random calls here and there. Nothing crazy. Remember? Nothing that was ever in a mean-spirited manner, but more so just random and disconnected messages. I know it sounds strange, but no one ever got hurt or even close to that until recently. That is, until Will's disappearance, which was partially his doing. I'm still not actually sure of the entire story. Then there was Molly getting abducted. I don't know, things just spiraled from there. It was one thing after another at that point. So, I don't know exactly what the turning point was, really. I am curious what made the glass tip over for him, though."

I paused for a brief second to catch my breath and then remembered Marla. Panic surged within me. "Is she okay?" I closed my eyes and then shook my head. "It's all so bizarre." My head was throbbing from the turn of events, my injury, or both. I rubbed my temples to ease the pressure building within me. Then I opened my eyes to see Alex just staring at me blankly.

"Well?" I said sarcastically, letting out a tiny laugh, then flinched at the laughter-induced pain. "Are you going to tell me what's up?"

Alex's mouth was agape in astonishment at the news of Will orchestrating his own vanishing act..

I looked at her. "You're going to catch a damn fly, Alex. Close your mouth." Like a small child obeying, she shut it and then let out a laugh.

"Sorry. So, wait, wait, wait. Will made it all up? Everything? He arranged his own disappearance. He purposely went over the rail and tried to fake his death? Why? For what reason? I'm so confused!"

I put my hands up to try and stop the crazy ideas forming in her head. Changing my tone to a serious one, I stared out of the window, reflecting on my sweet husband lying in bed somewhere in this hospital. "He was receiving threats, Alex, but didn't relay any of that information to me because he was trying to protect me and our kids. I understand that. He assumed that they were all coming from Baker. This whole time, Hannah was the semi-innocent one watching over Molly and Max. He didn't try to kill himself or fake anything. Someone cut his brakes. Who? Well, that I don't know. Was it Baker or was it Hannah? Surely it was Baker." Alex just stood there in disbelief.

"First off, Hannah is not innocent in this, but I understand why you are giving her a pass. Secondly, there's more. Marla is in the middle of all of this. It's so unbelievable. It sounds like a movie." My head was reeling. *Marla?* Then it came flooding back. Baker had mentioned someone who resembled Marla downstairs. "She was found downstairs, Charlie, unconscious. We have a feeling Hannah did it."

I shook my head, "No, Baker mentioned taking her out. I recall vaguely before I was pushed." Her eyes narrowed at understanding.

"From what we have been told so far, Marla was at the forefront of a lot of things that went down. They believe she took Molly into the woods that day. Not Hannah." I looked at her steadily, deep in thought. I could hear her words, but I was at a loss for what they all meant.

I closed my eyes, trying to replay those final moments with her—searching for anything that might hint at what she was truly capable of. Just then, Alex leaned in, as if about to share a secret.

"Marla is awaiting trial. She is in serious crap. Even her husband took the girls to live with his parents for a bit. Apparently, he had no clue about her involvement in all of this. We don't know anything, really. We must wait and see. As for Hannah, the only thing that she has told the cops so far is that she developed a relationship with Max and Molly. She had drawn a connection with Molly, mainly. It's like

something straight out of a twisted fairytale. She felt obligated to watch over them. Thankfully, she did, or Molly
might have wound up much worse that day. She told the
cops that she scared Marla away when you and Max found
Molly in the tree house. She had followed them into the
woods. It had been right when you and Max were walking
up."

I reflected on what she was saying and let my mind drift
back to my memories. I pictured Molly crying with tape
covering her mouth, helpless. That memory will haunt me.
The what-ifs taught me with plagued notions of not being
able to reach Molly in time.

"Wait, okay, this all makes sense. We saw a person in a
red hoodie, which now clicks because Molly's teacher had
said that Molly was talking to someone with the same
hoodie, but that the individual's face had been concealed. It
had been Hannah the entire time. Molly referred to her as
Anna." I sat there in deep concentration, my brain riddled
with fragmented knowledge. I focused on connecting the
pieces.

"Knock, knock." Sadie came into the room. She looked
exhausted, deep blue and purple shadows lining her eyes. I
felt awful knowing that this latest revelation—along with my
cancer—had likely affected her ability to conceive. I made a
mental note to follow up with her as soon as I got out of
there. I needed to be there for her, just as she had always
been there for me. She offered a weak smile.

"Hey, catching up on your very own soap opera?" She
handed me a green smoothie. No doubt it was infused with
every organic and natural concoction to aid me back to
health. Meanwhile, she got Alex a Diet Coke, oblivious to
the stark difference in drinks. I loved how well she knew us

both, and I felt blessed to know I have a strong support system in my family and that they can surround me during this tough time.

"Doesn't it just blow your mind?" She said as I took a sip of the smoothie. It was like heaven in my mouth, sweet and tangy at the same time. The refreshing hints of pineapple and ginger satisfy me.

"Thanks, Sadie."

She didn't even bat an eye, just sat on the other side of my bed. I was now flanked by both of my sisters.

"Can I ask you a question?" She paused. "Do you forgive Hannah for stalking you and your family? Now that you know she saved you, Will, and the kids."

I paused mid-sip and looked into Sadie's vivid green eyes.

"I just need more time to take it all in. I mean, it was weirdly invasive. To know that the stalker was always watching and not knowing who it was is bone-chilling. It's strange to swallow the idea of one stalker, but I apparently have more people who loathe me than the average person. I don't know how to feel about that and what that says about me as a person. I was never hateful toward her. If anything, I always felt like she deserved to hate me. She earned that resentment toward me for all that transpired. I mean, I don't really hate anyone, if I am being honest. I feel like that is not in my DNA to detest anyone. I understand that this situation is quite unnatural. I took something from her, and she was never able to receive closure. Maybe she felt as if she could gain that by seeing if he was truly happy? I don't know. I may never know.

"However, I can say that I am grateful to her for protecting my family. So, I suppose I do forgive her. I mean, if it wasn't for her watching over my kids, well, who knows what would have happened. Baker. Well, I'm more upset about Baker and his psychopathic, stupid, obsessive … I am going to have to lean on God to forgive him for everything. I don't know what to even think, but I know I can't let it weigh me down. I'm happy that he is gone from my life. I'm happy he will never hurt my family again. Long answer to your question, I think if I can defend her actions, then I can forgive her. Perhaps somewhere deep down, she has already forgiven me. Perhaps by seeing the family that Will and I created?"

Alex looked at me, doubtful eyebrows raised at my suggestion. Sadie smirked at the idea.

"Are we seriously thinking she has forgiven you?" Alex exclaimed, then Sadie continued.

"I wouldn't go that far, Char. I mean, she did stalk you like a stag at a hunting party, for crying out loud. She had an intention there, and that is enough to give me downright chills. I mean, you created a beautiful family together, but you also created this entire life with the very man she was supposed to have wed. Do not forget that part." Sadie took a sip of her own drink.

"I think, if anything, her heart has softened over the years, but do not be quick to think that she has forgotten."

Alex chimed in, "You will never truly know her intentions, even if you were to ask. No one ever will."

I sighed and shrugged. "That is fair to say. Now, Marla, on the other hand, that entire situation perplexes me. We don't know the motive. I am honestly at a loss. I have a variety of feelings when it comes to her. Betrayal is one word to sum it all up, though."

Alex stood and walked over to the window. "I never

trusted her. She gave me a weird vibe. I even told you all at the very beginning that something was off about her. She was always too close. Always in your business and offering to help. I wonder if the kids had a sense. I wonder if I asked if they would tell me."

I pondered that for a moment. *Did they?* I continued to go over events in my head. "There was that one time that Max said he ran into Marla in Molly's room after I had tucked her in. It was the night that we had everyone over to play games. Remember? We were playing cards, and the kids were watching a movie. I recall Molly had fallen asleep. I scooped her up and carried her to her room."

Sadie and Alex stared at me, concentration furrowed upon their brows. Then, click, like a lightbulb being switched on, they both recalled the memory.

"You're right. I do remember that. You mentioned the incident while we were having dinner at Mom's—you said you thought it was strange. Later, when you asked her about it, Marla said she had taken a stuffed animal that Molly had left downstairs. "

I wonder what other creepy things that woman did, and I was none the wiser. It freaked me out to even think about it.

"I guess we have to wait to see what else is uncovered."

Chapter 43

Charlotte - Behind the Glass

A couple of weeks had passed since Will and I were rushed to the hospital. I placed my phone down after disconnecting with the hospital nurse who informed me that Will had left thirty minutes prior. Which meant he was close to arriving home.

I walked into the family room where everyone had gathered to welcome him. "Come on, guys. Will should be here momentarily. We all need to be ready and outside to greet him." I scanned the room for the kids and noticed they were nowhere in sight. "Kids! Come downstairs. Daddy is almost home!" I motioned to everyone to go outside. I smoothed my dress and made sure my hair was in place. I wanted to be in flawless form for Will. My head still hurt, and I was on Tylenol most days, but it was getting better.

We all stumbled out of the house in unison. The children and Baxter led us in clumsy formation. I was followed by my mother, Alex, Sadie, and Geoff. Will's sister and her family were here, too. Her twin girls, Allison and Addison, were dressed in matching dresses. Picture perfect. Will's parents were driving him home, so we could all welcome him together.

My phone buzzed—a text from Will. "He's rounding the bend!" I said excitedly. The kids bounced up and down, balloons tied to their wrists, as the car approached. I glimpsed their white SUV curve steadily down the road. As it neared, I felt a surge of excitement. And with it, light-headedness. It had been only a few weeks since my last chemo, and I was still experiencing moments of fatigue and weakness. I discreetly grabbed onto Alex for support.

"Are you okay?" she whispered.

I smiled feebly. "Yeah, just nerves."

She squeezed my arm gently. "Try to take it easy today. Let us host."

I nodded and leaned into her shoulder for a second. "Thanks."

"Does Will know about your chemo yet?"

I pointed to my head. "Alex, I have on a wig. Of course, he knows. We spoke about it the night Baker shot him. It was emotional. He'd already noticed. He would sneak over to check on us, and he saw the signs."

She chuckled. "Could've been a tough conversation otherwise. 'Hi, hon, while you left us alone with stalkers, I also went through chemo.'"

I laughed quietly. "Thank goodness it's done. My hair is even starting to grow back."

I lifted the edge of my wig so she could see. "I've got a Sinead O'Connor thing going on. No razors needed anywhere. One perk of chemo."

We burst into laughter. The car came to a stop in our circular drive. Will's parents got out and helped him. His dad retrieved the wheelchair.

I approached slowly and realized I was holding my breath. I exhaled. "Hi, hon. How are you feeling?"

He gave me a coy smirk. "Oh, you know. Like I was shot and beaten. But Superman survives. How about you, pretty?"

I went to hug him, but stopped short as he grimaced. "Sorry!"

"You're fine. Come here. I missed you. Just sore on that side. You look good."

Geoff helped him into the wheelchair as the kids rushed over.

"Daddy! Look, I made you a Superman picture!"

Will laughed. "See? Max gets it."

Molly handed him a drawing of them holding hands. "I missed you."

"I missed you, too, sweetheart. I want to hear everything you and Max have been up to."

We all headed inside. The kitchen was filled with Will's favorite foods. The kids darted for the cookies. From the corner of my eye, I saw Max pocketing a few and then walking out to the lake swing.

"Kids! No crumbs!" yelled my mom.

Before joining the others, Will gestured for me to follow him into the office. I closed the door behind us.

"How are you holding up?"

"Hanging in. This ride's been intense."

He studied my face. I shifted on the desk, self-conscious. He smiled kindly.

"Losing Dad was one thing, but not knowing what happened to you... That was torture. The kids missed you. I tried to keep things normal, but it was never the same."

He wheeled closer, grimacing. "Charlotte, I love you. I

left that day thinking I could protect everyone myself. I was wrong. Every decision I made—reckless or not—was meant to keep you safe."

I whispered, "I know."

"You were sick and alone. I hate myself for not being there."

"It's okay. The cancer is gone. I was cleared."

He smiled. "Thank God."

"Will ... Did you see Hannah shoot Baker?"

He nodded slowly. "Yeah. I heard you fall. Baker was by the window. Then three shots. She got him in the chest, shoulder, and back. He broke the glass and fell. She ran to me, stopped the bleeding, told me she loved me, and said she was sorry. Asked for forgiveness. The cops rushed in after that. I never answered her. But I think I forgive her."

I nodded. "Me too. I hate how it ended. But I'm grateful."

I grabbed a book off the shelf—the one holding the glass bird. I showed it to Will.

"This was left once. I thought it was from Baker. But maybe it was Hannah. A warning. The bird in a cage. That was me."

Will took my hand. "You're the bird people admire for surviving."

I put it back. "I can forgive her. In some twisted way, I understand."

We exited the room. "Forgiveness is freeing. If I didn't bail her out, would I be any different than Baker or Marla?"

Will nodded. "Marla's another story. I'll need a stiff drink for that."

As we approached the kitchen, he paused. "What was Hannah's motive? Her endgame?"

I shrugged. "We may never know."

Inside, the kitchen hummed with activity. My eyes drifted toward the lake. Max was swinging alone under the oak tree as the sun dipped into the horizon. He looked deep in thought.

Will squeezed my hand, and I smiled.

I opened the patio door. "Max! Come inside to eat."

He glanced over. I stepped back in, closing the door behind me, surrounded by those I love. Peace finally settled over us.

Chapter 44

Charlotte - When the Fog Returns

I sat in the dim light of the living room, the flicker of the fire tracing lines of amber across the walls. Will was upstairs resting. The kids had been tucked in. Sadie and Alex were back at their respective homes. The house was finally quiet.

Still.

But my mind was anything but.

The truth is, silence doesn't offer peace anymore. It offers questions. Doubts. Images. So many images. Flashes of Baker's face. The thud of my body hitting the railing. The sound of Will crying out. The shattering echo of the gunshots.

And Hannah's face.

I leaned forward and rested my elbows on my knees. The ache in my bones from chemo was dull, ever-present, but tonight it took a back seat to the storm in my chest. I clasped my hands together. Prayed without words. Just movement. Just silence.

Forgiveness. That word again. It kept chasing me.

How do you forgive someone who made themselves a part of your life without permission? Who shaped moments, altered outcomes, manipulated narratives, and watched your children like a ghost in the walls?

But then, how do you not forgive the person who saved your life?

I didn't know what to feel. I couldn't fake closure. I couldn't wrap this up neatly in a bow, like it was some moral parable where the heroine learned her lesson and the villain was sent away. Because nothing was clear. Hannah was both. Villain and savior. Obsessive and guardian.

Will said she asked for forgiveness.

And he gave it.

That should be enough, right?

But then there's Marla. And Marla was different. Marla played a friend. Confidante. Godmother to my children. And yet the betrayals coming to light were growing in number and darkness. She may have taken Molly.

She may have planned more.

I felt a chill crawl up my spine despite the heat of the fire.

Marla lived in our lives as one of us. A wolf in sheep's clothing. Hannah was always an outsider looking in. There was a difference.

I reached for the small notebook beside me, a habit I'd picked up again since the hospital. I opened to a blank page and scribbled the word:

Discernment

The page stayed open on my lap, that single word staring up at me like a dare. I was trying. Trying to discern what God wanted me to do next. Trying to understand why this storm was allowed to come through my life and rearrange everything I thought I knew.

I could feel Will's presence behind me before he spoke. He limped softly into the room, his frame silhouetted by the hallway light.

"Couldn't sleep either?"

I shook my head.

He lowered himself next to me on the couch. We sat for a long moment in silence. Then he placed something in my lap. It was the bird. The glass bird.

"I thought it belonged here," he said.

I nodded, tears brimming.

"We can't go back to the way things were," I whispered. "But maybe we can start from where we are."

He squeezed my hand. "Then let's start here."

And in the hush of the room, with firelight dancing and shadows receding, I closed my eyes and inhaled the first clean breath in weeks.

Tomorrow, the reckoning continues.

But for tonight, I rest.

Chapter 45

Marla's Letter to Charlotte

I never intended to end up here. I never planned to wither away in prison for attempted murder, kidnapping, and a slew of other offenses. I have already been here a while, and it's miserable behind these metal bars. This bland diet and these icy nights were going to be the death of me. It's secluded here. The walls are chock-full of history. The murmurs of what each criminal went through play tricks on my head.

At night, when the wind howls, I swear I can hear the moans of my predecessors. It's damp and extraordinarily dismal. It mirrors my own psychological well-being. During the light hours, someone either wants to screw with you or screw you. I wasn't raised to be in this type of environment. My upbringing was rigid. I was in a boarding school all through high school. I was rarely even in the presence of my parents. I was always at home with my nanny. My parents were always working or out of town. I had what people call absent parents.

Although I am attention hungry and a self-proclaimed

enthusiast for love, this was not how my story was supposed to end. You see, I was unequivocally head over heels in complete infatuated love with Baker. One might even say I was slightly obsessed. Although it certainly didn't start that way. It ended intensely. My fixation on him grew over time. I had met Baker in college, right before Charlotte. We had all attended the same university. I had gone from the foreground, attached to Baker, to suddenly being shunned. I had always been there, in the background, like a prop on the Will and Charlotte show.

Baker had really done a number on me. I had gone to college early, always an A student. I made sure I was as perfect as I could be. I was sent to a private school as far away from my parents as possible. I had been sent to be raised by other adults, where sharp rules and stern tongues had been my daily routine. I had the best tutors money could buy and had always done extra assignments to ensure my GPA was the best. Even at sixteen, I had managed to graduate as valedictorian of my class and been voted most likely to succeed. I had it ingrained in my head that I was going to go to school and be something great. I had my whole life ahead of me, and then I met Baker.

I remember it as if it were yesterday. I can recall the good, the bad, and unfortunately, the brutally ugly. I had been studying on the beach outside my dorm. It had been the perfect autumn day. The leaves had begun to turn orange. Some seemed as though they had been lit on fire. It was such a contrast to the vivid green knolls. The landscape seemed as if it were out of a postcard.

He had walked by at the exact time the wind had blown. I had inhaled right at the very moment. The most intoxicating scent of pine, wood, and leather had filled my lungs. Pheromones had begun spinning their magic. He had been parading around in the middle of a boisterous group of young adults. The guys had all been big and brawny. Each with their own unique charming smiles and mop of messy hair. The girls had all been made up to resemble real-life Barbies. Each had a painted face, mask-like. They all had passed me, unaware of my curious eyes.

He offered me an effervescent smile. It had been a simple gesture, but it came at a time when I felt desperate and forlorn. Later, when he decided to split from his friends, I was in the same spot. I had been knee-deep in my thesis. Research was piled high while violins were weaving a classic melody in my ears. I was about to leave. An hour had already passed. I was famished from studying all day and had assumed he was going to go back to wherever he had come from.

However, just as I raised my nose from deep within my book, he came and sat right next to me, in an area that we called the quad. I remember he had leaned back against the wooden bench and feigned interest. His legs were spread wide, and his arms draped casually over the back of the bench. He radiated coolness and solidified my thought with a wily smirk. He reminded me of the Cheshire cat in *Alice in Wonderland*. I was hooked instantly.

He had tan skin and dark eyes, and I was in a complete trance. Hypnotic and aromatic, my senses were completely overwhelmed, inside and out. I remember he had casually touched my hair and had teasingly said, "I'm sorry, I had to; it's just that your hair is so beautiful. It has these golden flecks that gleam in the sunlight." Now, in hindsight, I know that had been a line to get me into his bed. I hadn't known at the time, though. I had not even reached eighteen. I was a well-versed imposter pretending to be more mature than I really was. I had never had a boyfriend, much less a group of real friends.

I had been craving socialization and attention. I never would have thought that I would be entranced by a boy based solely on his aesthetic appeal. I surely thought I was above that.

Then he had said to follow him. It had been as if he were the damned pied piper. The hidden garden was secluded and blocked from view. Once we were covertly hidden by the overgrown garden, he stopped and unexpectedly kissed me. It was long and hard. His lips were soft and tender. His taste had been sweet, with the remnants of strawberries.

Our relationship over the weeks had been amazing. I would either be at his place, or he would sneak into mine. At that point, we had yet to have sex. I had known it was coming. The notion of sex was daunting. I had been raised never to have sex prior to marriage, and that was something I had always intended on pursuing. The pressures of society, my friends, and my own securities kept escalating. My own vanity held a tight grip on me. It gave me anxiety at the mere thought of it. We had been doing everything but stopped short since I was still a virgin."

I had always been a good student. When I got to his place, there was a raging party going on. There were so many people scattered about his house. I felt out of place. The music vibrated loudly, so much so that the walls and floors felt like they were shaking. I remember he had come up to me and handed me a shot of vodka. He waited as I sucked it down. He had then spun me around toward his room, where we had stopped to meet a few of his friends on the way.

There was a fog of people mindlessly dancing. He then gave me two double shots as we shuffled through the black door. The music was loud. I reveled in the shelter of his room, away from the pulsating noise. The gray walls were bare except for a few rock band posters and a string of Edison bulbs. His sheets were rumpled, and his pillows in disarray. It was as if he had woken up in a rush.

He sat down and patted his lap for me to sit on. I was already feeling drunk and lacked control over my body. So, I had done as he instructed. Nerves shot up my spine. My heart was beating so fast it was as if in a race with itself. He immediately began to caress me. His hands wandered up my suede skirt while the other hand slowly crept up inside my shirt. He began to grab at my taut flesh, making me panic inside. My body was at war with my mind. Mixed signals clamored.

I recalled being into the idea at first. Then I would stop every few moments to catch my breath in hopes that I would be able to slow his pace. I was scared, knowing where it was leading. Part of me wanted to leave before I was too far in, but the other part of me didn't want to disappoint him either. That is when he whispered in my ear that he needed me. He needed to feel what I felt like. That he had been yearning for me ever since the day he had laid his eyes on me. That he wouldn't be able to continue if he didn't satisfy his desires and intense cravings for me.

I had been so enamored by his tongue that before I knew it, I was propped up on his bed facing the barren wall as he thrust himself into me. Desperation led me to grab at the sheets. I tried to focus on a lone nail hanging on to the vacant wall. I remember I had let out a stifled yell and had asked him to stop. I pleaded for him to get off me. He disregarded my defense. He rubbed my backside and instructed me that it would only hurt for a moment. Before I was able to protest again, he jammed himself inside of me. The pain radiated up my body. Tears poured out of my eyes. His eyes burned into my back. Then, in an instant, it was done.

He pushed me down, and I landed on my face, too scared to move. I turned to peek at him. He had begun to pull his pants up, then grabbed for his shirt and shot me a wink. I was stunned. I felt disregarded, like trash. "That was nice, right? Good girl." Before I could take in what had transpired, I was left there on the bed, naked and alone. I was shaking in fear, brokenness, and complete humiliation. I had been left vulnerable and exposed on a level I had never felt before. I laid upon his bed for at least an hour. I couldn't process what had happened.

I didn't understand how the months with Baker had led up to his night. I couldn't comprehend why he had left me as he had. Was this normal behavior for him and other guys? Had he done this with others? Then my mind, despite the disgust in myself, pondered the notion of us being over. I had so many questions running rampant through my mind. My head was in disarray due to my emotional state, and the rush of alcohol in my system had left my head spinning.

Then the door opened, and they walked in.

They surrounded the bed. Dread filled my body, and that was when I knew that nothing could stop what was about to take place. Through it all, I stifled a cry. I didn't want my tears to be mocked. I held them in; I zoned out almost completely. I let my head carry me to a different space. The smell was rancid, the perspiration thick. When it was done, I was covered in stains. My wounds were well beyond the physical.

When I finally limped to my feet and opened the door, you had been there. You saw my brokenness. You witnessed my frailty. My humiliation had morphed into what I thought was merely a nightmare for my own mind into a public joke. Then I later saw you with him, and my blood boiled.

You always thought David stayed because he loved me. That he was my protector. That's what he told himself, too. But it was a lie. David thought he stayed for me. He told himself he stayed to protect me. Lies. He stayed because Baker had him on a leash before I ever bled into their rituals. They were brothers in that house and not the kind you can run from. He knew what happened, what Baker made us do, and he knew if I ever spoke, the whole fraternity would burn. So he stayed. He build me a life, twisted as it was, but it was never his choice. It was obedience. Baker owned him. He owned us both."

Epilogue

The Final Silence

Charlotte's

"I received a letter penned by Marla–left behind before she was transferred into psychiatric care. Officer Cortez thought I deserved to read it, to understand what came before she slipped away from all of us."

Will inched closer, grabbing a pillow and stuffing it under his arm as he usually did. He was clearly intrigued by what I had just told him. It had been a few months since everything happened. Will was still healing, and even though things had settled, a feeling of unease lingered.

"Oh, yeah? What does the letter say? Have you read it already?" He looked at me with a mixture of concern and intrigue.

"Yeah, I have. I read it over a few times. Each time, things begin to make more and more sense. Her intentions become clearer, as well as her emotional turmoil. I don't understand her validation and motive. No one has the right to do what she did, regardless of the shit hand they have been dealt. It's never excusable." Wrinkling my nose, I closed my eyes and took a deep breath before opening the letter. I saw her loose scroll looped across the white paper and the lost girl who held the pen. An unexpected sadness overwhelmed me. Will grabbed my hand, squeezing it gently.

"It's okay, Charlie. You don't have to read it to me. Just tell me what it says as best as you can."

I nodded as I cleared my throat to begin.

"She was there. Marla. I don't know if she herself attended my college, but she was there alright. I remember her now. She was there, Will. She was there the entire time. I remember her so clearly now. It took me a while to digest her words. It took longer to fit her into my past and to place her. She didn't look like the Marla we know her to be. She was a completely different person back then. I never would have remembered her if it wasn't for this letter. Now, looking back, I can see her eyes. Her eyes have stuck with me for years, just at the time I didn't know they were hers. Those eyes were what initially made it all click."

Will perked up a bit, visibly confused.

"You remember her? Okay, can you explain because I am completely lost. I thought you met her after or during a stretch class or something."

I sat up a bit and slapped him gently on the arm. He loved to playfully tease me about my classes and knew that it drove me crazy. "Babe, it wasn't a stretch class, and you know it. But yes, I did. It was a Pilates class." He winked and offered me a sly smile.

"Anyway, as I was saying, after reading her letter, I now know this had all been planned. I recall the exact moment that she refers to. It was years ago. I had just arrived at college and had been settling into my new life as a young adult. I remember it had been rushing week. Just like any college campus, it was a big deal for all the frats and sororities. I had been working at the bar the night I got an invite from a few bar mates for a frat party. They described it as the party of the year. I honestly didn't even want to go. I had piles of homework and wanted to go straight home and bury myself in my books. However, I had been asked several times by various friends, and finally I decided, What the hell."

He let out a small laugh. "That's quite spontaneous of you." I grinned at him and playfully hit him again, careful not to punch too hard. He shrugged. "Such a bookworm then and more so now."

I smiled as I continued. "Well, I caved and ended up going. It was a spacious property. There were two living areas. I grabbed a beer when I walked in and headed to the other side, where not many were congregating. There had been just a couple smoking and making out in between puffs. So, I sat in the corner by the open window and cracked open a book. No surprise to you, I became wrapped up in the story and completely unaware of my surroundings."

He snorted with laughter. I ignored his amusement and continued.

"I kept looking at my watch, though, and pondered a respectable time frame in which I could bolt." I cleared my throat as I closed my eyes to remember the moment.

"Then I recall noticing a group of guys. There must have been at least five of them. Not sure if all of them were in the fraternity or what. I couldn't be sure. They went inside a room across from where I sat. I couldn't hear anything because the music was deafening. It was so damn loud. Looking back, I have no idea how I was able to read."

Will rolled his eyes dramatically. "Only you."

I stared down at my hands and willed myself to concentrate.

"Then, about thirty or so minutes later, all the guys bolted out. They were laughing and eyeing each other strangely. It was as if they shared a secret. It was very suspicious, and it caught my eye. From my spot on the window seat, I peered inside the dark room. I assumed they had been smoking dope or some other drug. I had this feeling that something was off, though. Call it intuition."

Will squinted his eyes as he tried to understand how this connected to Marla.

"Ten minutes had passed when I noticed a rail-thin girl slowly peek her head out. She had a white tank top, faded jeans, and a dark hoodie. The hoodie was pulled to the side. It concealed a portion of her face. As I stared at her, fixated on the scenario, she stopped and looked me straight in the eyes. It was then that I noticed she had been crying. I could see that her eyes were bloodshot even from where I sat. She had mascara smeared down her face. Before I knew it, she had rushed off into the crowd.

I remember that I attempted to follow her into the crowd. I had dropped my beer, spilling it everywhere in the process. I tripped as I raced to catch her. Something told me that when we locked eyes that something had happened. I had to know if she was okay. Something about that stare, that vacancy of life. Her tears that moment had felt incredibly heavy."

I hung my head in disappointment and regret at my inability to catch her.

"I can only imagine what went on behind those closed doors. I would have assumed what you did if I had seen her in that state," Will said as he shook his head in disbelief.

"Yeah, that is exactly what I had thought at the time. That was why I tried going after her, but I couldn't find her. It was as if she evaporated into thin air." I made a hand gesture to emphasize the effect.

"So, this letter explains that she had been assaulted by a group that night, and that she had seen me witness the entire thing, unbeknownst to me. Well, apparently, one of those boys had been Baker. Although he didn't participate when they assaulted her, he had been the ringleader. One of the others was her husband, David. He apparently stayed close to her, for whatever reason, I don't know." I paused, "I bet that is why he flew the coop. Cortez must have been on to him."

Will's eyes grew with bewilderment. "What the actual hell?"

I nodded my head in agreement. "Yeah, I know. I don't know the exact details, but I can only imagine the motive if everything else his this insidious. I didn't see him originally. He wasn't there when they walked in. I would have noticed because he always sat in the bar where I waited tables. However, I didn't know him yet, or rather, I hadn't been formally introduced by that point. She did make mention of it in the letter, though. It all makes perfect sense now, looking back at it all. She was a victim in so many ways, and honestly, it drove her mad. Rightfully so. I wish she had gotten help after it happened. I wish I had done more to try to find her."

I could feel myself starting to well up with tears. Emotions I held inside started to seep out.

"She became obsessed with him. She ended up pregnant. She wanted him to want her and their baby. She felt it was his duty. Just like me, Will. It makes me wonder how many girls he has done this to. I clearly hadn't been the only one if it happened to Marla, as well. How many had been before her? How many after? Was this some dark ritual initiated by the fraternity? And again, what part did David play in all of this? Was he in on it with Baker the entire time?"

Will ran his fingers through his thick hair. "Babe, she was out for revenge, and unfortunately, you got caught in the middle of it. I really don't think the trap was meant for you–it just happened. Frats can be a breeding ground for reckless, entitled guys who take advantage of the power and privilege that's been handed down to them for generations. That doesn't mean everyone in them is like that, but it's definitely been the root of a lot of messed-up stuff in college history."

Will's statement didn't baffle me. On the contrary, I had known Will's disdain for fraternities and their policies long before this. He saw more bad than good that came from the institutional organizations. I couldn't blame him. Especially after this situation.

"So, now what? What's next?"

I shrugged dismally.

"I honestly don't know. It does offer some form of closure. Baker is the one who should pay; his death should not have happened. That was much too easy. He needed to be put on trial and pay for the lives he's ruined."

Will drew me in for a hug. "Not necessarily. He has a

lifetime in hell to pay for his sins." I lingered in his arms, taking in his scent of wood and musk.

"She did admit to killing the private detective, Larson. She confessed to all of it. She even said where she left him. His poor family. I can't imagine their pain. Also, Officer Cortez told me to tell you that they found the file you had mentioned giving to Larson. It was located in Marla's house in her desk. They only found it because they secured a search warrant."

Will dropped his head in his hands. "I feel partially to blame for that. I hired him to watch you and the kids. What a disaster, and then her family. Ugh. I just don't understand why she would go through this entire thing and put her family at risk. She had it all."

I put my hand on his shoulder. "We will never fully understand her intentions, and it is anything but your fault. He had to know that with each client, he put himself at risk. As did his family."

Changing the subject, I mused, "Hannah, Marla, and I all share similar stories. All victims of despicable acts. We were all warped emotionally and still are from the inside out. Our histories will forever be tangled."

Will squeezed me tighter, "Yeah, except in this story, your adversity transcended into something good. I got lucky when I met you, and we have our kids. Hannah got lucky that I met you and our kids, as well, it seems. It made her heart yearn for something other than cold-hearted revenge. Last I'd heard, she'd left the States under a cloud of scandal, trading courtrooms for coastal villas. The trial had ended in acquittal, not guilty, but the stain of it would never be washed off. Spain became her exile. Maybe her escape. Or maybe even a chance to rebuild, depending on who you asked. From what I've heard, she's doing well there. It is, however, heartbreaking to know that Marla took her own life. I can't pretend to understand the full weight of her suffering, but I know the church teaches that God alone sees the depths of a soul and the burdens it carries. I pray He met her in that moment with grace and mercy. Despite it all, I will pray for the repose of her soul. It's even harder knowing her only daughter now has neither of her biological parents."

Will's eyes connected with mine, and I knew that he just made the connection. "She is better off."

I nodded sadly, "Yes, sadly, yes."

Some truths don't arrive with closure. They arrive like echoes long past the moment.

Our kids were asleep. The porch light was humming quietly in the distance. Baxter lay curled at my feet, the weight of him warm and solid. Comforting.

Cortez called earlier and stated that the case was mostly done. That word *mostly* hung in the air, something unresolved but no longer threatening.

Marla's gone, not dead, not arrested. Just … gone.

I still find her handwriting sometimes. On an old note in the pantry. On a gift tag tucked into Max's keepsake box. I don't rip them up. I don't throw them away. But I don't read them either.

Some part of me hopes she finds peace. That whatever drove her to this will lose its grip someday.

But the larger part—the mother, the survivor—hoped I would never see her again. Not every scar needs revisiting. Some are meant to stay closed.

But I still lock the windows.

But there was one part of Marla's letter I hadn't told

anyone, not even Will. She wrote it as an afterthought, a line almost hidden near the bottom:

"Only one person ever knew. And now, I suppose, you do, too. My daughter ... she wasn't David's." Just that. No elaboration. No name. But I didn't need more; I understood the depths that plagued her mind.

I knew whose child she meant, and I knew now what kept her bound all these years.

And even now, I don't know what to do with that truth except hold it in the quiet where all the old ghosts live.

I turned toward the yard. The fog was settling in low, hugging the grass. And then I heard it, light, airy, almost playful. A laugh I hadn't heard in weeks.

I told myself it was nothing.

Still, I locked the door twice.

Cortez & Martha

The lake is still again. Fog hovers low, catching the morning sun in silver threads.

No more search teams. No more sirens.

Just stillness and the quiet clink of a spoon against porcelain.

Cortez stood on the porch of Charlotte's house, a cup of coffee warming his hands. His badge was off. His gun was locked in the cruiser. He wasn't a detective at this moment. He was just Ray.

He reveled in this time of day. The off-duty cop, the neighbor, the friend.

Behind him, Martha stepped outside, balancing a tray with more mugs and a plate of lemon loaf.

"Charlotte's mother said they're all finally sleeping through the night," she said softly. "Even little Molly."

They sat side by side, their feet silent on the stained wood, watching the world hold its breath as the chatter of people gathering inside buzzed loudly.

Cortez nodded toward the trees. "Every time I look out there, I think about how close we came to losing her. If Mariam hadn't walked in ... if we hadn't followed the clues ... hell, if Charlotte hadn't trusted her gut, honestly ..."

"She would've died," Martha finished, her voice cracking, but she didn't cry. "But she didn't, thank the Lord."

"No," Cortez said, "that she didn't, and yes, thank you, Jesus."

They watched Max toss a stick to Baxter across the yard. Somewhere deeper in the woods, a bird called out. The world kept going.

"They are all gone now, though," Cortez murmured.

And, for the first time in a long time, he believed it.

Martha leaned across the small café table, her eyes soft but searching. "Cortez, whatever happened to David?"

Cortez's jaw tightened, the question hanging in the air. He set his coffee down, the steam curling between them.

"David and Baker weren't just old friends," he said finally. "They were part of something much darker. A string of assaults on campus, rituals tied to their fraternity. It went back decades. David was there the night Marla was hurt. Maybe not the hand that did it, but he was there. He knew. And he stayed silent."

Martha's lips pressed thin, her hands folding tight around her mug.

"It's turned into a full-blown scandal now," Cortez continued. "Girls ... women ... are coming forward, one after another. Some who never thought they's be believed. If it weren't for Marla's letter, we might never have had enough to crack it open."

"And David?"

Cortez shook his head. "Flew the coop. Disappeared before we could bring him in. The Bureau's looking, but so far, nothing. Maybe he's running from Baker's shadow, maybe from his own. Either way, justice has a longer memory than he thinks."

The silence stretched, heavy but not hopeless. For the first time in a long while, Cortez let himself believe that maybe, just maybe, the truth was finally louder than the lies.

Acknowledgments

I owe deep gratitude to those who made this book possible. To my husband and children, thank you for your patience, love, and encouragement through late nights and countless drafts. To my sisters and mother as well as close friends who read early chapters and believed in the story before I fully did, your support kept me writing when doubt crept in. To my late father who helped fuel the passion ignited within me.

I am grateful to my team at Red Penguin Publishing for their guidance and faith in this manuscript, and to my early readers whose insights sharpened both the story and my resolve.

Finally, I thank God, who redeems every fragment of our history and brings light into even the darkest corners. Without His grace, these words and characters would not exist. May You never leave me.

About the Author

Kathryn Nichols grew up a cradle Catholic, raised by parents who instilled in her the foundations of faith. Over the years, she walked through seasons of trial, including the loss of several loved ones and, at just thirty-one, a battle with aggressive ovarian cancer. That journey marked by suffering, surrender, and unexpected grace brought her to the foot of the Cross and back home to Christ.

Her debut novel, *It Was In Their History*, is a psychological suspense story of redemption through confession, suffering, and divine grace. Her current work-in-progress,

Cradled in Grace, is a pro-life novel inspired by true stories of women who chose life against the odds.

Her flagship project, the *Faith & Fire* series, is a YA fantasy grounded in Catholic Scripture, sacred tradition, and apocalyptic prophecy. Written with a heart to inspire and equip the next generation, Kathryn's stories bring spiritual depth to young readers in an age of distraction and doubt.

She resides in Texas with her husband and their two children, who continue to be her greatest joy and inspiration.